Praise for

THE CHRISTMAS NOVELS
of
ANNE PERRY

A Christmas Garland

"Perennial best-selling author Perry once again shows why her work resonates with readers in this short Christmas story that doesn't rely on all of the usual yuletide tricks to make it sing. . . . This tale will delight Perry's fans and bring her new ones."

—*Kirkus Reviews*

A Christmas Homecoming

"A gothic novel par excellence, Anne Perry's offering for this holiday season sets the dark forces of fear and evil against the light and goodness of the Christmas season. Terrifying, uplifting and thought-provoking by turns, *A Christmas Homecoming* is vastly entertaining."

—*The Star-Ledger*

A Christmas Odyssey

"[Perry] writes with detail that invades the senses."

—*Lincoln Journal Star*

A Christmas Promise

"Poignant . . . should be on the Christmas stocking list of anyone who likes a sniffle of nostalgia."

—*The Washington Times*

A Christmas Grace

"[A] heartwarming, if crime-tinged, complement to the holiday season."

—*Booklist*

A Christmas Beginning

"Intriguing . . . Perry's use of period detail is, as always, strong and evocative."

—*The Seattle Times*

A Christmas Secret

"A delightful little book . . . Perry's gift is that she can evoke a sense of place and time while still producing the thrills and chills expected of a modern-day mystery writer."

—The Orlando Sentinel

A Christmas Guest

"[A] satisfying tale."

—The Wall Street Journal

A Christmas Visitor

"Heartwarming . . . [Perry] creates excellent winter atmosphere in the wild, snowy lands of Northern England."

—The Arizona Republic

A Christmas Journey

"One of the best books to brighten the joyous season."

—USA Today

THE CHRISTMAS NOVELS OF ANNE PERRY

A Christmas Journey
A Christmas Visitor
A Christmas Guest
A Christmas Secret
A Christmas Beginning
A Christmas Grace
A Christmas Promise
A Christmas Odyssey
A Christmas Homecoming
A Christmas Garland
A Christmas Hope
A New York Christmas

ANNE PERRY'S
Christmas Crimes

ANNE PERRY'S
Christmas Crimes

TWO VICTORIAN HOLIDAY MYSTERIES

A Christmas Homecoming

A Christmas Garland

Anne Perry

BALLANTINE BOOKS TRADE PAPERBACKS

NEW YORK

2014 Ballantine Books Trade Paperback Edition

A Christmas Homecoming copyright © 2011 by Anne Perry
A Christmas Garland copyright © 2012 by Anne Perry

Published in the United States by Ballantine Books,
an imprint of Random House, a division of Random House LLC,
a Penguin Random House Company, New York.

BALLANTINE and the HOUSE colophon are registered
trademarks of Random House LLC.

Originally published in hardcover as two separate works entitled
A Christmas Homecoming and *A Christmas Garland* in the
United States by Ballantine Books, an imprint of Random House,
a division of Random House LLC, in 2011 and 2012.

ISBN 978-0-553-39359-0
eBook ISBN 978-0-553-39360-6

Printed in the United States of America on acid-free paper

www.ballantinebooks.com

2 4 6 8 9 7 5 3 1

A Christmas Homecoming

To those who face the unknown
with courage

*C*AROLINE FIELDING SAW THE HUGE MANSION RISING from the steep incline ahead of them as the carriage turned the corner, and felt an almost overwhelming sense of relief. It was the end of a very long journey and she was aching with tiredness and from the biting cold. First there had been the early morning ride to the station in London. The platforms had been crowded and it had been difficult to push their way to the train with all the luggage in tow, trying not to bump into people. She had been glad to find their seats for the journey to York.

In York they had disembarked. One piece of luggage had been mislaid and, as time was short, they were desperate to find it. She had been asking the same porter the same questions over and over, until at last it was found, safely stowed in the guards' car on the train to Whitby. Then she and Joshua had almost run along the platform as the carriage doors began to clang shut, the engine belching steam and smuts, and they scrambled on just as the train began to move.

3

Now in the dark, surrounded by the newly fallen snow, they rode in a two-horse carriage from Whitby up to the cliff edge and this house where they would spend the whole Christmas holiday, if you could call it a holiday.

Caroline turned to look at Joshua beside her. Aware of her movement, he touched her gloved hand lightly.

"A bit brooding, isn't it?" he said ruefully. "But I expect it'll be warm inside, and we'll be very welcome."

The coach lamps did not give enough light to see his face, but she could imagine it: gentle, mercurial, full of humor. She heard the half apology in his voice.

"It'll be excellent," she said without hesitation. She would never be as good an actor as he was, because she could not help but always be herself, and it was his profession to imagine himself inside another man's skin, even his heart. But she had long ago learned to mask her feelings for the sake of those she loved, and she did love him. However, there were fears that crowded her every so often because she was so much older than he, and she did not belong to the world of the theater as he did. She feared she would always be an outsider, too old for him in the eyes of his fellows, too ordinary, undramatic, and painfully respectable. Yet she would have been miserable had she not married him, if she had given in to conventionality and remained a widow after her first husband's death. And she loved Joshua so much. She felt no inner doubt or shadow about her second marriage although outwardly it had not been at all the right thing to do.

For a moment Joshua's hand tightened over hers.

They climbed the last hundred yards of the road, horses straining against the weight of the vehicle, and finally pulled to a stop in front of the magnificent entrance of the mansion. The doors were thrown open, flooding the portico and the gravel driveway with light.

"You are right," Caroline said with a smile. "We are welcome."

A footman opened the carriage door and Joshua climbed out quickly, turning to assist Caroline. She had been glad of the cloak and her huge skirts while on the journey—they provided the only warmth available—but now they were an encumbrance as she tried to step down elegantly. She grasped Joshua's hand rather more firmly than she had intended, and stood up straight to her full height just as their host, Charles

Netheridge, came out of his ostentatiously large front door. He descended the wide steps, holding out his hand.

Introductions were made and orders given. Footmen materialized to unpack the boxes and trunks and see to the horses.

Charles Netheridge was a stocky man, thick-chested, heavy-shouldered. His gray hair was still strong, but receding a little at the front as he moved into his sixties. In the flare of the outside lights, his features were blunt and vigorous, as was his manner. He had made a fortune in coal, and later also in jet. It was his pleasure to donate generously to the theater in London and to know that some of the best performances would never have found an audience without his intervention.

Now he had Joshua, one of England's most dynamic actors, in his own home, and he was brimming over with satisfaction. He led them inside, calling out orders for their comfort, refreshment, for luggage to be taken to their rooms, and anything they wanted taken care of immediately.

Caroline barely glanced around the hall, with its gray-and-white marble floor and high ceiling from which hung a splendid chandelier. The warmth now enveloped her and just at that minute, it was all she cared about.

"Mr. Singer is already here," Netheridge said cheerfully. "He told me he is to play the hero, Van Helsing." He looked a little self-conscious as he said this last, watching Joshua earnestly, as if trying to read his thoughts.

Joshua composed his expression in a manner Caroline had come to understand. He was concealing a very considerable amount of irritation.

"I think he will be," he agreed. "But we will make no final decisions until we have read through Miss Netheridge's dramatization."

"Of course, of course," Netheridge agreed. "All in good time. I hope Mr. Hobbs and Miss Carstairs, and Miss Rye will get here before too long. It's a nasty night, and set to get worse, I think. No doubt we'll have a good deal of snow by Christmas. Nine days to go before the performance." He looked at Joshua narrowly, with a steady, curiously unblinking stare. "Long enough for you to get it right, do you think? No idea if it's any good. Alice has no experience, you know."

Joshua made himself smile. "You'll be surprised how quickly a production can come together."

"Damn silly story, if you ask me," Netheridge murmured, half to himself. "Vampires, indeed! But it seems to be all the rage in London, or so they say. Who is this fellow, Bram Stoker? What kind of a name is 'Bram'?"

"Short for Abraham," Joshua replied.

Netheridge looked at him wide-eyed. "A Jew?"

"I'm told he's Irish," Joshua said with a slight smile, but Caroline saw the slight stiffening of his body and the tension in his shoulders. She had learned not to leap to his defense: To do so was patronizing, as if there were something about being a Jew that needed explaining. But it was difficult for her. It is instinct to protect those whom we love; and the more open to hurt they are, the fiercer our retaliation.

Netheridge did not even appear to be aware that he had been clumsy, and this was not the time to let him know. They needed him in the coming year of 1898. Without his support, their next play would not open. It was the promise of that support that had prompted Joshua and the lead actors in his company to agree to spend ten days over Christmas as Netheridge's guest, and perform his daughter's amateur dramatization of Stoker's new novel, *Dracula*. It was fitting; in the book, a storm had washed the coffin containing the vampire ashore at Whitby. The play would be performed on Boxing Day, the day after Christmas, for an audience of Netheridge's friends and neighbors.

Eliza Netheridge came hurrying out of the passage at the back of the hall. She was a small woman with a gentle face, her fair hair just beginning to turn gray. She looked concerned as her husband made the introductions; he spoke with a touch of impatience, as if he was annoyed that she hadn't been there already, waiting for them.

"You must be tired," Eliza said warmly, looking first at Caroline, then at Joshua. "And cold. I'm sure you would like to go to your room and rest a little before dinner."

"Thank you," Caroline accepted quickly. "That is most kind. It has been rather a long journey, and we very much wish to be at our best tomorrow."

"Of course." Eliza smiled. "Will dinner at eight be suitable to you? We can always serve you something in the breakfast room at a different time, if you wish?"

"Eight will be excellent," Caroline assured her, turning toward the stairs.

*T*he bedroom they were shown to was large and richly curtained in dark wine red. There were chairs near the fire, and the fire itself spread such light and warmth that it was unnecessary to use the candles provided, except on the bedside table.

"I told you," Joshua said gently, as soon as the door was closed behind the footman who had brought their cases. "We are very welcome." He was smiling, although his face, which concealed emotion so easily now, could not hide either his weariness or a degree of anxiety.

Caroline walked over to stand close to him, then reached forward and touched his cheek softly with her fingertips. "Don't worry about it tonight, my dear. You'll all work on the play tomorrow, and it may not be nearly as difficult when you rehearse it together as it seems now on the page. How often have you told me that about other plays?"

He leaned forward and kissed her. "But it's actually

awful," he said ruefully. "It's a very difficult thing to adapt a book for the stage, and Alice Netheridge really hasn't much idea how to do it. I wouldn't even attempt this if we weren't at our wits' end to find a backer for next year. But without Netheridge's support we would all be facing a pretty bleak spring."

"That's not true, Joshua," she corrected him. "The company might, but *you* could always find a part somewhere. I know of at least three other managers who would leap at the chance to have you."

He winced very slightly; it was just a tightening of the skin across the bones of his cheeks. "Walk away and leave the rest of the company with nothing?" he asked. "The theater is too small a world to do that, even if I were willing to. It's not only Mercy and James, or Lydia—not to mention Vincent, although he would probably find something else. It's all the others as well; the bit players who take on a dozen other tasks: moving scenery, fetching and carrying, building props, looking after the costumes."

She had known he would say something like that, but when he did, it still gave her a rush of warmth, stronger than any heat the fire could offer.

11

He was frowning a little. "Are you afraid?" he asked. She had been used to being provided for, more than adequately, all her life. First by her father, then by her first husband, Edward Ellison. This was the first time she had ever realized, more than in theory, that it was possible that she could become cold or hungry, or truly at the mercy of debt, to the point of being afraid when a knock sounded on the door. Should she lie and deny that she had thought about these things? Or was honesty between them worth more than the kindness of the lie, than taking heart and having courage?

"Not yet," she said with a tiny grimace, choosing the middle ground. "As for Alice, just don't expect too much. Can you steer some sort of path between her work as it stands and what you would consider good enough professionally?"

"Between the rocks and the whirlpool?" He said it with a twisted smile, but there was no laughter in his eyes. "I can try. And keep Vincent from taking over and hogging the stage, Lydia from giving up altogether, and Mercy and James from endlessly defending each other from attacks that no one has made, while at the same time teaching Alice Netheridge how to do all the extra

parts, and playing a credible Count Dracula myself?"
He shrugged. "Of course. My wife overrates me per-
haps, but she believes I can." His voice lowered a little.
"At least she says so."

❧

*D*inner was a very generous affair, but informal.
Joshua and Caroline arrived in the drawing room to
find Vincent Singer already there. He had been the first
to arrive, and had clearly rested and changed from his
traveling clothes. Caroline had known him off and on
since her marriage to Joshua, but she still felt uncomfortable in his company. He was very striking to look at:
tall and lean with a powerful face, and at present he
had a full beard, lightly touched with gray. It was
neatly trimmed, although he had allowed his shaggy
hair to grow a little long.

He turned from the fireplace where he was standing,
glancing first at Joshua without speaking to him before
coming forward to Caroline.

"Good evening, Mrs. Fielding," he said warmly. He
had a rich and exquisitely trained voice, and he never

spoke carelessly. "I hope the journey was not too arduous for you?"

She knew he intended to sound concerned, and yet she felt a tiny stab of self-consciousness, as if he was also reminding her that she was older than the rest of them, and an outsider, unused to the rigors of the theater, and the self-discipline that made the players always give their best. For them, weariness, hunger, fear, and private grief were mere irritations to be overcome. She admired that in all of the troupe and wanted to equal them; above all so Joshua would never be embarrassed for her, or of her.

So she forced herself to smile at Singer. "It was a most exhilarating journey," she lied. "I have never been to this part of Yorkshire before. I could see, even in the dusk as we approached the town, why Mr. Stoker chose to set his story here."

She had no idea whether he believed her or not, but then she had never been able to read his face. Perhaps instead of trying to read him, and failing, she should make more certain that he could not read her, either.

"Do you think so?" he said conversationally. "I would have preferred Cornwall, myself."

"Too easily associated with smugglers," she replied. "Besides, how would one pass Cornwall by sea from Transylvania, in order to be washed ashore, whatever the storm?"

"You are too literal, ma'am," he said with a tiny shake of his head. "The whole thing is . . . fantastical."

"Not at all," she insisted. "It is a story created out of the darkness of the nightmares within us. It must be consistent in itself or it loses its edge of horror." Her mind flickered back to the past, to the terror that had surrounded and devastated her own family, sixteen years ago. She forced it away and turned to face Alice Netheridge, who came forward from where she had been standing by the curtains. She was not pretty in the usual way, but there was great emotion in her face, and when she smiled—as she did now—there was a way in which she was quite beautiful.

"Mrs. Fielding." She held out her hand. "You are marvelously perceptive. That is exactly what I feel, too. Dracula is the demon within us. I wish I could convey it more successfully on paper. I'm Alice Netheridge." She turned to Joshua, standing slightly behind Caroline, and now she was clearly nervous. She had tried desperately hard to force her ideas into form, and she was waiting for his judgment. She might aspire to be an actress adequate enough for the very small parts she would have to play in the adaptation, but she hadn't the skill to conceal the vulnerability in her eyes at the moment.

Joshua took Alice's hand briefly and smiled at her. "We will see how it reads tomorrow," he replied. "There are always changes; please don't feel badly if we make a few. The spoken word is very different from the written one. If we are any good at our parts, we may need to say far less than you imagine." He turned to Singer. "Good evening, Vincent. How was your journey?"

"Tedious," Singer replied. "But mercifully uneventful. The weather is vile, and apparently likely to get worse."

"Then it is fortunate that the house is so comfortable and we shan't have to leave it," Joshua retorted.

The door opened and they were joined by Lydia Rye, the actress who would play the second female lead, Lucy Westenra, Dracula's first victim. She was pretty in a voluptuous way, and yet there was a delicate character to her face, and her slightly husky voice was unusually attractive. Caroline had often wondered why Lydia had not overtaken her fellow actress Mercy Carstairs in the leading roles.

"Too little hunger," Joshua had said of Lydia, but looking at her now, Caroline could not understand what he had meant. It was just another example of the way in which she would never quite be one of them. She could learn all she wished and ask Joshua a hundred questions, but she did not have the instinctive understanding of the way the world of the theater operated that the others shared.

Lydia knew Vincent, of course, but she was introduced to Alice, and then to Mr. Netheridge, and to Eliza Netheridge. She spoke to Joshua and Caroline with the warmth she had always shown them, and they were talking agreeably of nothing in particular when the last two of the players arrived. Mercy Carstairs and James Hobbs had been married for three years and seemed well suited to each other. She was very slender, wide-eyed, and filled with a restless energy that commanded attention on the stage. He was traditionally handsome, as tall as Vincent Singer but far less dynamic. He was good in romantic leads but he had no inner darkness at his command to play villains, and no silence within from which to summon tragedy.

They all exchanged greetings, expressed their satisfaction at the ample accommodations that had been provided for them, and then swapped a few stories about the journey from London.

They had already been shown to the dining room and had taken their places at the table when the last of the week's guests arrived. He was introduced as Douglas Paterson, fiancé of Alice Netheridge. He was in his late twenties with a keen face. At the moment he was clearly unable to hide his discomfort at the present gathering. He took his seat with a brief apology, directed first to Mrs. Netheridge, then to Alice.

Alice accepted it without comment.

Caroline glanced at Joshua, and saw that he, too, had recognized the first sign of disapproval. Paterson's glance at Alice, and then the strange tension in his face at her lack of response, made the situation clear. He did not wish his fiancée to be wasting her time at such inappropriate pursuits. He had probably expressed his displeasure earlier, and Alice had clearly chosen to ignore him.

The meal was generous and very well served. They began with soup, then fresh fish. Netheridge remarked that it had come in overnight and been brought up from the docks that morning.

"I doubt we'll get more for a while," he said, looking at the closed curtains, beyond which the sound of the rising wind was quite clear.

"They'll put it on ice," Eliza assured him. "We have plenty to last us." She looked at her guests one by one. "I always find a stormy Christmas quite enjoyable, especially if there is snow. I can remember some years when Christmas Day was so beautiful it was as if the whole world had been made anew while we slept."

"So it had," Caroline responded quickly. "At least in a spiritual sense, and that is how we should view everything."

Singer stared at her in amazement. "I thought you were a Jew," he said, pointedly looking at Joshua and then back at her, his eyebrows high.

There was total silence around the table. Alice dropped her fork and it clattered on the china of her plate.

Caroline hesitated. She knew everyone was looking

19

at her, waiting to see how she would react. All the players were aware of Joshua's race and religion, but were
the Netheridges? Caroline was so angry at Vincent that
she put down her own knife and fork and hid her hands
in her lap to hide the shaking.

But she forced herself to smile charmingly. "No, you
didn't," she said to Vincent. "You know perfectly well
that Joshua is Jewish and I am Christian. You made
the remark to be absolutely certain that our host and
hostess are also aware of it, although I can't think why,
unless it is a desire to embarrass someone. If they now
wish us to leave, then you have sabotaged the whole
project, and all that hangs on it. Surely that was not
your intention?"

For several pulsing seconds the silence returned.
The color washed up Vincent's face as he fought for an
answer. Beside Caroline, Joshua moved uncomfortably.
Lydia stared at the floor; Mercy and James looked at
each other.

It was Alice who finally spoke, turning to face
Joshua.

"It would be terrible if you were to leave, Mr. Fielding. You are most welcome here. In fact, we cannot pos-

sibly succeed without you—either with the play, or with being the kind of hosts we wish to be. How could we celebrate Christmas if we were to turn anyone away into the snow, let alone our own guests, who have come here specifically to help us?"

Netheridge winced, but so slightly Caroline would not have noticed it had she not been watching him.

Eliza let out her breath in a low sigh.

Douglas Paterson was clearly appalled.

"You'll make an actress yet," Vincent said drily. "I look forward to working with you."

"Liar." Lydia mouthed the word soundlessly.

"This pork is delicious," James remarked to no one in particular. "It must be local."

"Thank you," Eliza murmured. She did not correct him that it was mutton.

*T*he meal finished with stilted conversation and very occasional nervous laughter. Afterward, Caroline found herself being shown the rest of the very large house by Alice Netheridge and Douglas Paterson. The tour began very formally, as a matter of courtesy. None of them had been particularly interested, but it was an easy thing to do, and filled the time until it would be acceptable to excuse themselves and retire to bed.

Alice was clearly eager to make up for the earlier discomfort, although it had had nothing to do with her.

"Do let me show you the stage," she said eagerly. "It was originally designed for music: trios and quartets and that sort of thing. One of my aunts played the cello, or the viola, I can't remember. Grandmama said she was very talented, but of course it was not the sort of thing a lady did, except for the entertainment of her own family." She glanced at Caroline as she said the words, her soft face pulled into an expression of impatience.

"She was thinking of her daughter's welfare," Douglas pointed out from behind her as they walked along the broad corridor. The walls were hung with paintings of Yorkshire coastal scenery. Some were very dark but, looking at them, Caroline thought it was more probable that time had dulled the varnish, rather than that the artists had intended them to be so forbidding.

"She was thinking of the family's reputation for being proper," Alice corrected him. "It was all about what the neighbors would think."

"You can't live in society without neighbors, Alice," he replied. He sounded patient, but Caroline saw the flicker of irritation in his face—at least that was what she thought it was. "You have to make some accommodation to their feelings."

"I will not have my life ruled by my neighbors' prejudices," Alice retorted. "Poor Aunt Delia did and never played her viola, or whatever it was, except in the theater here." Without realizing it, she increased her pace. Caroline was obliged to lengthen her strides to keep up with her.

"I imagine she still gave a great deal of pleasure." Caroline tried to imagine the frustration of the young woman she had never known, and wondered if Alice had actually known her well, or whether she was simply projecting her own frustrations into her aunt's story.

Alice did not reply.

"She married very happily and had several children," Douglas put in, catching up with Caroline and walking beside her. "There is no need whatsoever to feel sorry for her. She was an excellent woman."

Alice turned around to face him, stopping so abruptly that he very nearly walked into her.

Caroline thought of her own second daughter, Charlotte, who was willful, full of spirit and fire like Alice, and impossible to deter from following her own path, however awkward the path may be. She had married far beneath herself socially, but since the marriage, her husband, Thomas, had risen spectacularly. Charlotte had always been happy: in her own way, perhaps the happiest of all Caroline's daughters.

Caroline looked at Alice facing her fiancé, head high, eyes blazing, and felt a protective warmth toward her. It was as if she had for an instant seen her own Charlotte as a young woman again, struggling to defy the rules and follow her own dream. She longed to be able to help Alice, but knew that to interfere would be disastrous. She did not know the girl. All kinds of arrogant mistakes could spring from even the most well-meaning intentions.

"Excellent?" Alice challenged. "What does that mean? That she did her duty, as her husband saw it?"

Douglas kept his temper with an effort that even Caroline could easily see, and she did not know him. To Alice it must have been as clear as daylight.

"As she saw it herself, Alice," he said. "I met her, if you remember? She was gracious, composed, a good wife, and a loving mother. You should not forget that. Playing the viola, like any other pastime, is a fine thing to do, in its place. Aunt Delia knew what that place was, and she still played occasionally at dinner parties and was much admired."

"For what? Playing well, or having given up being brilliant in order to be dutiful?" Alice challenged him again.

"Living a life of love and generosity mixed with duty, rather than chasing after self-indulgence and an illusion of fame," he told her. "Only to end up old, lonely, and probably destitute among strangers."

"Lie to yourself that you are happy, when what you really mean is that you are safe," she interpreted. "If you take risks then of course they may turn out badly. But if you marry that can turn out badly, too." She glanced at him, her lips closed tightly as if to stop them from trembling. "And so can having children. Not all children grow up to be charming and obedient. They can be anything: wanton, spiteful, spendthrift; they can drink too much, even steal. Nothing is certain in life, except that you should not be too afraid of it to accept its challenges."

"You are very young, Alice." He still kept his voice under weary control, but Caroline could see the edge of fear in him now. He did not understand her, and mastery of the situation was slipping out of his grasp. She felt a twinge of pity for him, even though it was Alice she was able to relate to, to understand.

"I am working on getting older!" Alice snapped, and swung around again to continue on toward the theater.

Douglas reached out to grasp Alice's arm, but Caroline prevented him. She stepped a yard or so in front of the path he would have to take, making it impossible for him to catch hold of Alice.

"Don't," she said quietly enough that Alice would not hear her. Her own footsteps and the rustle of her skirts drowned it out. "We probably none of us know whether Aunt Delia was happy or not. The point is that Alice imagines herself in Delia's place, and feels trapped for her. You see her as gracefully letting go of an unreality and embracing a better path."

He looked at her with surprise. "Of course I do. Wouldn't anyone, if they thought about it without theater footlights in their eyes?"

Caroline smiled at him; it was almost a laugh. "Perhaps. But then I can't say; I have the same lights in my eyes. Or had you not noticed?"

"Oh." He blinked. For a moment he looked far younger, and not at all unattractive. "I'm so sorry . . . I . . ."

"Think nothing of it," she said cheerfully. "Let us allow Alice to show us the stage, and all its charms and limitations. She will do it anyway. We may as well be gracious about it."

He did not move. "Do you think this . . . play . . . will come to anything?" There was a real anxiety in his eyes. "Is she . . . talented?"

Caroline read a world of fear behind the words. What he was really asking was, was Alice bored with Whitby, even with Douglas himself? To him the theater was a tawdry world of make-believe, while to her it was the gateway to freedom of the mind, the wings to carry her to an inner life far brighter than any outer clay could be.

"I don't know," she admitted, remembering that Joshua had said the play was desperately amateur, close to unworkable. "But if she has the courage to put it to the test, you will win nothing at all by preventing her from finding out."

The flicker crossed his face again. "She may be hurt. It's my place to try to save her from that."

"You can't," she said simply. "All you can do is comfort her if she fails. You will learn that when you have children. Nothing in the world hurts quite like seeing your child fail, and then watching as they try to face the pain of it. But you must not prevent them from following their hearts, just because there is the possibility of failure. All that shows is that you don't believe in either their ability, or their courage. Believe me, Mr. Paterson, I have daughters just as willful as Alice, if not more so."

He looked startled. "Did they want to write plays?"

"No, but one of them wanted to marry a policeman, and live on a pittance."

He swallowed. "What did you do?"

"I let her. Not that I imagine I could have stopped her," she admitted. "It was a matter of doing it graciously, or ungraciously. I am delighted to say that she is very happy indeed."

He was clearly not sure whether to believe her or not.

"Let us join Alice, and be shown the theater." She took his arm, so he was obliged to leave the subject and do as she commanded.

*A*fter seeing the stage, which was unexpectedly impressive, Caroline returned along the series of corridors to the main part of the house. She found that Joshua had apparently gone to discuss the following day's arrangements with the rest of the players. Only Mr. and Mrs. Netheridge were in the large withdrawing room. Caroline hadn't had time to really notice the décor earlier, as they had actually approached the dining room from the other side, and so had glimpsed this room only through its open double doors.

Inside it was awe-inspiring, certainly the central

room of the house. The ceiling was unusually high and ornate. She tried to imagine how long the scrolled and curlicued plasterwork must have taken, and gave up before her staring became too obvious to be good-mannered. The walls were separated into panels, but the most remarkable feature of the room was an enormous window of almost cathedral-like proportions with panes of delicate leaded glass, most of it in rich autumnal colors. It was clearly seen because the curtains on either side of it were drawn back and held by thick silk ropes. Lanterns outside the window shone through the colored glass.

Mr. Netheridge saw her looking.

"My father had that built," he said proudly. "Talk of the town, it was, back then. And folk take it for granted now, least from the outside they do."

"I can't imagine that's true," Caroline said truthfully. Whether you cared for it or not, the window was certainly impossible to ignore.

Netheridge was pleased. "Whole room designed around it, of course," he went on. "My mother did it all. Had a wonderful eye, didn't she, Eliza?"

"Wonderful," Eliza agreed drily. Caroline caught the look of sudden loss in her face, but Mr. Netheridge was looking the other way. His gaze was wandering over the richly colored walls—too richly colored for Caroline's taste. She found the shading oppressive, and longed for something cooler, less absorbing of the light. She wondered if Mrs. Netheridge senior had been as dominating in personality as she was in her ideas of design, and if Eliza as a new bride had felt obliged to subordinate her own tastes because of it.

Caroline looked at Eliza again and saw a momentary unhappiness in her face that was so sharp as to make Caroline feel that she had unintentionally intruded. She wanted to make amends for it immediately.

"It is quite unlike anywhere I have been before," she said with forced cheerfulness. Perhaps she would make as good an actress as Lydia or Mercy, one day? "And it is so extraordinarily comfortable. For all its richness, it still feels like someone's home." That was a total lie, enough to make her teeth ache, but she saw the pride in Netheridge's face, and the relief in Eliza's.

"We're glad you came," Netheridge said with satisfaction. "It'll give our Alice a real chance. Bit of fun for 'er, before she settles down to married life."

Eliza said nothing.

*C*aroline slept well, too tired to even move. Even when she heard Joshua's voice speaking her name, and felt his hand on her shoulder, she had to battle to the surface of consciousness. She opened her eyes to sharp, white winter daylight, and it took a moment or two for her to remember where she was.

Joshua was smiling. "Sorry," he said gently. "Have I landed you with a wretched Christmas?"

"Probably," she replied. "But listening to Eliza Netheridge in that awful drawing room yesterday evening, I thought of my mother-in-law, and blessed your name for having rescued me from her."

"Oh, Grandmama." He rolled his eyes. "I was just doing my impersonation of St. George, rescuing the maiden from the dragon. Was she pretty awful, old Mrs. Netheridge? I believe she died over ten years ago."

"She's still around in spirit," Caroline said, sitting

up in bed and pushing her long hair out of the way. It was soft and shining, and still mostly dark brown. She rinsed it in a solution of cold tea and iron filings, but she would rather that Joshua did not know that. "She designed the décor, and it has remained untouched since then," she went on.

"It must have been redecorated in ten years!" he protested.

"Certainly, but not changed." She looked at him. "It's awful, isn't it!"

"Ghastly." He leaned forward and kissed her softly, intimately, then stood up. "After breakfast I have to read through this play again. I don't know what on earth I'm going to do with it to make it work. It's bad on the page, and I've an awful fear it's going to be even worse when it's read."

"We have a week to work on it." She pushed the bed-clothes away and swung her feet out. "Let's at least enjoy breakfast. I shall probably eat far too much while I'm here. Judging from dinner last night, they have an excellent cook, and nothing in the kitchen is my re-sponsibility. That in itself makes it all taste better."

The meal lived up to her every expectation. The

sideboard groaned under the weight of chafing dishes of kidneys; bacon; sausages; potatoes; and eggs boiled, scrambled, poached, and fried. There was porridge for those who wished it, and racks of toast with butter, jam, and marmalade, and pots of tea. It was only the temper of the guests that was sour.

Vincent barely spoke, but that was usual for him in the mornings. Lydia was cheerful, but for some reason, this irritated Mercy.

"I don't know why we are bothering," she said for the third time. "Look at the weather. Nobody's going to be able to come for the performance, even if they wish to." She reached for the marmalade.

"Why wouldn't they wish to?" Lydia asked with exaggerated innocence. "*Dracula* is all the rage in London. Everyone is reading it, if only to not be left out. It will be enormous fun. Don't you want to be Mina, and fall into the arms of the vampire, become one of the 'children of the night'?" She sipped her tea delicately.

Mercy glared at her. "All I can say is thank God you die near the beginning!"

"But then I am 'undead'!" Lydia said with a grin. "It isn't until much later that I can go into the audience and watch all the rest of you without having to worry about remembering any more lines."

"That's if we can make it workable in the first place," James said darkly. He had taken a liberal breakfast and was still eating it: kidneys, bacon, eggs, and sausage.

"We must," Joshua reminded them. "A good deal of our company's survival next year depends on it. And I suggest that next time you find a line difficult or an entry or exit clumsy, you remember that, and try a bit harder to make do."

At that moment, Alice appeared. The conversation instantly became polite and trivial.

❖

*H*alf an hour later they were assembled in the theater with copies of the script, ready to begin. Joshua was on the stage both to direct and to play the part of Dracula.

Caroline watched as they began a trifle awkwardly. In the original story, there had been several more characters. Principal among them were Doctor Seward, the

father of Mina, the female lead, who was played by
Mercy; and Renfield, the unfortunate man who became
the creature of Dracula, obsessed with eating flies and
small rodents in the belief that their life force was necessary to his own survival. Alice had adapted the story
so that Seward could be cut entirely and Renfield only
referred to in passing.

Joshua understood and approved the reduction in
the number of characters. They only had so many cast
members, and an unfamiliar audience would find too
many people confusing to identify and remember. They
were left with only Van Helsing, the hero; Jonathan
Harker, who was in love with Mina and yet helpless to
save her; Mina; Lucy, who was Mina's friend and Dracula's first victim; and of course Dracula himself. Alice
had kept Whitby as the setting, for the most obvious of
reasons.

But even Caroline, who now knew the story better
than she had any real wish to, found the reading difficult to follow.

For the first reading there was no movement, although they were all reasonably familiar with their
lines. As it had been adapted, Harker was telling Mina,

his fiancée, about Renfield's travels to Transylvania, and how they had subsequently resulted in his present tragic condition and his confinement to the insane asylum. She was listening, appalled and sympathetic.

Caroline had not watched many rehearsals before. Were they always so wooden? James was reading Harker as if he were half-asleep. Was he saving his emotion for later, when there were actions to go with the words?

She turned to Alice sitting beside her and saw the tension in her face, the tightness where she was biting her lip. Did the words sound stilted to her also? Was she embarrassed by her adaptation now?

On the stage, Mercy responded. Her voice rose and fell with emotion that sounded totally artificial, ridiculous when coupled with the banal words she was saying.

Caroline began to feel more and more uncomfortable. She found herself fidgeting in her seat, unable to relax. She knew Joshua well enough to see his frustration in the way he moved and hear it in his voice when he told James to read his lines again.

At that, Mercy came to her husband's defense instantly.

37

"There's no point yet," she said sharply. "We'll only change it. We'll have to. Nobody speaks like this."

A flicker of anger crossed Joshua's face. Caroline could see the difficulty with which he controlled his tongue.

"Most dialogue sounds inappropriate if you read it like a railway timetable," he replied. "You're describing how a normal, decent man has changed into an insane, disgusting creature. We are supposed to be giving the audience a taste of the horror to come."

"All so we can be appalled when you appear," Vincent said drily. "Rather an old trick, don't you think?"

"Well there's not much point in Van Helsing's battle against Dracula if Dracula isn't appalling, is there?" Joshua shot back. "I won't ask you if you want to direct, because I know perfectly well that you do. But right now it's my responsibility, so concentrate on your own job."

Vincent shrugged elaborately and sighed.

"Move on to the next scene," Joshua instructed, his voice strained.

It was no better than the first. It was the initial appearance of Dracula, washing ashore in a violent storm that had wrecked his ship and sent his coffin to the shore. There was no possible way of showing all this on the stage, however, so it had to be recounted by one of the actors. Thus it had been built into Lydia's part as Lucy Westenra. But when she spoke the lines, she too sounded as if she barely believed what she was saying, though there was no sharp disdain in her voice as there had been in Mercy's.

"For heaven's sake, Lydia, act it!" Mercy said furiously. "How do we know if it works or not if you don't try?"

Lydia read it again, with more emotion, and even Caroline had to admit it sounded better. She glanced at Alice Netheridge and saw some of the embarrassment slip away from her expression.

The addition of Dracula's presence improved the drama considerably. The next couple of scenes were quite good. Until Van Helsing made his appearance.

"I don't think that's strong enough," Vincent commented. "He sounds as if he doesn't know what he's doing."

"He doesn't, yet," Joshua argued.

"Yes, he does," Vincent answered immediately. "He's

a genius and he's made a life study of vampires. He has to be powerful. After all, he destroys Dracula, the greatest vampire of all." He sat back a little in his chair, smiling.

"That's at the end," Joshua said with markedly less patience. "If we know all that about him at the beginning, then there is no story."

"Everybody knows the end anyway," Vincent argued. "Most people have either read the damn book or they've heard people talking about it."

Lydia rolled her eyes. "Vincent, you're an actor. Pretend you don't know, for heaven's sake, or we'll be here all day and go nowhere."

Vincent turned to her. "And where exactly is it that you think we are going, my dear?" he asked sarcastically.

"I have no idea," Lydia replied. "Any more than you have."

"I know I'm going quietly mad!" Mercy put in very distinctly.

"That won't be a very long journey," Caroline muttered. She was embarrassed when she realized Alice had heard her, until she saw the sudden smile on Alice's face.

"You said 'quietly,' " Joshua said, looking at Mercy. "Make that a promise, will you!"

She glared at him.

"Page thirty-nine, from the top," Joshua resumed. "Van Helsing to Harker."

"We really need another character here," Vincent pointed out. "It doesn't make sense like this. Harker's an idiot, completely ineffectual. Van Helsing would neither turn to him nor try to use him."

"He'll use what he has," Joshua snapped. "And at the moment he has no one else. Just read it; we'll make what amendments we need to later."

With elaborate patience Vincent did as he was told. It sounded ridiculous, just as he had intended it to.

*T*hey stopped at lunchtime, after having read through the entire hour-long script twice. The meal was awkward, everyone concentrating on their food, which again was plentiful and excellent. They spoke of trivial things: places they had traveled to at one time or another; books they had read; even the weather—although that last subject became less trivial as the wind increased and the snow that had been falling intermittently became heavier. It was clear from the almost horizontal angle at which it was streaming past the windows, and the thrashing of the trees beyond, that the storm was increasing in violence.

"It makes me think of those at sea," Eliza said unhappily, staring at the snow-coated glass. "I feel almost guilty to be so safe."

"I can't imagine why anyone wants to go to sea, especially in the winter," James observed.

"They probably don't." Vincent looked at him witheringly. "Poor devils have little choice. We can't all be actors."

"Indeed we can't," Joshua retorted. "Not even all those of us who try."

Lydia laughed, then winced as apparently someone kicked her under the table.

Douglas Paterson looked at her with quick appreciation, then straightened his face again and pretended he was not amused.

After the meal Joshua asked if he and Caroline might speak with Netheridge. He showed them into his study, a large, extremely comfortable room with leather-covered armchairs and a fire burning briskly in the hearth. A huge oak desk was littered with the implements of writing: pens, papers, two inkwells, a sand tray, sticks of sealing wax in various shades of red, matches and tapers, and several penknives and paper knives. The walls were lined with books, set by subject rather than size, as if they were there for use.

Caroline wondered why Joshua had asked her to accompany him.

"I can't help," she had said, meaning it as an apology, not an excuse.

"Yes, you can," he had told her with a tiny, twisted smile. "If you are there at least he will hesitate to lose his temper. So will I."

Unfortunately Douglas Paterson had also decided to join them. Since he was Alice's fiancé it was difficult to protest his presence.

Netheridge stood in front of the fire. Joshua accepted the invitation to be seated, even though it placed him at something of a disadvantage. Caroline sat opposite him, already feeling defensive, in spite of the agreeable smiles on everyone's faces. Douglas Paterson stood by the window, his back to the ever-increasing storm.

"Well, Mr. Fielding, how is it going?" Netheridge asked. "Do you have everything you require? Is there anything else we can provide for you?"

Caroline felt her throat tighten.

"We have read through the script a couple of times, to see how it works," Joshua replied. "That is customary for a new piece. What seems powerful on the page does not always translate to natural speech."

Netheridge grinned but he did not interrupt.

It was Paterson who spoke. "Is that the beginning of an excuse to say you cannot perform it?"

Joshua swung around in his chair to face him. "No, Mr. Paterson. If that was what I had meant to say, I would've been plainer about it. Mr. Netheridge deserves the truth, as far as we can discern it."

"The truth is that Alice has some rather impractical dreams, and it would be better if you didn't indulge her in them," Paterson said bluntly.

Caroline remembered Alice's face as she sat in the audience and listened to her words read on the stage: the awe, the excitement and hope, the embarrassment.

Joshua must make the play work, she decided, although she had no idea how.

"As I see it, it is a work that needs some attention. Possibly the order of certain scenes should be changed, so that we can give it the passion and drive it requires to move it from one medium to another," Joshua answered Paterson quietly but firmly.

"So are you saying you can do it?" Netheridge asked directly.

Joshua hesitated for only a second, but Netheridge saw it. His jaw hardened. "You doubt it!" he challenged him. "Be honest, man. Alice is my only child. She's willful, a dreamer, perhaps a little naïve, but I'll not have her made a fool of, by you or anyone else."

Paterson smiled, and the tightness in his shoulders eased a little. The shadow of a smile softened his face.

Netheridge looked at Joshua. "Are you prepared to work at this thing and make it right? Give me a straight answer, man."

Joshua took a deep breath, then let it out slowly. The clock on the mantelpiece over the fire moved two seconds. "Yes, I am."

"Right! Then what is it you want from me, Mr. Fielding? The party is set for Boxing Day, December twenty-sixth. Can't change that now," Netheridge said with a frown.

"I understand," Joshua replied. "We will have to work very hard. I will need the time with no interruption, other than for meals. Possibly I might request to eat in the theater room, if the cook would be kind enough to make something simple that can be served there. And perhaps Mrs. Netheridge would help my wife to find a few articles we might borrow as props to dress the stage?"

"Done," Netheridge said. "She'll be delighted. What else?"

"A good supply of paper and ink, more than I thought to bring with me. But most of all I would appreciate your assistance and even support in explaining to Miss Netheridge that all this is necessary if we are to make the play a success—"

"A success?" Paterson interrupted. "We're doing this as a Christmas gift for Alice, not to see it performed on the London stage. How on earth can you judge what is a success? If it pleases her that's all that matters. If it isn't going to work, then perhaps the most honest thing would be to tell her so now, to save her from being humiliated in front of her friends, and her family's friends, the people she will mix with long after you all have gone back to London, or wherever it is you come from." There were two spots of pink in his cheeks, and he had moved a step closer to them.

"I judge a success as something that entertains and enthralls an audience, Mr. Paterson," Joshua replied, his voice gathering emotion. "Something that suspends their disbelief for an hour, makes them laugh or cry, think more deeply about their lives or create new dreams in their minds. And a failure is something that bores them, has no integrity within itself, and does not for a moment take them somewhere they have never been before. If we are to capture and hold their imagination, then we must iron out the inconsistencies and improve on the strengths."

"Then why are you here instead of in the theater doing that?" Paterson asked, but his tone had lost its belligerence. He looked puzzled and anxious.

Caroline realized how far out of his depth he was. He did not know Alice as well as he had imagined he did, and realizing this frightened him.

"Because Alice needs your support," she answered for Joshua. "When you have created something as she has, there is so much of yourself in it that it becomes very hard to accept criticism. We all need praise, even when we are being shown how our work could be better. Why, everyone needs their loved ones to believe in them, to believe that they can succeed."

Douglas chewed his lip, glanced at Netheridge, then back not at Caroline but at Joshua. "If you change it into your work, what will be left of it that is hers?" There was uncertainty in his eyes, and still a degree of challenge.

Netheridge nodded. "Yes, Mr. Fielding. Douglas is right. If you change it as much as you say, whatever our friends think, she'll know it isn't hers. And she's honest, Alice is. She won't take the credit for your work."

Caroline looked at him still standing in front of the fire: a self-made man who owned more than all his ancestors put together, a father who loved his only child but did not believe in her talent. And perhaps he was right not to. Joshua had said the play, as it stood, was unperformable. What answer could Joshua give that would be even remotely honest?

"I'm not going to rewrite it for her," Joshua said softly. "I'm going to help her rewrite it herself. It will still be hers, but with a lot more knowledge of what stagecraft can do."

"Ah." Netheridge looked pleased. "Good," he said firmly. He turned to look at Paterson. "Told you, Douglas, got a good man here. Right you are, Mr. Fielding. You'll get everything you need from me. Thank you for your honesty."

Joshua rose to his feet and straightened his shoulders. Perhaps only Caroline, who knew him so well, could see the overwhelming relief in him.

When they were outside the door and it was closed again behind them, he turned to her with a shaky smile.

"Thank you," he said in a whisper.

She found herself suddenly absurdly emotional. Her own voice was husky when she spoke. "How are you going to do it?"

"I have no idea," he admitted. "But God help me, it's probably beyond anyone else's ability."

She moved a little closer to him and slipped her hand into his. She felt his fingers tighten, warm and strong against hers. She wanted to say something encouraging, full of certainty, but it would have been a lie. He would have known it, too, so she said nothing, just held on to him.

Caroline found Eliza delighted to help.

"I'm sure we can find all sorts of things," she said eagerly when Caroline asked her. "Just tell me what you need."

Caroline had already given it much thought. It was of great importance to her that she help Joshua, because their success mattered so much to the company, but also because she had a hunger to be a real part of the production, not merely an onlooker. Too often she had participated only in the role of Joshua's wife, permanently on the fringes of the emotion and the companionship.

"We need something to suggest Mina's home," she replied, and Eliza led the way to one of the box rooms where unused furniture was stored. "Chairs, perhaps? And a spare curtain, if you have one. It would suggest warmth, and height. I think that would be good. We can't have anything too heavy to move."

"Oh, yes, I see." Eliza opened the door to the box

room and led the way in. It was piled with all kinds of discarded chairs, tables, cupboards, cushions, curtains, a couple of cabin trunks, and two or three carved boxes. There were also a lot of jardinières, lamp brackets, and some large and colorful vases that would not have fitted anywhere in the parts of the house Caroline had seen.

Eliza saw her glance and give a tiny, rueful smile. "Choices I shouldn't have made," she said quietly.

"I like them," Caroline responded before she thought. The colors were warm and unusual.

"So do I," Eliza agreed, biting her lip. "But they don't fit in with my mother-in-law's taste." She did not offer any further explanation, but it was unnecessary. The stamp of that dominant personality was heavy in every room Caroline had seen so far.

"My mother-in-law's taste would have been good for a funeral parlor," she said sympathetically. "She made one quite naturally feel in mourning, whether they had lost anyone or not."

Eliza gave a little giggle, and then stifled it quickly, as if she felt she should not have been amused. She met Caroline's eyes in a glance full of humor. "Just right for a vampire story, then, don't you think?" she asked, then blushed.

Caroline found herself liking this side of Eliza immensely. "Perfect. But thank goodness she's safely in London with my younger daughter. If we could use that red vase with the flowers, it would give Mina's house something warm and bright, and the audience would remember it and know immediately where the characters are when they see it again." She looked around the room. "And we could use that dark curtain over there to suggest the crypt where Lucy is buried."

Eliza gasped, then burst into laughter, her hands flying to her mouth to quiet it.

"I'm sorry, is that not . . . acceptable?" Caroline felt awkward.

"No, no, it's perfect!" Eliza shook her head, dismissing the apology. "It was my mother-in-law's favorite. It took some five years to get it out of the withdrawing room. Charles and I still have disagreements over it." The laughter vanished.

"Would you rather not remind him of it?" Caroline asked. "Or maybe it would hurt his feelings, do you think? I mean, if we use it to suggest . . . a crypt?"

"It's perfect for a crypt," Eliza said decisively. "It looks like grave hangings anyway. Let's see what else we can find."

Caroline took a deep breath and followed Eliza through the piles of furniture. She hoped she was not going to cause this warm and vulnerable woman more heartache after they were gone.

❖

*J*oshua spent the afternoon attempting to rewrite at least some of the major outline of the play. It was a difficult work for an amateur to adapt, particularly because, like many novels, much of the tension came from the characters' inner thoughts, and was impossible to dramatize without creating scenes that did not exist in the original book. There were also a great many letters in it, impossible to translate into action.

Alice had done a good job of cutting the story to exclude these while still keeping the story intact, but there were many awkward transitions that needed quite a lot of work.

The weather became worse, the wind rising so that

the snow drifted, piling up into banks and leaving the lee side almost bare. Trees leaned dangerously, cracking under the weight. Some lighter branches broke.

Joshua barely noticed, but Caroline, staring out of the windows at the leaden sky late in the afternoon, realized that there was a great likelihood of them being snowed in, perhaps for several days. Though they had intended to be there until well after Christmas, she still found the notion curiously imprisoning.

It was almost evening and already dark when the doorbell rang. It was so startling, considering the weather, that Caroline stopped where she was at the bottom of the stairs, watching as the footman appeared to answer it. He pulled the door wide open, peering forward a little as if he expected to see no one on the step.

He was mistaken, and Caroline heard his gasp from twenty feet away. She, too, stared at the man who stood silhouetted against the snow-whirled darkness. He was of at least average height, his hair smooth and black, and the shoulders of his cloak were covered in pale, glistening snow. The lamplight from inside made his cheeks hollow, his eyes under the dark brows so black as to seem without pupils.

"Good evening," he said softly, but his voice carried with startling clarity, his diction perfect. "I apologize for disturbing you on such a night, but circumstances have forced me to seek your help. My name is Anton Ballin, and my carriage has broken down in a drift some way from here. I have left my coachman at the wheelwright's, but I must ask for shelter for myself."

The footman had no civilized alternative but to ask the man in.

"Please step inside, Mr. Ballin. Give me your cloak, sir, and warm yourself by the fire. I shall inform my master of your situation."

"You are most kind." Ballin came inside, as requested. As he crossed the light it was possible to see that he was carrying a small case, such as one might have for a single night's stay somewhere. He looked at Caroline.

"Madame," he inclined his head. He was striking in appearance. He would have been handsome were his cheekbones not a little too prominent and his skin unnaturally pale. "I regret imposing on your hospitality," he added with a very slight shrug. "The weather is far worse than I had anticipated."

She realized that he spoke with a very faint accent. It was more a precision of diction than any alteration of vowels.

She came forward. "I am Caroline Fielding, another guest, but I am sure Mrs. Netheridge will make you welcome for as long as this weather lasts." She offered her hand.

He took it gently. His hands were gloved, and freezing. He raised hers to his lips in the gesture of a kiss, then let it fall. He regarded her curiously. Even inside, under the lights of the hall, his eyes were as black as they had seemed in the shadows.

"Not another orphan of the storm, I hope?" he asked curiously.

"Not at all, Mr. Ballin. My husband and I are here as Mr. Netheridge's guests, with a very small company of actors, who are to perform a play for such friends and neighbors as are able to come, on Boxing Day."

"Fielding," he rolled the name on his tongue. "Mr. Joshua Fielding?"

She felt a distinct flush of pleasure, even of pride. "Yes. Do you know him?"

"Of course." He smiled. He had excellent teeth, even and very white. They gave his face a power she had not appreciated before because it was so dominated by his eyes. "A fine actor," he went on. "He has the ability to convey many moods, many types of people, and carry you with him while doing so. It is a rare gift. What are you to perform for these fortunate guests of Mr. Netheridge's?"

Now she was not so certain that telling him about the play had been a good idea, although if he were to be islanded here by the storm, as seemed inevitable, then he would know soon enough. Still, she felt self-conscious in answering.

"An adaptation of Bram Stoker's novel *Dracula*," she replied, wishing she could have said it was a few scenes from Shakespeare, or even a reading from Mr. Dickens's works.

"Really?" His voice held no incredulity, and certainly no suggestion of disappointment. "I did not know such a thing had been written. That interests me greatly."

She felt even more embarrassed, but there was no way to avoid answering him.

"Miss Netheridge has made an adaptation," she said with as little hesitation as she could. "The work is not complete yet, but we are progressing quite well." That was a massive overstatement. She knew that Joshua's afternoon had been frustrating. He had said he felt even less hopeful now than he had when he made his promises to Charles Netheridge, and by implication to Alice, the evening before.

She was saved from Ballin's reply by the appearance of Netheridge himself. He introduced himself to Ballin and made him welcome, offering him hospitality for as long as he should need it. This included a change of clothes from those he was wearing, which were obviously soaked through. Small pools of water glistened at Ballin's feet in the light from the chandeliers.

Caroline excused herself and went to tell Joshua of Ballin's arrival, and that he knew of Joshua and admired him.

❖

*B*allin joined them for dinner that night. His clothes had been dried and ironed by Netheridge's valet, and, if he was exhausted by his carriage ordeal, or his long walk in the snow, he showed no sign of it at all.

"I hope you were not hurt, Mr. Ballin?" Eliza inquired with concern.

"Not at all," Ballin answered gravely, and yet a certain amusement flickered in his eyes. "Except my dignity, perhaps. To be riding in comfort, if also in anxiety, at one moment, and then scrambling to arise out of a drift of snow the next, makes one appear more than a little ridiculous. However, there was no one to observe me, except my coachman, and he was in no better circumstances than I."

"Where is he?" Lydia asked, her soup spoon arrested halfway to her mouth.

"In the servants' quarters, I imagine," Mercy answered her. "Did you expect to see him in the dining room?"

Ballin looked at Mercy with interest, his eyes searching her delicate, pretty face as if trying to observe something deeper. "Actually, he is staying at the wheelwright's cottage, Mrs. Hobbs," he answered softly. "He bruised his legs rather badly, and I fear this walk would have been distressing for him."

"Where were you hoping to go?" James asked. However, there was no interest in his face; it was clear that he inquired only to be polite.

"To stay with friends on the farther side of Whitby," Ballin replied. "I regret that it will be some time before that is possible, judging from the weather. No doubt they will have deduced that I was obliged to seek hospitality elsewhere, and they will not be overly anxious."

"Sorry." Netheridge shook his head. "Can't get a message to anyone through this storm. The snow is several feet deep in some places on the road. And if this wind gets worse, we could have trees down."

Even as he spoke the howling outside increased. Mercy shivered, glancing toward the rich red curtains drawn across the windows.

" 'Listen to them, the children of the night'," Vincent quoted from the book, a line Alice had kept in the play.

Mercy gave another, even more convulsive shiver.

"You're not onstage now!" Lydia said sharply. "There are no bats or wolves out there. This is Yorkshire."

"Dracula came to Yorkshire," Mercy retorted instantly. "This is exactly where it all happened! Didn't you read the book, for heaven's sake?"

"I read it," Lydia said with a sigh. "I don't believe it. It's my job to believe it onstage, not at the dinner table."

"It's only the wind," James said to no one in particular. "The whole thing is an excellent horror story, but there's nothing real to be frightened of."

"Bravo," Vincent observed sarcastically. "That's perfectly in character. Harker didn't believe in vampires until Dracula had already taken Lucy and turned her into one."

Alice looked from one to the other of them. Her eyes were bright, and there was a slight flush on her cheeks, although it was impossible to tell if it was embarrassment or excitement. Perhaps a little of each.

Douglas Paterson regarded Alice's face with a distress that was close to exasperation. "Really—," he began.

Alice cut him off, looking toward Ballin. "Can we make you believe in vampires, just for a season?" she asked him.

"Alice!" Netheridge protested.

Ballin held up his long-fingered, powerful hand, moving with uncommon grace. "Please! It is a game we must all play, the suspension of disbelief, just for a while. Surely Christmas is the season in which to believe in miracles? The Son of God came to earth as a little child, helpless and dependent, just as we all are, even when we least think so. Does it not follow that the creatures of evil must also be knocking at the door, waiting for someone to allow them in?"

Mercy gave a little gasp.

Lydia rolled her eyes and glanced momentarily to Douglas before turning away again.

Alice was looking at Ballin intently, her expression keen with interest. "I've never heard anyone say something like that before," she said.

"Of course you haven't," Douglas responded. "It's nonsense."

"No, it isn't!" Caroline said quickly. "Haven't you seen Holman Hunt's painting of Christ, *The Light of the World*? He is standing at the door, but the handle is on the inside. If we do not open it ourselves, then he cannot come in, either. So maybe the final choice is always ours?"

"What about Halloween?" Mercy asked. "Aren't demons supposed to be abroad then? Can't they come in?"

"Fairy stories," Netheridge said briskly. "Anyway, demons are not the same thing as vampires. The Church might have a reasonable argument for the devil, but vampires are strictly Bram Stoker's imagination. Damned good story, but that's all."

"If you will forgive me saying so, Mr. Netheridge, vampires are a lot older than Mr. Stoker, vivid as his imagination is," Ballin said apologetically. "And they are not demons, which are essentially inhuman. Vampires are the 'undead,' who were once as human and mortal as you or I, but who have lost the blessings of death and the resurrection to eternal life. They are damned, in the sense that they can never move on."

"What the devil are you talking about?" Douglas demanded hotly. "You are speaking as if they were something more than the creation of some opportunistic writer with a desire to make a name and a fortune for himself by trading on the unhealthy fears of a part of society who have time on their hands, and overheated imaginations."

Netheridge gave him a heavily disapproving look. "Nonsense," he said tartly. "You are making far too much of it, Douglas. A little fear sharpens our appreciation for the very real safety and comfort that we have. Don't spoil the entertainment by sounding so self-righteous."

Douglas blushed deep red, but said nothing at all.

Eliza looked uncomfortable.

Joshua drew in his breath, but found that he had nothing to say, either.

It was Ballin who spoke. "You give Mr. Stoker too much credit, and too much blame, Mr. Paterson. His work is very fine. He has created a story that will no doubt entertain readers for decades to come, but he is far from the first to use the ancient figure of the vampire as a literary device. But perhaps Stoker's novel will be even more successful than John Polidori's *The Vampyre,* published eighty years ago. Polidori's vampire, Lord Ruthven, was actually based upon his illustrious patient, Lord Byron."

"I think we very safely presume there is no truth in that," Joshua put in.

Ballin smiled at him. "I agree, unequivocally. However, the history of the vampire, real or imagined, goes back even beyond the ancient Greek to the Hebrew, and the blood-drinking Lilith. The pedigree is not perhaps respectable, but it is certainly rooted in mankind's knowledge of good and evil, and what may become of a human soul when darkness is chosen over light."

Alice was fascinated. The color in her cheeks had heightened, and her eyes were brilliant.

"You know!" she whispered. "You understand. The evil is real." She turned to Joshua. "You are right, Mr. Fielding: We haven't caught the essence of the novel yet. I am so grateful to you for not humoring me and letting me go ahead with something so much less than good, let alone true. We must work harder. Perhaps Mr. Ballin will help us?"

Lydia looked at Alice, then at Douglas, and her face registered a gamut of emotions. Caroline thought she saw in it more compassion than anything else. Was it for Douglas, or for Alice? Or had she misread it altogether? Perhaps it was only fear, and a degree of embarrassment?

"If I may be of assistance, without intruding, then I would be honored," Ballin replied, first to Alice, then to Joshua.

Caroline watched Joshua, uncertain of what she read in his eyes. Was it amusement, desperation, or aware-

65

ness of his own inadequacy to mend a situation that had run away from him like a bolting horse?

"Have you any experience in stagecraft, Mr. Ballin?" he asked.

Ballin hesitated, for the first time Caroline had seen since he had stepped through the front door out of the storm and into the light and the warmth.

"I think I should leave that to you, Mr. Fielding." He bowed his black head very slightly. "I can speak only of the legend of the vampire, and what it says of mankind."

"Legend is just what it is," Netheridge agreed. "Like all that Greek nonsense about gods and goddesses always squabbling with each other, and changing shape into animals, and whatever."

"Ah," Ballin sighed. "Metamorphosis. What a wonderful idea: to change completely, at will, into something else. Such an easy dream to understand."

"Not if it's wolves and bats." Lydia shuddered. "Why would anyone want to turn into such a thing?"

"To escape, of course," Ballin told her. "It is always to escape. Bats can fly, can steer themselves without sight, moving through the darkness at will."

Mercy gave a cry, almost a strangled scream.

"Stop playing to the gallery," Lydia muttered. She said it under her breath, but Caroline heard her quite clearly. She wondered who else had. James looked pale. Joshua was exasperated.

The evening was clearly going to be a very long one.

$\mathcal{I}$t did not end as Caroline expected, although looking back on it, perhaps she should have. She was standing at the top of the stairs speaking to Eliza about further pieces for the stage that they might use when a nerve-jangling scream ripped through the silence, instantly followed by another, and then silence.

A door flew open along the landing and James burst out, his hair wild, his shirt half-undone. He stared at Caroline and Eliza, then swiveled around to face the opposite direction.

Vincent opened one of the other doors and put his head out. "What the devil's going on?" he demanded.

"Mercy!" James all but choked.

For a cold instant Caroline thought he had been attacked, then she realized it was not a plea, but his wife's name.

Joshua was coming up the stairs from the hall. He turned on the step and started down again, increasing his pace to a run as he reached the bottom.

Eliza was ashen. "What is it? What's happened?"

Vincent came out onto the landing and closed his bedroom door.

James rushed past Eliza and Caroline and ran down the stairs, all but falling in his haste to take them two at a time, grasping on to the rail close to the bottom to steady himself. He followed Joshua into the passage that led to the stage.

Caroline started after them, Eliza behind her.

There were no more screams, only a thick silence, almost smothering the sound of their footsteps. Caroline could feel her heart beating and she knew she was clumsy, afraid of slipping on the stairs, afraid of being too slow, too late for whatever terrible thing had happened. What were they going to find? Blood? Someone dead? Of course not. That was ridiculous. A maid had tripped and fallen, at the worst. Perhaps a broken ankle.

She was hampered by her skirts. Joshua was well ahead of her. She could hear James still shouting for Mercy.

She bumped into a large Chinese vase filled with ornamental bamboo and set it rocking. She stopped to replace it upright, and Eliza caught up with her.

"Never mind that!" she said breathlessly. "I always hated it anyway. Come on!" She shoved the whole thing out of her way and it crashed to the floor.

Caroline hesitated, then went after her.

They swung around the last corner before the theater to find Joshua and James facing Mercy. She was leaning against the wall, gasping for breath, her face flushed scarlet.

Mr. Ballin was standing some seven or eight feet away from her, perfectly composed, his hands at his sides.

"You have a superb theater, Mrs. Netheridge," Ballin said frankly.

They all looked toward Eliza, who flushed at the attention.

"Even the sound is flawless. It was designed by someone with the most excellent taste and technical knowledge. I came to look at it, and I regret that Mrs. Hobbs did not expect to find anyone else here. Quite understandably, I startled her. I am so sorry."

Joshua swore under his breath with a couple of words Caroline had not heard him use before. She would not have heard them at all had she not been standing close enough to almost touch him.

He steadied himself quickly. "You have no need to apologize, Mr. Ballin. I am sure you intended no harm. Mrs. Hobbs's imagination seems to have gotten the better of her." He looked at Mercy without trying to conceal his impatience. "For goodness sake, Mercy, go to bed and get some sleep. We all need it."

"Are you sure you are quite all right, Mrs. Hobbs?" Eliza asked anxiously.

James moved closer to Mercy, then glared at Ballin. "Of course she isn't all right! He comes creeping around here, uninvited, and frightens her half to death. How could she possibly be all right?"

Vincent spread his arms wide. "Perfect," he said sarcastically. "The black-cloaked stranger comes out of the storm, no doubt washed ashore in his coffin, and then stalks young women in the vast heart of this elaborate house with its stained-glass windows and private theater. I couldn't have designed it better myself. For God's sake, stop being such a damned actress, Mercy. Be a human being for half an hour."

Lydia, who was standing next to Caroline, started to laugh, and choked it off only with difficulty.

Alice appeared, breathless. "Is anyone hurt?" she asked anxiously.

"No, of course not," Vincent snapped. "Mercy met Mr. Ballin around a corner and imagined she met a vampire so she screamed like a banshee, in order that no one in the entire house, and probably half of Whitby, would miss her moment of high drama. Go to bed and don't worry about it. It's a rehearsal." He stalked away from the group and disappeared around the corner back to the main hallway.

Mercy started to tremble.

Eliza went to her. "Please let us take you back to the withdrawing room. Perhaps a hot cocoa would warm you. You have had a terrible shock."

"So must poor Mr. Ballin," Caroline said. "If he was walking along the corridor quietly and someone came out of the shadows screaming at him at the top of her

71

lungs, it's lucky he didn't have an apoplexy. Mr. Ballin, I'm extremely sorry we are all behaving like mad people. We have been rehearsing a play of considerable horror, and we are all worried that we will not be able to do the subject justice. We are tired and rather highly strung. I hope you will be quite all right. Perhaps you should have a hot cocoa as well. It will settle your nerves after what must have been a terrible shock for you."

"If you wander uninvited around other people's houses at night, you must expect to cause terror and distress," James said angrily.

Joshua clenched his teeth. "He is not uninvited, James. He offered to help us improve the script and we accepted . . ."

"*You* accepted!" James snapped back.

"I did, and so did Miss Netheridge. It is her play, and I am directing it. And Mr. Ballin is a guest here." He turned to Ballin. "I hope you will sleep well, and still feel like giving us whatever assistance you can in the morning."

Ballin bowed. "Of course. Good night." He walked away slowly, elegantly, clearly conscious of everyone watching him.

Caroline let out a sigh of relief and leaned closer to Joshua. His arm tightened around her.

❦

*I*n the morning they were all considerably subdued. It was still snowing and, although no one said so, it was apparent that they were effectively imprisoned in the house. The drifts were deep. No vehicle could make its way through them—and a man on foot might easily slip and fall, and the snow would bury him. One of the footmen had been as far as the bend of the road, and reported that there were several trees down. They could not reasonably expect to be able to get a even a dog cart past for a couple of days, even if the weather improved within hours—and it showed no signs of improving. The sky was leaden, and every so often there were fresh squalls of snow.

"Is there any point in rehearsing?" Mercy asked Joshua when she found him walking toward the theater with Caroline. "You can't imagine that anyone is going to come to an amateur play in this weather!" She ignored Caroline.

"Have you a better idea how we should spend our time until we know whether we are to perform or not?" Joshua asked her.

"Perform for whom? The kitchen staff?"

"If we can entertain the kitchen staff it would be a good indication that we had made a passable drama out of it," he said. "But Christmas is still half a week away. A rise in temperature and a day's rain, and the roads will be open again. What else do you want to do?"

"Not play Mina in this damned awful play!"

"And not play on the London stage in the spring, either, I presume?"

"All right! I'll do Mina! In fact, get that horrible man to play Dracula and we'll scare the wits out of half the neighborhood," she retorted, increasing her stride and moving ahead of him. She barged past Caroline as if she was nothing more than a curtain on the wall.

The rehearsal began quite well. They started at the scene just after Mina has been attacked once already and Van Helsing discovers the puncture marks of the vampire's teeth on her throat.

Mercy was suitably wan and exhausted. Caroline hated to admit it, even to herself, but she did the scene rather well. Even James, Douglas, Lydia, and Alice, all sitting in the audience, did not feel inclined to interrupt. Only Joshua seemed weary of it, as if something still did not satisfy him. Caroline did not understand what it was. Once, she looked at Mr. Ballin, and saw for an instant the same weary expression echoed in his face.

At the end of the scene they stopped, waiting for instructions as to the next place to work on.

"That was excellent," James said enthusiastically. "We are beginning to catch the mood of it."

"She's still terrified from last night, aren't you!" Lydia challenged, looking at Mercy with amusement. "If you had met the real Dracula, you would have died of fright. Not much use to anyone then, even him."

Ballin turned toward her.

"I think perhaps you miss the point, Miss Rye, that Dracula is repellent only when one sees his soul. In human form he is greatly attractive, especially to women."

"He's evil!" Douglas said sharply. "We can all see that. That is why it horrifies us. That is the point, surely?"

"No, Mr. Paterson." Ballin spoke gently, caressing the words. "The very power of evil is that it is not recognizable to us most of the time. It is not repellent at all. It does not attack, it seduces."

Caroline felt a sudden chill, as if a cold hand had touched her.

Douglas's mouth curled with disgust, and, for an instant, with something that looked like fear. "It's a fairy story, Mr. Ballin," he said gratingly. "An entertainment for Christmas, one I think is in very poor taste. But if we must have it, then let us at least be honest about it. The whole idea of vampires is disgusting. If we make that clear, then at least we will have achieved something."

"We will have lied." Ballin smiled. "Do we not all feed upon each other, at times, in some fashion?"

Lydia laughed and gave a brief applause. "You're wonderful, Mr. Ballin. You are giving us exactly the frisson of genuine fear we need to make this play come alive." She shot a look at Douglas, her eyes bright and gentle. "And you play to him perfectly. Did you arrange it?"

Douglas was clearly nonplussed, but he enjoyed the

compliment. After a moment's hesitation he decided to make the best of it and smiled slowly, neither confirming nor denying.

Alice was startled. She saw Douglas's gratitude to Lydia, and even a spark of admiration in his face. But what surprised her most was that she felt no jealousy at all.

Watching them all, Caroline was also surprised. Had she been Alice, she would have wanted to be the one to charm Douglas, and she would've resented another young and very pretty woman who had done it instead.

But Alice was clearly thinking only of the play. She turned to Ballin. "I haven't caught that essence of evil yet, have I?" she asked. "I wanted Dracula to fascinate the audience and make them afraid, but the whole point of the story is that he fascinates Lucy and Mina as well, in spite of their being good people. It's the potential weakness in all of us that is the really frightening thing."

"You have to invite the vampire into your house or he cannot enter," Ballin added. "That is the heart of it. Perhaps you might make the point a little more forcefully. The way it is now, the audience may miss its importance."

"Yes. Yes I will! Mr. Fielding is so much more correct than I realized, even yesterday. We have a lot of work to do."

Douglas looked pained. "It's only a play for the neighbors, Alice."

A shadow of annoyance crossed Alice's face. "I want to do the best I can for the play's own sake," she said a little angrily, as if he should have known her well enough to know that much.

"You were upset yesterday by all the work that needed to be done. You were nearly in tears," he pointed out.

She stood up, her cheeks flushed with embarrassment that he should have made her humiliation so public. "Well, I'm not now! I'm grateful. You may not care whether I succeed or not, but I care. I want to do the best I can. I want to capture the power and the meaning of the book as well as the more superficial horror. I'm sorry you think I'm not worth that, and that I can't do it. But perhaps it's as well I know that of you now." She walked stiffly past Douglas and Lydia and stopped at the foot of the stage, a couple of yards from where Joshua was standing with the script in his hand.

"I shall come back in a few moments," she told him. "I'm not walking out. I just need to think a little."

Joshua nodded and watched her leave. Then he looked at Ballin, his face registering both curiosity and respect. Caroline imagined that she saw a moment of bright, almost luminous understanding between them.

Douglas looked wretched. Lydia put her hand on his arm, very gently.

"Don't worry so much," she whispered to him. "She's nervous because she is trying to do something very difficult, and she wants to do it well. Wouldn't you, especially when you have everybody you care about looking at you? I would."

He looked at her intensely for several seconds. "Do you love acting?" he asked impulsively. "I mean . . . I mean, really love it? So you would be wretched if you couldn't?"

She lowered her eyes, then looked up at him with a sweet smile. "No, not at all. It's quite fun, and I like the friendship we have, almost like a family, but I'd still rather have a real family, a husband and children. I think most women would, perhaps not all . . ." She left the idea unfinished, as if it were too indelicate to complete.

He sighed and leaned back in his seat.

Caroline heard Eliza Netheridge breathe in sharply and turned to meet her eyes, feeling as if she knew her thoughts. She had had three daughters herself. Sarah, her eldest, had died some time ago, in circumstances that still touched her with horror. Charlotte, the second and by far the most awkward, had met the man she would eventually marry because of the manner of Sarah's death. Caroline had almost despaired of Charlotte's happiness, and yet in some ways Charlotte had enriched all their lives through her choice of husband in a way that no one else in the family had. Emily, the youngest, had married brilliantly the first time, then had been widowed, and was now happily married again. But Caroline knew exactly what Eliza was suffering. She smiled at her now.

"I wouldn't bother saying anything to her, if I were you," she said very quietly, so there was no chance of anyone else overhearing her. "Just now, it would only make it worse. I have a daughter whose nature is not unlike Alice's. She is about as biddable as a domestic cat. I don't know if you have ever tried to make a cat do anything it didn't wish to?"

Eliza smiled in spite of herself. "Quite pointless," she replied. "But I'm still fond of them, and they are both affectionate and very useful in the house."

"So are willful daughters, when they are good at heart." Caroline nodded.

Eliza sighed. "Alice is good, but she will lose that young man if she is not kinder to him. I'm sorry if she is a friend of yours, but that young Miss Rye has her eyes on Douglas—I don't know with what intent, to win him, or merely for the fun of playing, like a cat with a mouse, to continue your domestic likeness."

"From what I know of her, quite possibly to win him." Caroline surprised herself by the sincerity of her answer. She realized as she spoke how many times she had seen Lydia a little apart from the others, in mood if not in physical presence. The stage, and even the admiration and love of the audience, did not satisfy some far greater need in her. And quite possibly she wanted what Alice had more than Alice wanted it herself.

"Do you really think so?" Eliza asked. "And then what will Alice do?"

Caroline smiled, but there was an edge of apprehension in it. "Judging from what I have seen of her so far, whatever she wants to. And if the cost is high, she will have the courage to meet it."

"Oh, dear," Eliza said, biting her lip. "I was afraid that was what you were going to say."

*H*alf an hour later they were back rehearsing again. This time Caroline was taking notes for the lighting that would be required, as well as any further props that could be used to suggest a scene. They had bright limelights with them, and Joshua had shown her the equipment, and how to use it. It was a strange contraption with little taps to turn on the hydrogen and oxygen, and a screw for rotating and raising the calcium oxide. Just at the moment, all she wanted to do was make decisions about where in the script the lights needed to be focused, or changed.

Joshua and Alice had done some further rewriting,

and they began with a scene from earlier in the play. They had cut out Jonathan Harker's account of Renfield's travels in Transylvania, and given the speech referring to Renfield's circumstances to Van Helsing instead. With the other character cuts, the changes worked far more smoothly than the earlier version had.

Vincent was reading from the new script. Even though he described the reduction to insanity of a previously decent man, it seemed to Caroline to be without either honor or pity. She found her attention wandering, and was very much afraid that the audience's would also. Was Alice's writing really so poor?

She looked at Joshua's face and saw his frustration. Alice was standing just below the stage; her pale face and tight jaw betrayed that she also knew it was not working.

Ballin stood up.

Vincent stopped reading at once and glared at him. "Does your superior knowledge of vampires, or of good and evil, suggest how this could be better written?" he asked sarcastically.

"Not at all. But I have a suggestion about how it could be differently played," Ballin replied mildly.

83

"Though it would alter the character of Van Helsing somewhat."

Vincent spread his arms wide. "By all means. After all, what does Bram Stoker know about it? Or about anything?"

"We can't avail ourselves of his knowledge," Ballin replied. "At least not before Christmas, and we need a remedy rather sooner than that."

"In what way would it alter Van Helsing, Mr. Ballin?" Alice asked, cutting across Vincent.

Ballin moved toward the steps up to the stage. The lights shone on his coal-black hair and his unnaturally pale face with its powerful features.

"By giving him a little lightness," he replied, glancing at her, then at Joshua. "It is possible to be very serious about fighting evil without taking yourself so . . . pompously. Allow him a sense of humor, some eccentricity or talent other than his obsession with vampires."

"That's the whole point of him." Vincent was really angry now. "If you can't see that, then you have missed the essence of the character."

"That he has but one dimension?" Ballin concluded.

"Do you you truly believe so?" Again he looked at Alice. "I do not."

Vincent opened his mouth to retaliate, then decided against it. He abruptly threw the script down on the floor, leaving its pages scattered.

Joshua was pale, the lines around his mouth deep-etched. He looked so weary that Caroline longed to help him, but could think of no way at all to do so.

Ballin climbed up the steps onto the stage, picked up the fallen script, and found the place where Van Helsing described Renfield.

"May I?" he asked.

Alice nodded.

"If you wish," Joshua conceded.

Ballin began, using exactly the same words as Vincent had, but in a totally different voice. He was not Van Helsing using language to tell the audience how Renfield had caught flies and eaten them, or pulled the heads off rats to drink their blood: He was Renfield doing it in front of them. He buzzed, mimicking the flies. His hand moved so fast it was barely visible, as if he had caught the insect on the wing. The buzzing ceased. He put it to his mouth and crunched his teeth.

In the audience Lydia gasped and stifled a cry. Eliza Netheridge groaned. Mercy put her hand over her own mouth as if to prevent anything from entering it.

Ballin went on. He described a rat, clicking his fingernails on one another like rat feet on the floor. He wrinkled his nose, sniffing. He pounced on an imaginary rat, squeaking as the creature might, and made a movement as if tearing off its head.

Caroline felt her stomach clench and was glad she had not just eaten her luncheon. In her mind's eye she could clearly see the miserable Renfield, reduced to an insane caricature of the man he had been, so in thrall to the vampire that he imagined he could survive only by such means.

Ballin handed the script back to Joshua and straightened his back. The obscene pleasure left his face.

"There is nothing wrong with Miss Netheridge's words," he said quietly. "Although perhaps fewer of them are needed, if the actor portrays Renfield himself rather than Van Helsing telling us about him. Why should Van Helsing not be a man of imagination and empathy, even if it is for such a poor wretch as Renfield? That would enable the audience to see for themselves the man's decline as Dracula's ascendancy over him strengthens. It must be emotionally more powerful. And perhaps it also explains Van Helsing's greater ability to understand the vampire itself: an empathetic imagination, no?" He made it half a question, but the answer was obvious.

Joshua was smiling. He took the script back and made a brief note in the margin. "You're quite right, Mr. Ballin," he said graciously. "We can create a far more powerful image with imitation rather than mere description, and in doing so, cut out a page or so of words. And we can use the same device later on, to show the cause of his decline. Thank you."

Ballin bowed. "It is my privilege to take part in your work, even if by so small a contribution."

"It's not small," Joshua replied. "It is always difficult to reduce a cast drastically, and this helps us to conjure for the audience the characters we can't afford to play, but also cannot cut entirely."

They read on through Lucy's death scene. The man she loved was one of the many characters who had been cut out, and without him the scene lacked emotion, witnessed and felt only by Harker and Van Helsing. It appeared as if a stranger had died rather than somebody loved and cherished; there was nothing moving about it.

"We can dim most of the stage here?" Joshua said, frowning. "Perhaps create more deliberate shadows?"

Alice was not happy with the idea. "But at this point, it seems Lucy has gone peacefully, to escape the pain she had," she said. "We don't know yet what has really happened to her. Wouldn't dimming the stage to darkness be too much of a hint at what's to come?" Then she blushed at her boldness in challenging him.

"For heaven's sake," Douglas said irritably. "Nobody's going to be so involved that it'll matter! It's a story, a piece of make-believe to entertain. I'm sorry, Alice, but it just doesn't matter."

She ignored him entirely, as if he had not spoken at all. But the pallor of her face and the muscles of her neck, which showed rigid above her lace collar, gave away the fact that she had heard him.

"I don't think we should create more shadows," Alice said to Joshua, as if they were the only two present. "I think we should keep Mina here. After all, she is one of the strongest and most sympathetic characters, and she and Lucy were friends all their lives. Mina's grief can be ours. It wouldn't be difficult to write her in. I can do it this evening."

Joshua hesitated only a moment. "Good. We don't need much in the way of words, just the sight of her face. Give it to Mercy when you've finished." He turned to Vincent, who was standing at the back of the stage looking elaborately bored.

"Let's run the bit where Lucy attacks the children. That needs more work. It's still awkward. We'll go through the scene in the script, and also the part where the stake is put through Lucy's body in the coffin. James, we'll have to see most of the horror of that moment in your face."

They obeyed. Caroline watched and took notes until a late luncheon was served, then again all afternoon. They could not resolve all the slow patches, or the technical difficulties, but they continued into the search for Dracula after the destruction of Lucy's vampire form in the coffin. As Joshua had suggested, they put another excellent piece of mimicry into Van Helsing's speech recounting Renfield's death and final release from his terrible state; even in his very last moments, as his body contorted, Renfield could not completely forget his lust for the life force in the flies and rats, so tight was the vampire's control over him.

They began to work on the first part of the play, where Dracula attacks Mina, establishing the bond with her that would ultimately bring about his own destruction.

"It's coming," Joshua said wearily, his voice cracking a little. It was nearly six o'clock in the evening and they were all exhausted. The snow was still streaming past the windows in the darkness, glistening briefly in the reflected light before the curtains were pulled closed.

He repeated the same belief again to Caroline when they were at last alone in their bedroom. The fire burned hot in the hearth, the guard set in front of it so no coals could fall out and set light to the carpet. It was warm, silent but for the rushing of the wind outside, and filled with a rare kind of comfort, as if they were uniquely safe.

"Is it truly?" she asked him. She sat on the bed brushing her hair, finding the rhythm of the movement soothing.

He smiled. "Yes. Alice is really quite good, you know. She's perceptive and she learns quickly."

"Mr. Ballin was brilliant." She watched his face to read whether he minded or not. She saw only admiration.

"It makes me wonder if he is an actor himself," he agreed. "Or even a playwright. I didn't think of having Van Helsing virtually play Renfield, but as soon as he showed us, it seemed so obvious."

"Will Vincent do it?" she asked with sudden anxiety. "What if his vanity prevents him from taking the advice?"

Joshua smiled widely, almost a grin. "You don't understand him yet, do you? He'll do it, believe me, and take credit for the idea. It's far too clever, too good a showcase for his talents for him to turn it aside. I won't have to persuade him, which is what you are afraid of."

"Am I so easy to read?" she demanded, putting the brush down on the bed and letting her hair fall loose around her.

He looked at it with obvious pleasure. "Yes, a lot of the time," he answered. "But only because I care enough to watch you."

She smiled back at him, feeling more than the warmth of the room inside her, a safety deeper than the stone walls of this huge house on its hilltop defying the storm.

*I*n the morning the wind had subsided but the snow was conspicuously deeper. Although the sky was clear overhead, there were dark clouds shadowing the land to the north and far out over the sea. No one bothered to say that there was worse to come: It was obvious to anyone who looked.

"We'll spend today running it through from beginning to end," Joshua announced after breakfast.

"The whole play is only an hour long!" Vincent said, already short-tempered. "For God's sake, why would the run-through take all day?"

"It will with your additions," James snapped. "There won't be a fly left in Whitby by the time you get around to Renfield's death."

"There aren't any actual flies, you fool!" Vincent shot

back at him. "It's imagination. That's what acting is about."

"Then we'll all try to imagine that you're making a good job of it," James said. He was not going to be beaten easily. "At least until Mr. Ballin comes back again and shows you how to do it better."

"A pity he hasn't shown you yet!" Vincent retorted.

"No doubt he will," Joshua cut in. "But until he does, let's see what we can do on our own. We'll start with thunder and lightning effects . . ."

Vincent stared around the room and then toward the windows. "Probably unnecessary," he observed.

"So was that remark," Joshua said tartly. "The coffin will be on the stage and dimly lit, and I will climb out of it. Then the lights will go out, and come on again to be moonlight. Caroline, can you manage that?"

"Yes," she said immediately. She had practiced with the limelight contraption and she felt more confident, though not quite as confident as she sounded. She too could act!

Joshua smiled. "Good. Lucy will be sitting on the seat or by the shore. I will attack her—"

"Are we going to go through that?" Lydia asked. "Please? We haven't done it yet."

"Yes, I suppose we'd better," Joshua agreed. "Then we see Lucy at home with Mina and Harker. She is ill. Harker sees the bite marks on her neck. She gets worse and Mina cares for her. Dim lights to see Dracula at the window. He comes in and bites her again. In the morning she is far worse."

"I thought Harker was supposed to be in Budapest?" James interrupted.

"In the book he is," Joshua answered. "But since we have written Arthur and Dr. Seward out of the play, we have to have him here. We've altered the storyline appropriately."

James shrugged.

"Van Helsing arrives and tells Harker about Renfield," Joshua went on.

"When do Mina and Harker get married?" James interrupted again. "It's supposed to happen in Budapest."

Joshua glanced at Alice.

"They'll have to be married before we begin," she answered. "I didn't think of that, but I can't see that it matters."

"Good." Joshua looked at his notes again. "Lucy is attacked again and gets worse. We don't need to see the attack—"

"Yes, we do." Lydia was the one to interrupt this time. "Otherwise it doesn't make sense."

"No, we don't," Joshua told her. "If we show Dracula attacking too often it loses impact. The audience can deduce what has happened. One really dramatic and powerful scene is better than two weaker ones."

"They aren't that powerful," Vincent pointed out. "You need to be far more sinister. At the moment you look like a lover coming up the garden ladder to elope. Or a burglar caught in the act!"

Alice was frowning. "There is something else important that we missed—"

"*You* missed," Lydia corrected her.

"I missed." Alice accepted the rebuke.

"What?" Joshua was puzzled.

"Mr. Ballin said that the vampire cannot come in unless he is invited. Someone has to invite him, and the audience needs to see that."

"Mr. Ballin says?" Vincent allowed his contempt to darken his voice. "Since when has he been in charge?"

Alice blinked, but she did not retreat. "The suggestion is a good one, Mr. Singer, and that is all that matters. It is an important point that evil cannot come in unless we invite it. It is our choice."

"But none of the characters had the faintest idea what he is, or that he's evil," Vincent argued. "Or did you miss that point?"

"Perhaps they should have known," she countered. "It is naïve to imagine anyone is so good that they are immune to evil. Or perhaps it isn't a lack of goodness, but a total lack of humility that makes one vulnerable?"

"Vincent wouldn't know anything about that," Mercy remarked. "Humility, I mean. He probably has no idea what you are talking about."

"Neither have you, my dear," Vincent said to Alice. "This is supposed to be drama, not a schoolgirl philosophy."

Joshua drew in his breath. Caroline knew it was to defend Alice, but she spoke for herself before he could say anything.

"I did not invent vampire lore, Mr. Singer. I am simply quoting what Bram Stoker wrote. Since it is his book, and it greatly adds to the power of the drama, I wish to keep it in." She looked for a moment at Joshua, to make sure he approved, then turned back to face Vincent.

Joshua was amused. He tried, and failed, to hide it.

"Then we will add it, even if it requires another scene," he agreed. "You are quite right. It makes moral sense, and it will be good for the audience to see it. Then we will do Lucy's death scene, as witnessed by Mina. We will dress her in white and keep the light on her to suggest that Lucy is still innocent in appearance and still beautiful."

Lydia smiled.

"Then we will move to the scene of Lucy attacking the children," Joshua continued. "We haven't got any real children so we'll have to have Alice create children's voices for us offstage—high-pitched and terrified." He looked at Alice. "You'll have to practice that. Then Lucy appears with blood on her mouth and face, and walks through the gravestones to return to her coffin."

"How are we going to get gravestones on the stage?" James asked.

Joshua looked at Caroline.

"Eliza and I have found some very good old cabin trunks," she replied. "They are solid and about the right size, stood up on end. We can easily cover them in paper and paint on them appropriately. We can get some stones and a little bit of earth from the kitchen staff."

"Very good," Joshua said with satisfaction.

"We may have to condense this next scene a bit for the sake of time; instead of finding the coffin empty multiple times, we'll just have her in it, serene and lovely. Then empty, to get the point across."

"It will be stronger if it is shorter," Alice agreed. "But we should see her smile a terrible smile."

"We will." Joshua did not even think to argue. "We'll see Lucy as a vampire quite clearly, and the struggle that Harker, Van Helsing, and Mina have to kill her. Then, with lights, we can make her seem to return to herself and finally be at peace in death. That is really the end of the middle act."

"Bravo," Vincent said sarcastically.

Joshua ignored him. "Then we move into the beginning of the climax, the search for Dracula. We start to see that Renfield's behavior reflects Dracula's being nearby." He looked at Vincent now. "Van Helsing will recount that, with the mimicry," he instructed. "Including Renfield's death, with appropriate sadness from Mina and Harker. We'll include his reference to rats and flies. I know that's a repeat of his previous references, but this time his manner will be different, and it should be a nice counterpoint."

No one interrupted, but looking around at them, Caroline saw that he had his troupe's complete attention. Even Douglas Paterson had nothing to say, as if at last, despite himself, he was drawn into the story.

"Then we have the series of scenes where Dracula appears and attacks Mina. The audience knows it, but Harker and Van Helsing don't . . ."

Eliza Netheridge was sitting next to Caroline. "This is getting rather exciting, isn't it? I begin to understand why Alice cares so much." She looked across at Alice, who was standing at the far side of the stage, her eyes on Joshua.

"Van Helsing realizes the awful truth of Mina's condition when he places the holy wafer on her forehead and she screams with pain. It leaves a red scar," Joshua went on. "They corner Dracula, but he escapes."

Eliza shuddered.

"Mina tells them that at sunrise and sunset Dracula loses much of his control over her." Joshua continued the narrative. "Van Helsing hypnotizes her and she says that when Dracula calls her—and he will—then she will have no choice but to go to him, wherever he is, and whatever it costs her." Joshua smiled. "At that point we should have the audience on the edge of their seats. Then we have the climax." He glanced at Caroline, then away again.

"This will call for some clear lighting to create the illusion of movement," he went on. "And then of a screaming wind and a snowstorm in the Carpathian Mountains. Our three remaining characters are huddling together as darkness falls, waiting for the coach that holds Dracula in his coffin, as he is returning to his native soil to regenerate his power. They have to drive a stake through his heart to destroy him forever, or else he will destroy them. We have to make certain that all the necessary information is given without slowing down the action or breaking the sense of doom and terror."

Vincent grinned. "Actually, it sounds quite good," he

said reluctantly. "It might even be passable, by the time Boxing Day comes. Let's just hope there is an audience."

"If there isn't, we'll put it on for the servants," Joshua retorted. "Now let's get to work."

❖

*F*or a time as they worked, the challenge of creating a story in which they could all believe overtook their personal differences. There was a spark of excitement in the air.

Caroline leaned forward in her seat as they put more energy and movement into their positions on the stage. It was beginning to come alive. She forgot she was sitting on a chair in a stranger's house in Whitby, working to make something good out of something poor. Bram Stoker's characters became people; the dark shadow of the vampire reached out and chilled them all.

Vincent was enthusiastic about Van Helsing's new and larger role. As Joshua had predicted to Caroline, he grasped at the chance to play Renfield as well. He did not do it exactly as Ballin had, but he did it slyly, at moments pathetically. In spite of her dislike of Vincent, Caroline was forced to be both fascinated and moved by his performance. Renfield became not a device to further the plot but a real person, revolting and pitiful. Vincent Singer was Van Helsing, and Van Helsing, in his portrayal, was Renfield. The magic was complete.

When they changed the scene, stopping for a few minutes to talk about movements, Caroline turned to Eliza sitting beside her. She saw the awe in Eliza's face, the naked emotion.

Aware of being looked at, Eliza colored a little and smiled apologetically. "I'm sorry, did you say something?"

"No. And please don't be sorry. You were caught up in it. So was I. It is the greatest compliment you can pay an actor," Caroline replied.

Eliza looked startled. "I suppose it is. You know, for a moment I believed it as if I were there. Do you suppose there really are people like poor Renfield?"

"I fear there are." Caroline shivered. "But I am quite sure that there are no actual vampires."

"Actual?" Eliza stared at her. "But such seductive

art is real, isn't it! People who prey on one another, even who live by feeding on each other in some emotional way."

"I think that is the whole point," Caroline agreed. "It would hardly frighten us if the danger were only imaginary. We jump at shadows the first time, and then we laugh at our own foolishness and feel silly, but happy that there was no substance to it. If at heart we know the evil is real, then the feeling is completely different."

Eliza looked at her with anxiety. "Should we be dealing with such ideas about real evil at Christmas? Isn't it . . . inappropriate?"

"But isn't the good real as well?" Caroline countered simply.

Eliza swallowed hard, her throat tightening.

"I used to believe the battle between good and evil was something of a fairy story," Caroline went on seriously. She remembered Sarah's death. She felt the horror again, as sharp as if it had been yesterday.

"Now as I get older and have seen more, I believe it is real. We need redeeming so desperately. We need hope because without it we have nothing. If there is a God, then mercy and renewal must be possible, even if we understand only a little of them, and nothing at all of how such redemption works. We get so much wrong, make so many rules, because it deludes us into thinking we have control of what goes on around us. We don't, and we shouldn't want to.

"For heaven's sake, we are so limited!" she added with sudden ferocity. "We need a force infinitely bigger and wiser than we are in our lives. But we cannot have good without also the possibility of evil, so if there are angels, then there must be devils as well. If we are even remotely honest with ourselves, we know that. So . . ." She looked at Eliza's face and wondered if she had already said too much. "So in a way devils and demons are good," she finished. "Because if we are reminded that there is evil, even supernatural manifestations of it, then we will believe in and love the good even more."

Eliza was smiling. She put out a hand very tentatively, resting it on Caroline's arm. "My dear, you are a remarkable woman. I could never have imagined that watching a group of actors working would have taught me something I so badly needed to know. Thank you so much." Then, as if embarrassed by her frankness, she stood up and excused herself to go and speak to the cook about dinner. "I fear we shall have to be a little more sparing with our rations than usual," she added, by way of explanation.

Caroline thought that the cook would have noticed for herself that the snow was impassable, but she only nodded agreement.

On the stage they were proceeding with some of the later scenes; Vincent Singer was elaborating on Van Helsing's intellectual brilliance.

Caroline watched Joshua, and knew he did not like it. She agreed with him. Glancing at the faces of those who were watching, she could see that they were bored as well.

Mr. Ballin came in silently, bowing briefly to Caroline, and to Alice and Lydia, who were both sitting in the audience. Douglas ignored him, but Ballin did not seem to see anything untoward about Douglas's manner.

Caroline watched Joshua standing on the stage holding the script in his hand. He had asked Vincent to make more of Van Helsing's character, his humanity. But now that Vincent was trying to add depth, the character was not coming alive. But Joshua needed a solution before he risked interrupting Vincent's monologue. They could not afford the time or the emotional energy for tantrums, and Singer was crucial to the drama.

Vincent continued on, making Van Helsing seem a smug genius, and Alice sat wincing, looking more and more perplexed.

Finally Joshua interrupted. "Vincent, this doesn't work. It's taking up too much time, and half of it is irrelevant."

Vincent stared at him. "I thought you wanted Van Helsing to be more of a character? As Miss Netheridge has written him, he's flat, and even tedious. And more important, he's no match for Dracula. How many times have you told us that a hero has no validity if the villain has no menace and no power? Surely the reverse must also be true?"

"Yes, it is," Joshua conceded. "But telling us he is clever doesn't convince—"

"What do you want?" Vincent demanded. "I'm an actor, not a conjurer or a contortionist. You want the music halls for tricksters!"

"It's too many words," Joshua said flatly. "We stop listening."

Ballin walked over toward the stage. "No one cares for a man who boasts of his achievements," he said quietly but very clearly. "And we have to like Van Helsing, even if we do not always understand or approve of what he does until after he has done it. Then we see the necessity."

Vincent started to speak, and Joshua held up a hand to silence him.

"What do you suggest?" he asked Ballin.

"Let him solve a problem, a difficulty of some sort," Ballin replied. "Then his quick thinking, his knowledge and improvisation will be evident, and useful. He will not need to boast; in fact, he will not need to speak at all."

"Oh, bravo!" Vincent applauded. "Such as what? I'm sure you must be overburdened with examples."

Ballin thought for a moment. "Well, the use of light and mirrors is always interesting," he replied. "Especially with vampires, who traditionally have no reflection."

"We already know who the vampire is." Vincent dismissed the suggestion with a degree of contempt.

Ballin ignored him. "Van Helsing could arrange mirrors that reflect from each other, magnifying light and sending it around corners. Vampires are creatures of the shadows. At least to begin with, Dracula does not wish to be exposed."

"Brilliant," Vincent said sarcastically. "Then we lose all the tension because we defeat the poor devil right at the beginning. So how is it then that we let anyone fall victim to him? Are we all just blazingly incompetent?"

Ballin was unperturbed. "We do not succeed because Lucy is bitten outside, in the night, before Dracula ever enters the house. Van Helsing doesn't know that. Nor, at the beginning, does he know the depth of the vampire's seduction. Lucy moves the mirrors, just as later Mina will lie, and even become violent, when Dracula calls her."

Joshua was smiling slowly.

Ballin continued. "Later Van Helsing could suggest an alarm to warn them all if anyone enters Mina's room through the window. A chemical device, of magnesium dislodged by the movement of the window so that it lands in water. It would give off a brilliant white light, which could be seen by anyone watching the window from another part of the house."

"And they don't come running to the rescue be-cause . . . ?" Vincent asked, but his voice was now in-terested rather than dismissive.

Ballin smiled very slightly. "Because Mina has drugged their wine. That is already in the story. Again, clever as we are, we have underestimated the strength of the vampire's hold over our minds."

This time, Vincent agreed, but reluctantly.

"Good," Joshua said firmly. "Now there is the prob-lem of lighting the scene where we peer into Lucy's tomb in the crypt. I haven't worked out yet how we can do that so the audience can see. The sense of shock and dawning horror is crucial there."

"Any ideas for that?" Vincent asked Ballin.

"Do not show the audience," Ballin answered.

"Oh, superb!" Vincent jeered again. "What shall we do? Recite it to them in the rash of words you are so much against? I'm sure that will frighten them out of their wits! Very dramatic."

Ballin kept his patience. He smiled, as if amused at Vincent's contempt. "Most emotions are the more pow-erful for being shown through the characters we iden-tify with," he said calmly. "Open the tomb with a creak, a sigh of hinges, and let us see the horror dawn on the faces of Van Helsing and Mr. Harker, even Mina, whom we admire so much. Let us see her grief for her friend Lucy. Perhaps you need an additional scene earlier on so we may observe how fond they are of each other? We will know that something is terribly, hideously wrong, but for a space of seconds time will stand still and we will not know what it is. Our imaginations will fill it in with a score of different abominations. Then one of you may say that the tomb is empty." Ballin spread his hands in an elegant gesture, his pale fingers catching the light.

They went on discussing, adding to and taking out, and by the end of the afternoon they were exhausted. Caroline and Joshua went up to their room, Caroline grateful for an hour's respite from the subject before they all met again for dinner.

But when they were in the bedroom and the door closed, she could see that Joshua was still worried. He certainly would not rest as she had hoped.

"It's not working," he said bleakly, standing at the window and staring out at the light catching on the pale blur of snowflakes in the darkness beyond. "Not yet."

She bit back her impatience. The disappointment in his voice was enough to pull at her emotions, crushing the irritation she had felt mounting inside her.

"I thought Mr. Ballin's suggestions were very good," she said, knowing she risked making him feel as if he should have thought of them himself. Just now she believed the rescue was more important than its source.

He turned to face the room, the lines around his mouth deeply etched, his eyes pink-rimmed. "They are," he agreed. "But they are only cosmetic. There is still a lack of cutting edge to it. Dracula isn't . . . isn't terrifying. We can feel the horror, but not the evil."

She wanted to be helpful but nothing came to her mind that was honest, and he did not deserve to be patronized with false comfort. "I'm not certain if I know what evil is, onstage," she said unhappily.

He pushed his hands into his pockets. "Ballin is right: It will only become real to us, and to the audience, when we see the effects of such evil in others. I wish I could think how to show that."

"Who is Mr. Ballin, I wonder?" she asked curiously. "He seems to know a lot about vampires, and about acting. How can he? *Dracula* was only published this year."

"I've no idea who he is," he replied, walking toward the bed and lying down, hands behind his head. "I could sleep until tomorrow," he said. "Except that I can't afford to."

"Mina," Caroline said suddenly, with certainty.

"What about her?" Joshua was confused.

She turned toward him. "Jonathan Harker is a usual sort of hero, but he's . . . I don't know . . . a bit cardboard, terribly predictable. He isn't like any real person I know, because he has no faults, no vulnerabilities— unless being a crashing bore is a vulnerability? It isn't, is it?"

He smiled. "Not onstage. Bores don't feel hurt, they just drive everyone else to drink. What are you getting at?"

"We don't really care about Harker," she explained. "We know he's good, but we don't care. And Van Helsing is a 'know-it-all.' We need him to defeat Dracula, and we believe he's going to. In fact, I suppose we take it for granted. But Mina is good, really good—but vulnerable, too. She cares about other people. She's brave but she has enough sense to be frightened as well, and later on when the holy wafer burns her, we know that Dracula has finally gotten to her. She is the one we need to care about, to see slowly pulled further and further down into the darkness, despite everything. I would mind terribly if anything happened to her, anything that Van Helsing couldn't save her from."

He sat up. "Would you?"

"Yes. Yes I would."

He leaned forward and kissed her, gently and for a long time.

"Then we shall let them think Mina will not survive," he said at last. "Thank you!"

❖

$\mathcal{B}$allin attended the morning rehearsal the following day. Now he was quite open about his suggestions, and Alice was eager to adapt them. Douglas seemed less displeased, and Caroline noticed that when Lydia was not onstage playing the character of Lucy, they quite often stood together. They did so awkwardly at first, but then with increasing ease. They might have simply been commenting on the play and its progress— Caroline was not close enough to hear—but the unspoken communication between them told quite a different story. She had learned from Joshua the difference between text—the words on the page that actors spoke—and subtext—the emotional meaning that they conveyed and (if the acting was any good) that the audience understood. For Douglas and Lydia, the subtext was that they were increasingly drawn to each other. Alice either had not noticed, or else she had, and was not as disturbed by it.

Did Alice believe she could undo any damage as soon as Lydia left? Was she so confident of herself, or of Douglas's love for her? Or had it perhaps to do with her father's wealth and the opportunities that it would offer Douglas in the future? Was she really so shallow? So vain?

Caroline found herself hoping very much that the latter was not so. She liked Alice. She was highly individual, and perhaps she reminded Caroline rather a lot of her own daughter Charlotte, another young woman full of impractical dreams.

Or was it really that Alice reminded her of herself? After all, what kind of a woman with any sense would abandon a respectable and financially safe widowhood in order to marry a Jewish actor seventeen years her junior? Caroline shook her head and turned her attention back to the stage, where the drama was beginning to form a coherent whole. At last Joshua himself was acting, not merely reading his part and watching the situation and the details of others. The entry of Dracula made a world of difference.

Very carefully Caroline dimmed the lights, then brightened them slowly as the coffin lid opened, the creak of the wood pausing for just a moment before Joshua emerged.

She almost stopped breathing as he uncurled his body and stood up, his face wreathed in a terrible smile.

There was a gasp from Alice, sitting close in the front row, and Mercy gave a little shriek.

"Ah!" Ballin said with satisfaction. "But one small suggestion. May I show you? It might be simpler than trying to explain."

Joshua's jaw tightened, but he stepped aside. "Of course."

Caroline dimmed the lights and began again.

Ballin climbed into the coffin and lowered the lid. There was a moment's silence. Everyone was watching. Very slowly the lid rose again, perhaps two or three inches, then long, white fingers emerged, curling like talons, feeling around as if in search of something.

"Oh, God!" Mercy breathed, her own hands flying to her face.

The coffin lid continued to open very slowly. A full arm was visible. Then, still carefully, noiselessly, Ballin climbed out and stood up, his head peering from side to side.

There was no need for anyone to comment; the difference was too clear to require it.

Caroline found herself tense when they resumed, picking up as Dracula crept up on Lucy, sitting on a bench overlooking the sea. They went through the attack, but it lacked that vital knife edge of terror. After the power of Dracula's emergence, it was anticlimactic.

"The book says a bench, a 'park seat,'" Joshua said unhappily. "But it's awkward. It's just physically clumsy."

"You are right," Ballin agreed. He turned to Alice. "Have you any better ideas, Miss Netheridge? Something less . . . pedestrian? Certainly something less impossible to relax back against."

"Relax?" she said in astonishment. "She is attacked by a vampire just risen from the grave!"

"No, no, no!" Ballin shook his head. "She is seduced, Miss Netheridge. We have seen him walk from his coffin but she has not. We watch the horror, helpless to prevent it. That is your tension. Never forget it. We know he is something hideous, risen from the dead, but to her he is a lover, bewitching her, filling her dreams."

"Ugh!" Alice shuddered, but there was no denial in her face. On the contrary, her eyes were bright with a kind of luminous excitement.

From the back of the room, Douglas looked at her with a distress quickly mounting into anger.

"Perhaps it isn't the path above the cliff at all," she suggested, watching Ballin. "What if she has gone to the graveyard to pay her respects to her dead father, or mother?"

"A gravestone?" James said in disbelief. "You want

her seduced on a gravestone? Miss Netheridge, that is . . . vulgar, even blasphemous." His face showed his distaste very plainly.

Alice blushed, but she did not retreat. "It is her neck he bites, Mr. Hobbs. I was not imagining an overtly"— she swallowed—"sexual scene. I am surprised you were."

Now James blushed scarlet.

Ballin smiled. "An excellent idea, Miss Netheridge. I assume you had in mind one of the taller stones. If she were to lean back against it, all the symbolism would be perfect, the suggestion without the gross detail." He swung around to Joshua. "Do you not think so, too, Mr. Fielding?"

There was only an instant's conflict in Joshua's face, then the resolution. "Of course," he agreed. "It might be difficult to make something suitable. For now we can use one of the upended trunks."

It took ten minutes to find such a thing and prop it up, with weights at the bottom so it would stand. They replayed the scene, and suddenly it was transformed. The gravestone worked perfectly, allowing Joshua to raise his arms and spread his shielding black cloak.

The audience could imagine anything they wished. When he moved back, slowly, as if sated, Lydia leaned half-collapsed against its support.

From the audience Mercy gave almost involuntary applause. It was as if she was so wrapped up in their performance that, for a moment, her professional enthusiasm overrode her personal need to be in the limelight.

Dracula's first entry to the house, with Mina's invitation to him to come in, had to be done several times. It was mostly in order to place the lighting in exactly the right position so he stood first in dramatic shadow, and then emerged out of it, transforming from a figure of menace to one of increasing charm, even grace. The final time they ran the scene, even Mr. Netheridge could not help but be fascinated. He had come in quietly and was watching from the back.

"Aye," he said grudgingly. "It's gripping, I'll grant you that." He turned to Alice. "You've done well, girl. I begin to see what you're on about."

She smiled and said nothing, but the pleasure was bright in her face. She looked across at Ballin, and he gave a tiny nod of acknowledgment. It was so small that had she not been looking at him directly, Caroline would barely have seen it.

The scene with Van Helsing acting as Renfield worked superbly. Vincent was excellent. He would not have admitted it, but he copied almost exactly what Ballin had done, although his own sense of timing also asserted itself. The result was both chilling and pathetic, and very real.

By the time they came to Lucy's death scene, they were all caught up in the story. Even James, as Jonathan Harker, displayed a sensitivity Caroline had never seen in him before. Mercy's grief as Mina reduced the audience to a throat-aching silence, and Eliza, who had also returned to watch, quickly dabbed at her eyes to hide her tears.

They took a break only for luncheon: cold meat sandwiches, pickles, and hot apple pie with cream, all served in the theater.

"I think we should see more of Harker and less of Van Helsing in the tomb scene," Mercy said suddenly. She had just finished the last of her pie and was reaching for the excellent white wine that had been served with it. "It would improve the pace. Van Helsing is the intellect; Harker is the heart and the courage of the pursuit. Apart from Mina, of course."

"Of course," Lydia answered. "But actually the core of the scene is Lucy. She is the one who has become a vampire. And we still don't know what we are going to do about the children." She looked at Joshua, then turned to Ballin. "Perhaps Mr. Ballin, who seems to have been sent here by the storm to solve all our problems, will be able to answer that for us?"

"We are reduced to illusion," he said thoughtfully. "We have no way of physically representing a child. Alice could—" It was the first time he had used her given name.

"That's stupid!" Douglas cut across him at once. "She is nothing like a child; she couldn't play one. She's a full-grown woman, at least in appearance."

Ballin's face tightened with anger, whether for himself or for Alice it was impossible to tell. "She is also quite a passable actress, Mr. Paterson," he said very softly, very precisely. His voice was oddly cold, as if there was some threat in it. "We can make a dummy, something of pillows, with the appearance of arms and a head. I'm sure Mrs. Netheridge's maid can give us a dress that will do. The minds of the audience will create for them what they expect to see."

Joshua gave a sigh of relief.

Douglas snorted with what seemed to be contempt, although Caroline was certain that it was actually frustration.

"The master of delusion and deceit, aren't you!" Douglas spat the words.

It was Alice who sprang to Ballin's defense. "Stagecraft, Douglas. I'm sorry you don't know the difference. It is causing you to be unnecessarily rude to our guest."

"He is not our guest," Douglas insisted. "He is a stranger who landed on the doorstep out of the storm, melodramatically, asking for help, and he has been aping Dracula ever since."

"Don't be ridiculous!" Alice said angrily. "He told us what happened. His carriage overturned and broke a wheel in the snow. He won't be the only person stranded in this weather. What on earth would anyone do except invite him in, especially at Christmas? What would you have done? Tell him there is no room?"

"Invite the vampire into your house," Douglas answered, his own voice louder and more strident. "He told you himself: Evil can come in only if you invite it."

Alice paled a little. "No one can come in unless they are invited," she said, glaring at him. "Don't tell me we've done this so well you actually believe in this vampire stuff?" She tried to laugh, and failed. It came out as a gasp of breath, with no humor and no conviction.

"I believe in evil. And in stupidity," he said bitterly.

Her eyes raked him up and down. Her lip curled a little. "Don't we all?"

"Of course we do." Lydia moved closer to Douglas's side. "If we didn't before, we should now." She faced Alice. "You are fortunate to have the love of so fine a man, Miss Netheridge. I think he is something like Jonathan Harker, brave and modest, not knowing how to fight evil because he has none within himself, to be able to understand it."

Alice went even paler. She started to say something, then changed her mind and walked away.

"Perhaps you'd like to attack the children again after we've finished lunch?" Joshua suggested to Lydia with an edge of sarcasm that was breathtaking. "Just pretend you have the dummy in your arms. Leave it in the shadows. Drop it, if it seems right to you, and then come forward to Harker and Van Helsing."

Caroline put her hands over her face and pretended she was somewhere else, just to give herself time to regather her strength.

*T*he crypt scene and Lucy's final scene, as a vampire, went quite smoothly. They moved into the last act: the hunt for Dracula. Vincent was slightly overplaying Van Helsing's mimicry of Renfield, but he added some details that were very vivid, and truly tragic, evoking Renfield as a man once decent, now a helpless victim of the terrible vampire. Joshua told him very firmly to keep all that he had added in; if the play ran five minutes longer because of it, then so be it.

"It's not necessary," James protested. "We're ten minutes over time already. We'll lose the audience."

"No, we won't," Joshua told him. "It's a superb piece of acting."

"We're here to entertain, not show off," Mercy said

defensively. "Vincent's just trying to impress Mr. Netheridge. He's looking for another lead in the London West End."

"On that performance, he deserves it," Joshua said. "And it's important to the play. He makes Renfield matter to us."

"Renfield's trivial, a plot device," James said with disgust.

"He's a plot device that works extremely well," Joshua said gravely. "His degradation from decent man to fly- and rat-eating lunatic shows us more clearly than any words what the power of the vampire is. Through Van Helsing we watch him die, but for an instant return to the man he once was. This is the only time we get to see that, to understand how far he fell. If we're not frightened of Dracula after that, then we are truly stupid."

James drew in his breath to argue, then let it out again. He was actor and dreamer enough to know the truth of what Joshua said.

They followed the script through to the end. They even tried the effect of the lights to create the illusion of a snowstorm, and cut down the words used to describe the last chase of the coffin carried through the mountain pass as the lights dimmed in imitation of the sun sinking in the west. They killed Dracula in its last rays, and the unearthly scream that rang out as the light faded and the curtain came down drew a moment's total silence, and then a roar of applause.

"It will work," Joshua said simply. "Thank you for your ideas, Mr. Ballin. You have helped us enormously. Without you we might never have succeeded."

Ballin bowed, smiling. "It was a great pleasure," he said. "A very great pleasure. Miss Alice, I think you have a happy future ahead of you."

"Thank you," she whispered, her eyes shining.

*D*inner was quiet. Everyone was tired and ready to retire early. There were no more problems to solve; all that was left was for the script, much amended, to be learned by heart so there were no mistakes, no hesitations. In fact, several of them would write out a new copy of the script, clean, without the scratchings-out and scribbled margin notes. Many actors found writing out the script was an excellent way to commit the words to memory.

Caroline wrote out the script as well, not every word, but the key phrases that cued the light changes. The prompting script would be with Alice, though Caroline had often taken on that task. Alice's parts onstage were only a few words here and there: a servant or a messenger. It would not be difficult to fill all the roles and still act as prompter. The lights were crucial, and Caroline wanted to focus entirely on them.

Joshua was sitting at the small desk in the bedroom and Caroline was on the bed, reading her cues over again, when she remembered a note she had written hastily about the lighting of Lucy's death scene. She had left it on the stage.

"I'll just go and get it," she said, slipping her feet off the bed and standing up. "I won't be long."

"Shall I get it for you?" Joshua offered.

"No, thank you." She walked over to him and touched his cheek lightly. "You're busy." She looked down at his half-written page. "There's another hour's work you have to do still. I'm not afraid of vampires in the dark. I'll be back in ten minutes or so."

Joshua smiled and turned back to the desk. She was right; it would take at least another hour or so to complete.

Caroline went out onto the landing and down the stairs to the main hall. The lights were always left burning low—but quite sufficient for her to move swiftly toward the passage to the theater. The hall seemed even more magnificent in the shadows: the ceilings higher, the checkered marble floor bigger, the stairs sweeping up on either side disappearing dramatically into the dark corners where they turned and curled back to the gallery above.

The long passage to the theater was even darker, leaving the distance between the niched candles heavily shadowed, the outlines of pictures barely visible. She walked briskly. Luckily there were no chairs or jutting tables to bump into. Not even the vase of bamboo was there now, she remembered, with a small smile.

She turned the first corner, then the second, her eyes on the wall ahead, searching for the next candle along the corridor. Then she tripped over something and pitched forward, landing hard on the floor on her hands and knees. She got up slowly, shaken and bruised. How could she have been so clumsy? She turned to see what she had fallen over, and at first did not understand what it was. She was in the shadow between the lights, and the object looked like a pile of curtains dropped on the ground.

Then as she stood dazed, her heart pounding, her eyes became more accustomed to the darkness, and the form came into focus. It was a man lying crumpled on his side, his legs half-folded under him. Was it a drunken footman? What on earth was the stupid man doing here?

She bent to shake him, and only then did she see the long handle of the broom slanting upward. Except it was only half of the handle. The brush was missing, and the shaft ended abruptly in the man's back. She felt the shadows blur and swim as if she were going to faint. She closed her eyes for a moment, then opened them again. It was not a footman, it was Ballin. His eyes were open and his mouth was open, as if he had screamed when the makeshift spear had struck him. She had no doubt whatsoever that he was dead.

Should she yell for help? It seemed ridiculous to scream now, deliberately. Added to that, her mouth was as dry as if she had been eating cotton. She should stand up, control herself, make her legs walk back up the stairs to Joshua. Please heaven no one come along this corridor in the meantime.

Her legs were wobbling. It was all she could do not to fall again. What had happened? Was there any imaginable way it could have been an accident?

Don't be absurd, she told herself, crossing the hall as silently as she had the first time, a world and an age ago. Nobody takes the head off a broom and spears themselves with the handle by accident. In fact, it must have been sharpened into a purposeful weapon, or it wouldn't have even penetrated the skin anyway.

She reached the stairs and clung to the newel post, climbing up hand over hand, pulling and balancing. She had seen murder before. One of her sons-in-law was a policeman.

She was at the top of the stairs. She reached her own bedroom door and opened it. She saw the light on Joshua's brown hair, the fair streaks in it shining.

"Joshua . . ."

He turned around slowly, smiling, the pen still in his hand. Then he saw her face.

"What is it?" he asked huskily, starting up from the desk. "Caroline!"

"Someone has killed Mr. Ballin." She gulped, struggling now not to sob, not to let her knees buckle. He was beside her, arms holding her.

"I tripped over his body in a dark stretch of the corridor to the theater," she went on. "Before you ask, yes, I am sure he was killed . . . murdered. He has been stabbed through the chest with the broken-off handle of a broom. You could say . . ." She gulped again and the room swam and blurred in the corners. "You could say down through the heart with a stake." She wanted to laugh but it ended in a sob.

He was guiding her to the bed, still holding her.

"Have you told anyone else?" he asked, his voice unsteady.

"No. I . . . I thought of screaming, but it seemed so stupid. We must tell Mr. Netheridge. Do you know which is their bedroom?"

"No. I shall call one of the servants to wake him." He glanced at the window, then back at Caroline. She was sitting on the bed now, and he still held both her hands. "We will have to deal with it ourselves . . . without the police."

"Joshua, it's murder!" she protested. "We can't just . . . just deal with it, as if it were some kind of domestic accident!"

"Caroline. Who's going to walk through that snow to fetch the police?" he asked very gently.

"Oh . . . oh." She took a deep breath. "Yes . . . I see. How stupid of me. We'll have to . . . Oh, heaven!" Now she leaned against him as her body began to shake. "That means one of us must have done it."

He touched her hair gently, pushing the long strands away from her face.

"I'm afraid it does. There won't be any more strangers out in the night coming here, or anywhere else." He let out a long, shaky breath. "I'll go and get one of the servants. Butler, I suppose. He'll call Mr. Netheridge. At least we must provide a little decency for the body, for the time being." He took a step.

"Joshua!"

He turned. "You stay here," he told her. "Perhaps you had better not let anyone else in."

"Put a blanket over the body, if you like," she told him. "But you'd better not move it until someone has looked at it. We have to find out who killed him." She smiled bleakly and it felt like a grimace. "I've been around rather a lot of crime scenes, one way and another. Thomas is a policeman, if you remember."

"We can't leave it there until the thaw," he protested. "We'll have to find a better place for it, somewhere cold. But yes, perhaps we should take a very careful look at it first. I don't know who, Netheridge himself, I suppose. It's his house. You know, I have the odd feeling that Ballin would have been the best person to take charge in a situation like this."

He looked very pale. For a ridiculous moment she thought, what a disappointment it was that they would hardly be able to put on the play now. It really had become very good.

"Yes," she agreed. "He was very able. I'm . . . sorry he's gone." It sounded so inadequate, and yet it was all she could think to say.

"Stay here," he repeated, then he went out the door.

133

*I*t was nearly half an hour later when Joshua returned. Caroline insisted on going down with him to the withdrawing room, where the rest of the company was gathered. All had dressed again, but hastily, and none of the women had bothered to pin up their hair. Everyone was clearly shocked and frightened. James and Mercy sat together on the couch, holding hands. Douglas stood behind the big armchair in which Alice was hunched up. Her face was white, and she was clearly distressed. Lydia sat alone, as did Vincent.

Eliza sat close to where her husband stood with his back to the fire, which had been stoked up again. The huge stained-glass window made the room look like a church.

Joshua and Caroline took places on the other sofa.

Netheridge cleared his throat. "It seems we have a very ugly tragedy in the house," he said with deep unhappiness. "No doubt you all know by now that the stranger, Mr. Ballin, has met with a very sudden death." He glared at Vincent, who had seemed about to interrupt him. "We don't yet know what happened, whether it was some sort of accident, or worse. If anybody has anything they can tell us about it, now would be the time to do so. Obviously we can't call a doctor, or the police. We have no way of getting out to do it, and they have no way of coming to us until the weather improves. No doubt they will clear the roads as soon as they can." He looked around the group.

No one said anything.

"Come now. Who was Ballin?" he demanded. "He appeared out of the night and asked for shelter. We gave it to him, as we would. Who knew where he came from? Did he talk to any of you? Did he say who he was going to visit here in Whitby? Why? What does he do? Where does he live? We don't know anything about him!" His glance embraced Eliza, Alice, and Douglas.

"For heaven's sake, we don't know him, either," James said heatedly. "We don't even know anyone else in Whitby."

"Well, why would anybody kill him, then?" Netheridge asked.

"He was an objectionable, interfering, and arrogant man." Douglas pulled his mouth into a thin, hard line. "He was not difficult to dislike."

Caroline lost her temper, which happened very rarely indeed, largely because she had been brought up to believe that ladies never did such a thing.

"Mr. Paterson, this man has been run through the chest with a broom handle. The fact that you did not care for him is irrelevant. Unless you are saying that your dislike was sufficiently intense for you to have murdered him? And I do not think that is what you mean. Somebody here obviously had a far deeper hatred or fear of him, beyond simple dislike. One does not take another human being's life violently, in the middle of the night, without a passion that has slipped out of all control. Your resentment of his generosity in working with Alice, and his assistance in helping her believe in her ability, is surely not of that order, is it?"

There was a stunned silence.

Douglas was white to the lips. "Of course it isn't!" he said savagely. "How dare you say such a thing? The man was arrogant, and probably a charlatan, but I didn't do anything to him at all. Look at your fellow players. It has to be one of you."

It was Vincent who answered, his eyes wide in disbelief. "One of us? Why, for God's sake? It was this house he came to. It is entirely conceivable that he had actually heard that Mr. Netheridge was entertaining his friends with a group of professional actors in his daughter's drama, even though he claimed he had no idea. Maybe that was why he showed up. Even if it were not, how would Ballin know specifically who we were? One has to assume it was someone here he came for, someone he expected to find."

Netheridge's face flushed dark. "I've never seen the man before, or heard of him!" he protested. "Neither has anyone in my family, and that includes Douglas." He was clearly horrified, but also afraid. His big hands clenched at his sides and he started to take a step forward, before changing his mind.

"There is no point in trying to lay blame on one another," Caroline said as levelly as she could. "We would all rather it be a crime committed by someone who broke in from outside, a random act that had nothing to do with any of us, but that would be childish and naïve. No one has come or left. Either it was a sudden quarrel so violent that it ended in death, or else he already knew someone here—who either lives here or is visiting—and an old quarrel was renewed. It doesn't matter. I doubt anyone is going to admit to either."

"Maybe he attacked someone, and they had to defend themselves?" Eliza said shakily. "That would mean it wasn't their fault, wouldn't it?"

Caroline slowly looked around at them all. For a moment her heart was pounding and her mouth dry with the hope that that could be true. Then the dead man, beyond all further hurt, would be to blame. Even as she thought that, she knew it was likely a false hope, but one she could not give up on easily.

"No one looks to be hurt," she said at last. "No one is dirty or torn, as if they had been in a fight for their lives. And surely if that were the case, the party would now admit it?"

"One of the servants?" Mercy said immediately.

Caroline gave a little shrug. "Why would Mr. Ballin be in the corridor to the theater in the middle of the night, attacking one of the servants with a broken-off and sharpened broom handle?"

"How do you know it was sharpened?" Douglas challenged her.

"Because it wouldn't have speared him if it were blunt," she said with weary patience. "This is not a play, this is real. It has to make sense; we have to look at facts to figure out what's true."

"We must wait for the police," Netheridge said, taking command again. "Until then there's nothing we can do. Please, everyone, go back to bed, and get whatever rest you can. Douglas and I will go and move the poor man so that none of the servants find him. They're a sensible lot, but this will distress them, naturally. I think it would be a good idea if we merely say that Mr. Ballin was taken violently ill and died. We can amend that when the police come."

Caroline rose to her feet. "You can't do that!"

"I beg your pardon?" It was a rebuke, not a request.

"Of course he can," Douglas said sharply. "You've had a shock, Mrs. Fielding. Let your husband take you upstairs and perhaps you have a headache powder you can take . . . or something . . ." He trailed off lamely.

Caroline remained where she was. "You can tell the servants whatever you think is best to keep some sort of calm in the house," she said to Netheridge, ignoring Douglas. "But Mr. Ballin was murdered. I quite see that you have to put his body somewhere more suitable than where it is, but not tonight in the dark. If you bolt the door to that part of the house it can be done in daylight, but it would be most unwise to do it alone . . ."

"My dear Mrs. Fielding, it will be unpleasant, but there is absolutely no danger whatever, I assure you," Netheridge said patiently. "He is a perfectly ordinary man of flesh and blood, and the dead do not hear us. There are no such things as vampires, or the undead—"

"Of course there aren't!" she cut him off angrily. "But he was murdered. Anyone moving him before the police get here may be accused of altering the evidence . . ."

"What evidence? We can't leave him there, woman! He'll . . . smell! The natural—"

"I'm not suggesting we leave him there," she corrected him. She was beginning to tremble. "But we need to be there, all of us, or at least several of us, when we move him. One of us did that to him. We don't want the police to accuse any of us of tampering with evidence that would have indicated guilt . . ."

"Such as what, for heaven's sake?" Netheridge pretended to be outraged, but understanding was already beginning to show in his eyes.

"Such as proof that Ballin knew his attacker on a more personal level, or that there was some quarrel that took place between them," she answered. "Something on his clothes or his person that would indicate who was the last one to see him alive. All sorts of objects are possible to discover at a crime scene, either because they were left accidentally, or because they were left on purpose by someone wishing to implicate someone else; or, conversely, not to discover, because they have been purposely removed."

"She's right," Mercy said incredulously. "But how on earth do you know these things? Who are you?"

"I am Joshua's wife," Caroline replied. "But I have a son-in-law who is a policeman, and he has solved dozens of murders—scores. Please . . . let us use sense as well as compassion. We'll all go together, in the daylight, when we can see the body, the floor around, anything that can tell us what happened. We need to protect ourselves from unjust suspicion by the police, as well as anything else." She stopped, swallowing hard, her mouth dry.

141

"You are quite right, of course," Netheridge agreed more calmly. "Thank you. Fielding, perhaps you would come with me while I lock the door from the hall to the corridor. As Mrs. Fielding points out, we need to take the proper care to be above suspicion. I shall see the rest of you at breakfast at the usual hour. Until then, please take whatever rest you can."

Caroline sat up in bed waiting for Joshua to return. It seemed like ages, although it was probably little more than five minutes before he came in and closed the door. He looked very shaken.

"The corridor has been locked," he said quietly. "Are you going to be all right?" He looked at her anxiously, trying to read beyond the calm words she was saying.

"Did you look at him?" she asked.

He sat down on the edge of the bed.

"Only briefly. I suppose Netheridge wanted to make sure you hadn't had a nightmare or something. I'm afraid it's definitely Ballin, and as you said, someone killed him. That sort of thing couldn't have happened by accident." He touched her hair, then her face. "I wish I could have protected you from this. I knew there'd be difficulties, quarrels in the cast, but I never imagined it could end in violence."

"Of course you didn't," she said, surprised at how calm she sounded. "It's probably to do with Netheridge, not us, but we must be prepared to deal with whatever happens." She smiled bleakly. "You know, I'm really very angry. We had finally made a decent play of it, and now we can hardly perform it, given the circumstances. Added to which, I very much liked Mr. Ballin, odd as he was."

$\mathcal{T}$hey were all present at breakfast, which was a silent and unhappy meal. It was clear that no one had slept well. When it was completed, Mr. Netheridge announced that it was time to move Ballin's body. There was an appropriately cold room on the outside wall of the house, he said, that was often used for storing meat, at times when the icehouse would have been too cold.

Obediently they rose and followed him across the

hall to the corridor door. He turned the lock, swung the door open, and then—after taking a deep breath—set off at a brisk pace. They followed obediently, Mercy and Lydia a step or two behind the rest. For the first time that Caroline had observed it, they seemed to cling to each other as if they were the friends that Mina and Lucy were in the play.

They rounded the last corner and saw the stretch of linoleum floor ahead of them; the pool of dark blood on the floor; the long shaft of the broom handle, sharp, scarlet-ended; but no corpse.

Netheridge stopped abruptly.

Douglas Paterson swore.

Mercy screamed, loud and piercingly sharp.

Lydia quietly slid to the floor in an awkward heap.

Douglas swiveled around, saw her, and went to her anxiously, calling her name and trying to raise her in his arms.

James went to Mercy, catching her hands, which she was waving around. "Stop it!" he said loudly. "It's all right! He's not here. There's no danger at all."

"No danger?" she shrieked. "He was dead, someone murdered him, with a stake through the heart, and now he's not there anymore, and you say there's no danger? Are you mad, or stupid? I told you there was something wrong with him, terribly wrong. He came here out of the night and during a storm just like the one that brought Dracula's coffin ashore." Her voice was getting louder and more high-pitched. "He knew everything about vampires, more than we did, more than Bram Stoker did. He was dead and locked in, and still he escaped. He wasn't dead, you fool! You can't kill him, he is the 'undead.'"

White-faced, Eliza turned to Caroline.

Caroline stepped forward. "Mercy!" she said abruptly. "You are not helping anyone by being hysterical. If you really want to step out of reality into Mr. Stoker's book, then for goodness sake live up to the character you chose to play. Mina Harker would never have been so peevish and cowardly, and she was faced by a real vampire who was determined to kill her. Mr. Ballin, poor man, is dead and can do you no possible harm, even if he wanted to. Take hold of your emotions and stop making such an exhibition of yourself. We need to think very clearly what to do if we are to defeat whatever evil is lurking here."

"Evil!" Mercy repeated the word with a loud wail.

"Stop shrieking!" Caroline commanded. "I would be delighted to have an excuse to slap your face. If you insist on giving it to me, I shall take it, I warn you."

Mercy fell instantly silent.

"Thank you." Caroline's voice was tart. She turned to Netheridge. "There is no point in our standing here. Clearly the body has been moved. Since there is no one in the house except us and the servants, you had better find out if one or two of them came here and found him and, perhaps out of decency, felt obliged to move him somewhere else. One thing is absolutely certain: He did not remove himself, either as a man, or as a bat or a wolf, or anything else supernatural. If you don't want all the maids in hysterics, and possibly the footmen as well—or, worst of all, the cook—then you had better be very circumspect as to how you do it."

"Yes," he agreed, as if he had thought of it himself. "Of course." He turned to Joshua. "I'm sorry, but under the circumstances I don't believe there is any point in your continuing to practice for the play. I . . ." He shook his head. "Just at the moment I hardly know what decisions to make about anything. Please . . . look after yourselves. Do as you please. I'm sorry, but as such it is quite impossible for you to leave, or even to walk outside. The snow must be a couple of feet deep, and it is bitterly cold. There are books in the library, quite a good billiard table . . ." He did not bother to finish.

Caroline felt sorry for him. The party he had planned with such care for his daughter had collapsed in a tragedy no one could have foreseen. Now instead of celebration he had a crime, and a group of strangers in his home without a purpose, one of them possibly a killer.

She stared at Joshua, then at Netheridge. "Mr. Netheridge."

He turned toward her, simply out of good manners. His face was weary, and he looked ten years older than he had when he welcomed them to his home. "Yes, Mrs. Fielding?"

"Alice has written a play that we have all worked extremely hard on, particularly she. We will perform it one day; if not here, then somewhere else. Possibly even in London, at the very least in the provinces. Considering how much he contributed to it, we could do it in memory of Mr. Ballin. Our time and her efforts have not been wasted."

He swallowed, sudden emotion filling his face. It was a moment or two before he could master his voice.

"Thank you, Mrs. Fielding. You are a generous woman, and brave. I hope one day that will indeed be possible." Then, before he embarrassed himself by a display of his vulnerability, he made his excuses and left.

One by one they all went: either to their bedrooms, the billiard room, the library, or the room set apart for letter writing with desks, inkwells, and ample supplies of paper.

Caroline walked away from the corridor and up the stairs to go back to her bedroom. Then she changed her mind and went to the window seat in the long gallery from which she could see across the snowbound countryside. The hill fell away, covered by trees bending under the weight of last night's new fall. Some of them looked precariously close to breaking. There was no mark on the landscape of human passing: no wheel tracks, no footprints. It was impossible to tell how deep the snow lay, except that all the smaller features— rocks, low walls, and fences—had disappeared. They were alone.

Far out toward the sea more clouds were piled up, ominous and heavy gray. There was worse weather to come.

She realized as she sat there that they must solve the crime themselves. They could not remain here day after day knowing nothing, doing nothing. One of them had killed Anton Ballin. They had to find out which one of them it was, and be strong enough to deal with the answer together, whatever that answer was. Of course, it must also be done with caution and care. They could not risk anyone else being killed. A person who would spear Ballin to death might not hesitate to do the same to anyone else who threatened him or her.

How had this happened? It seemed unimaginable that it was one of them, from the slight vanities and squabbles they had, no more than pinpricks to the self-esteem: The play made no difference to any one individual's career. It was a lesser part on the small stage, no money involved, nor any critical review to care about.

And yet someone had cared about or feared something so intensely that they had driven a broom handle through a man's body. Why? What was it that lay below a surface that appeared so normal? They had all been

149

deceived, ignorant, walking a razor's edge across an abyss, and never thinking to look down.

She shivered, although it was warm in the house. Fires burned in every room. Candles blazed. Food was plentiful and excellent. There were servants to attend to every physical need. What lay hidden behind such apparent ease?

How could she find out, and so discreetly that she did not get herself killed in the process? If she had any sense at all, she would take very great care indeed. For a start, she would tell no one what she was doing, and that included Joshua. In fact, more than anyone else, she absolutely mustn't tell Joshua.

She was speaking to herself as if she had accepted that identifying the murderer was her responsibility. But who else was there who could possibly do it? None of them had any experience of murder, except herself. Douglas Paterson was possibly guilty! He had loathed Ballin, and made no secret of the fact that he thought Ballin was deluding Alice that she had talent when she did not. And even if she did, it was not a talent Douglas was willing for her to use. It would mean her leaving Whitby, where his future lay. If she did not marry him, then perhaps he did not have a future—not in the way he had imagined, and intended. Charles Netheridge was a very wealthy man indeed. The house more than attested to that, quite apart from his frequent and large investments in the London theater. Alice was his only child. That was why he had been willing to invite an actor of Joshua's fame and quality up to Yorkshire for the whole Christmas period, and pay his expenses and those of his company, on the understanding that he, Netheridge, would stake them next London season.

But could Douglas have hated Ballin so much for helping Alice? Or could anyone in the company have hated Ballin so much? He was a stranger to all of them. What danger could he present? Surely nothing in the four days since he arrived had given birth to a passion so violent it had ended in that terrible act in the corridor?

He must have known one of them before. Had he come intending to seek revenge for some old wrong?

Caroline watched the sky. The dark clouds over the sea were closer now, and heavier. A gust of wind stirred the bare branches, sending piles of snow falling off into the deep drifts beneath.

Was it possible that Ballin had not been the intended victim? In the uncertain light of the corridor could the killer have mistaken Ballin for someone else? He was tall, but so were Vincent and James. With his back to the candlelight, would such a mistake be possible? If so, they must not have spoken; Ballin's voice was too distinctive.

Netheridge was of average height, and broader than any other man here. He walked quite differently. Douglas Paterson was a good height, but he had not the practiced grace or elegance of Ballin.

No. She could not believe there had been such a mistake.

The sharpened broom handle was a very carefully prepared weapon. It had been created, not used in any spur-of-the-moment anger or self-defense. Nobody possessed such a weapon offhand, never mind carried it around with them in the middle of the night, unless they had an attack in mind.

Was it possible someone really did believe in vampires? Was anyone so crazy? Surely not? They were actors; they played all sorts of parts, real and fantastic. They could take up roles as they stepped onto the stage, and discard them again as they left it. She had seen Joshua as every character imaginable, from a pensive hero like Hamlet to a blood-soaked tyrant like Tamburlaine; as philosopher, cynic, and wit in the works of Oscar Wilde; and the lover Antony to Mercy's Cleopatra. None of them was the real Joshua, the man she knew.

Had Ballin known his killer? Had they intended to meet there in the middle of the night? It was ridiculously unlikely that the meeting was purely a chance encounter, surely? Which meant that Ballin knew his attacker at least well enough to be willing to keep a midnight tryst.

Why was the body moved?

She thought of Mercy's fear of the "undead," which she had dismissed as a vain woman's pretense to get attention. But the fact that the body had apparently disappeared now made her fancies seem less ridiculous. Was it likely that someone had hidden the body to cause and heighten that very fear?

Possibly. But it was more likely the body was moved because there was something about it that would give away the truth of the crime. What could that be? Either something of the identity of whoever had killed Ballin, or something about Ballin's own identity, which would betray whom he had known well enough for them to hate or fear him with such passion.

Whom could she ask for help? The only person she trusted without question was Joshua. However, he would be fully occupied trying to keep up morale and sensible behavior among the cast, especially now that there would be no performance, at least in the foreseeable future. He would have to find them something to do, to keep them at bay and hold them together as a group. Any old jealousies or squabbles that surfaced now might result in near hysteria, and things could be said or done that could not be mended.

Someone must find out who had killed Ballin, and prevent the wrong person from being accused. She, Joshua, and the rest of the players were strangers here in close-knit Whitby. Who would suspect Douglas Paterson, never mind Netheridge himself, when they had the perfect scapegoats in a group of strangers, and actors at that?

She must squash down her own emotions and think clearly. What would her son-in-law, Thomas Pitt, do?

He would ask questions to which there would be precise answers and then compare those answers. If she did the same, with luck a picture would emerge, even if it was merely an understanding of who was lying and who was telling the truth.

Maybe she would be better equipped if she knew more about everyone present. For a start, she would definitely need the help of Eliza to speak to the servants. She did not imagine for an instant that any of them had killed Ballin; why on earth would they? But they should be eliminated as suspects all the same.

She found Eliza in the housekeeper's room. After waiting several minutes for her to complete her conversation, she followed Eliza as she walked back to the main part of the house.

"I was wondering if I could be of help in any way," Caroline began. "I don't know if you have told the servants or not."

Eliza looked very pale in the white daylight reflected off the snow outside. The fine lines around her eyes and mouth were cruelly visible.

"Charles said I should not," she replied. "He has told them that Mr. Ballin was taken ill. We were going to say that he had died and we had placed him in the coldest storeroom until the authorities could come, but of course now we don't know where he is." She stopped and turned to Caroline, her face tight with misery. "Where on earth do you think he could be? Why would anyone move him?" She was trembling very slightly. She seemed to want to say more, but some discretion or embarrassment prevented her.

Caroline longed to be able to help her. Eliza looked frail and a little smaller than she had seemed only yesterday. Had she been about to ask Caroline if she had any belief in the supernatural, but stopped because she feared seeming ridiculous?

"Perhaps to frighten us," Caroline answered with a very slight smile. She meant it to be reassuring, but was suddenly anxious in case Eliza imagined that it was out of mockery, or amusement at her superstition. "And they've succeeded," she went on hastily. "We are all unnerved by it. But honestly I think it is probably for a more practical reason. If we were to look at the body more closely we might learn something that would indicate which one of us killed Ballin."

Eliza looked close to tears. She stood still and stared

at the huge hall with its magnificent decoration and its oil portraits of various Yorkshiremen of note, portraits that were the choice of a rich man who had local roots, but no ancestry of which he was proud.

Eliza gazed at them one by one on the farthest wall, her face filling with dislike.

"I don't even know who they are," she said softly. "Charles's mother chose them, and there they hang, watching us all the time."

"There aren't any women," Caroline observed.

"Of course not. They're councilors and owners of factories who gave great gifts to the poor," Eliza told her. "I think they look as if they parted with their money hard."

"They look to me as if they had toothache, or indigestion," Caroline answered. "Perhaps they were very bored with sitting still. I don't suppose they could even talk while they were being painted." Then another thought occurred to her. "Didn't any of them have wives, or daughters? A woman with a red or yellow dress would brighten the hall up a lot."

"Charles's mother chose them," Eliza repeated. "Nothing has ever been changed since her day. Charles won't have it. He was devoted to her." There was defeat in her voice, and a terrible loneliness, as if she were a stranger in her own house, unable to find anything that was hers.

"What about a painting of you?" Caroline suggested. "And surely he would love to have one of Alice? She has a lovely face, and if she wore something warm in color, she would draw the eye away from all those sour old men."

"I don't think so," Eliza said, but she was clearly turning the idea over in her mind. "But you know, I think I'll try asking him anyway. Tell me, Mrs. Fielding, was Alice's play really any good? Please don't make up a comfortable lie. It would not be kind. I think I need a truth to cling on to, even a bad one."

"Yes, it was," Caroline said honestly. "And by the time we had worked on it and rehearsed it that last time, it had become really excellent. There were some moments in it that were unforgettable. Above all it touched on the real nature of evil, not of attack by the supernatural, but seduction by the darker side of ourselves. Mr. Ballin was very clever, you know, and Alice could see that. She had both the courage and the honesty to learn from him."

"Thank you. That comforts me a great deal, although I don't think Douglas will allow her to write another, or indeed to have that one performed properly, by people with the talent to understand it. It is . . . it is a great pity that it will not happen this Christmas."

"Yes, it is," Caroline agreed. "But please don't give up hope for the future."

"Douglas doesn't like it. He won't allow it. He has said so." There was the finality of defeat in her eyes and in the downward fall of her voice.

"Are you sure?" Caroline asked with a growing fear inside her. Was *that* perhaps the reason for Ballin's death? It would not only ensure that Alice's play was not performed, but also be a kind of punishment for Ballin because he had been the one whose suggestions had brought the work to life, the vivid depiction of fear and the reality of evil.

"Oh, no!" Eliza breathed the words more than said them, following Caroline's train of thought. "He wouldn't—"

"Who wouldn't?" Caroline asked, knowing Eliza had no answer.

Eliza gave a tiny gesture of helplessness but said nothing.

Caroline touched Eliza's hand, and then went into the hall, leaving her a few minutes of privacy before the next demand on her time came from one servant or another, with their domestic concerns.

She found all the cast in the large withdrawing room, sitting around in various chairs reading or talking quietly to one another. Douglas Paterson was there as well, listening to Lydia describe something to him. Caroline could not hear the murmured words but she saw the animation on Lydia's pretty face, and the delicate gestures of her hands as she gave proportion to the scene of her recollection. Douglas's eyes never left her. He was oblivious to everyone else in the room, including Alice, who was talking with Joshua near the window.

Vincent, Mercy, and James were all reading, grouped close together as if only moments before they might have been involved in some discussion. None of them looked up as Caroline came in. Suddenly she felt the same sense of exclusion that she knew Eliza must constantly feel. She was here, this was the right place for her to be, and yet she did not belong. She had never stood on a stage in her life, never played a part so convincingly that a vast sea of people in the shadow of an auditorium listened to her words, watched her face, her movements, while she held their emotions in her hands, moved them to laughter or tears, to belief in the world she created with just her presence. It was a magical art, a power she was not gifted with to share.

She turned away again and went back out into the hall with its grim portraits. Maybe she would never be a part of their art, but she had a skill they did not have. She would find out who had murdered Anton Ballin, and why.

❖

*S*he continued to struggle with the problem of where to begin. She had no authority to ask questions, no physical material to examine—not even the body, at the moment, although that would no doubt be discovered eventually. It could not be far away because no one could possibly go far from the house, let alone with a body.

She would have searched Ballin's luggage, but he had brought nothing with him except a small hand case. Why not? Presumably he'd had cases with him in the carriage that had been overturned. Presumably they were too heavy to carry in the snow. What had he brought in his hand case? At the very least a razor and a hairbrush? A clean shirt and personal linen? It meant that there were at least a few things that she could look at to get some sense of the man: quality, use, place where they were made or bought, anything that told of his personality or his past.

What would Thomas have done? Well, for one thing, being a policeman, he would have had the authority to question people.

She would probably learn nothing if she went to Ballin's room and searched, but she would be remiss not to try. She could even ask one of the servants if they had noticed anything. But better to look herself first.

She knew where the other members of the cast had rooms, so she could deduce which Ballin's must be. The family slept in a different wing. Of course it would be possible to misjudge and end up in Douglas Paterson's room, but she thought his was a little separated from the main guest wing, and so his room ought to be easy enough to avoid. It was really a matter of not being caught by a housemaid.

Ballin's room turned out to be a very pleasant one, overlooking the snow-smothered garden. It was not as large as the one she shared with Joshua, but then Joshua was the most important guest. Ballin had been no more than a stranger in trouble, given shelter because the storm had left him stranded.

Or was that all it had been?

She stood at the window and stared out at the white lawn and the trees so heavily laden as to be almost indistinguishable one from another. Not a soul had passed that way in the last twenty-four hours, at the very least, perhaps not since the first storm struck.

She looked around the surfaces of the dressing table and the tallboy, the two chests of drawers. A hairbrush, razor, and strop, as she'd expected, but no pieces of paper, no notes. She turned to the bed. It was slightly crumpled, but not slept in. The sheets were still tucked tightly at the sides. He had lain on it, but not in it.

She looked at it more closely, but there were no pieces of paper, even between the folds of the sheets, or under the pillows.

She tried the drawers, and found only clean, folded underwear, presumably mostly that lent to him by Netheridge. There were two shirts hanging in the wardrobe, and a jacket, also borrowed. Ballin had died wearing his own clothes: the black suit and high-collared white shirt in which he had arrived. There was nothing in any of the pockets of the clothes in the wardrobe.

Where else was there to look?

There was a carafe of water on the bedside table, and an empty glass. She could not tell if he had drunk anything because the glass was dry, but the carafe was little more than half-full.

She bent and looked to see if anything could have fallen onto the floor and slid under the bed. She lifted the heavy drapes, but found nothing, not even dust.

Lastly she looked at the coal bucket by the fire, and into the cold grate. If she had received a note to keep an appointment at night, secretly, she would have burned it. It was the easiest and surest destruction.

There was a faint crust of gray ash at the edge of the cinders. But whatever the paper was it had burned through and curled over, subsiding on itself. If she touched it at all, even breathed on it, it would collapse into a heap of ash. However, she was sure it must have been a small note. But there was no way to prove it.

So Ballin had received the invitation, or the summons. The other person had come prepared, carrying the weapon.

She stiffened as she heard footsteps outside in the corridor, and a maid's laughter. Surely Mr. Netheridge would have told the servants not to come into Ballin's room?

Or would he? Would he even think of it? He had probably never experienced anything to do with murder before. Very few people had. Caroline must do something before the maid disturbed anything, and then tell Mr. Netheridge that the room ought to remain untouched.

She opened the door and came face-to-face with one of the housemaids, a tall girl with dark hair. The girl gave a little shriek and stepped backward sharply.

"I'm sorry," Caroline apologized. "I wanted to make

sure that nothing had been disturbed here. Mr. Netheridge requests that you do not come into this room, under any circumstances. Do you understand?"

"Yes . . . yes, ma'am," the girl said obediently.

Caroline wondered whether she should ask Eliza to lock the door. But if she did that, the maids would wonder where Ballin was. Perhaps it could be explained as an infectious disease? Would that be enough, or could curiosity still get the better of someone, driving them to look around the room?

Then again, how much did it matter? There was nothing in there, except the curled-over ash remnant of a note, which no one could read now anyway.

"Thank you." She smiled at the girl and then came out into the passage, closing the door behind her. She would find Eliza immediately and apologize for giving her staff orders, and explain to her the necessity.

Eliza looked surprised when Caroline told her. "I . . . I never thought of it," she admitted. "Mr. Netheridge thought it better not to tell them anything, which I find very difficult. They will not see Mr. Ballin, and they know perfectly well that he cannot have left. No one could." She bit her lip. "If they ask me, and the butler certainly will, what should I say?"

"I think perhaps that Mr. Ballin is ill and must not on any account be disturbed. Also that we are not certain if what he has might be contagious. But I would add that only if necessary."

"Then why do we not feed him?" Eliza said reasonably. "Even the sick need to eat and drink, and also have their bed linen changed."

"Perhaps we may know the truth before such an issue is obvious," Caroline said gravely. "If not, perhaps then it will be time to tell them the truth we have."

"Where could he be?" Eliza's voice dropped to a whisper.

"Well, he has not returned to a mysterious coffin somewhere," Caroline assured her. "But we do need to know as much of the truth as possible, for our own safety, and to prevent any further tragedies."

"Will it prevent tragedy?" Eliza looked at her candidly. "One of us here in this house must have killed him. There's no one else, and there is no possibility whatever that it was suicide or accident. He could not have done that to himself; even I can see that. Who carries around a broom handle carved to a spear point in the middle of the night, unless they intend to kill someone?"

"Nobody," Caroline agreed. "And we will all be afraid and wondering until we find out who did it. Do you think there is any chance we can forget it and carry on as normal until the snow thaws and the police can arrive, and ask us all the same questions we can ask now, except days later when we don't remember anything as sharply?"

"No. So what can we do?"

"There are three things we can agree about," Caroline answered. "Who had the ability to kill him: that is, the means? Who had the opportunity: In other words, where were we all at the time it must have happened? And who would want to: Who believed they had not only a reason, but no better way of dealing with it?"

Eliza frowned. "Can we really find all that out?"

"We can certainly try," Caroline said with more conviction than she felt. "We know that Mr. Ballin was killed some time after we parted to go to bed, and when I went down again to fetch the note I had left behind on the stage."

"What times were those?" Eliza asked. They were standing on the landing at the top of the stairs, talking quietly. No one else seemed to be around. Housemaids were busy. Footmen must have been in the servants' quarters and would come only if the doorbell rang, which at the moment was impossible. Kitchen staff would be busy preparing luncheon for the household, which—including servants—was well over twenty people.

"We went to bed at quarter to eleven," Caroline answered. "I went down to get my note just before midnight."

"An hour and a quarter, roughly," Eliza said. "Everyone would be in their bedrooms, or say they were. How does one prove that?"

"Well, I know where Joshua was and he knows where I was," Caroline reasoned. "You and Mr. Netheridge could account for each other, as could Mercy and James." She stopped, seeing a shadow in Eliza's face. "What is it?" she said more gently.

"Charles and I do not share a bedroom," Eliza confessed, as if it were some kind of sin. She looked deeply uncomfortable. She seemed to be struggling for an explanation, but no words came.

"I'm sorry," Caroline apologized. "In a house this size of course you would not need to. In the later years of my first marriage, I did not share a bedroom with my husband." She smiled briefly; the memory no longer hurt. "He was very restless. I share with Joshua now because we're both happy doing so, and also we do not have the means to do otherwise most of the time, especially when we are traveling."

Eliza smiled and blinked. "You are very generous. It must be an interesting life, going to so many places, meeting people, performing different plays. You can never be bored."

"I'm not." Caroline wondered how much of the truth to tell. "But I am quite often lonely, because I am not part of the cast."

Eliza looked amazed. "But you are. You are involved."

"Not usually. This is in many senses an amateur production . . . or, it was. We were to make our own scenery, and I was taught how to work the lights. In an ordinary professional production there is no work for me, except sometimes to help Joshua learn his lines. I speak the other parts to cue him. Otherwise I have nothing in particular to do, and we are away from home a lot."

"But you are happy," Eliza said, smiling. "I can see it in your face, and in the way you look at him, and he at you."

Caroline wanted to thank her, make some gracious acknowledgment, but the sudden rush of gratitude she felt had brought tears to her eyes and a tightness to her throat that made it momentarily impossible to speak. She had risked so much in marrying Joshua: the horror of her family, the outrage of her former mother-in-law, the loss of most of her friends and certainly any place in the society to which she had been accustomed through most of her life. She had been respectable, and financially safe. Now she was neither. But she was certainly happier, and she was very aware that Joshua loved her in a way Edward Ellison never had.

She also realized that Eliza Netheridge had never experienced those gifts of happiness and love. Even now she felt a stranger in her own house, as if her mother-in-law still watched her every choice with disapproval.

Caroline made a sudden, rash decision. "Eliza, I wonder if you can help me. We may at the very least be able to make certain that some among us could not have killed Mr. Ballin. I imagine it could not have been any of the servants, but let us save them from police questions and suspicion by making certain ourselves. I have no authority and no right to ask them, but you do. If you are careful, and precise, you may be able to find some sort of proof that clears them all. Especially if you promise them that whatever they were doing, there will be no blame in this instance. You may need to tell them that something very unpleasant occurred, and it is absolutely necessary that they tell the truth, whatever that may be."

Eliza took a deep breath, but she seemed perfectly steady. "Yes, of course I can do that," she said with determination. "I shall begin immediately. Will you speak to your own people?"

Caroline smiled at the thought that the players could be seen as "her" people. "Yes. I'll begin with Mercy and James. That should be easy enough."

But it was not. She found Mercy in the writing room busy with what looked like a pile of letters. Caroline was quite blunt about what she was asking, and her

172

reasons. She had already decided that an attempt at deviousness would be highly unlikely to fool anyone.

"Between half past ten and midnight?" Mercy repeated, blinking rapidly. "I was in my bedroom, reading a book for a little while, then I went to sleep. You can't imagine that I killed Mr. Ballin. I wouldn't have the strength, apart from the . . . the violence of mind."

"No, I didn't really think you did," Caroline agreed. "But I have to ask everyone, or else it will look as if I think only certain people are guilty."

Mercy smiled. "I can see how that would be very awkward. Why do you want to know? The police will ask all those questions anyway. Why are you bothering?"

Caroline had already prepared an answer to that question, as it was one she had anticipated. "Don't you think it would be much less unpleasant if we can tell them that some of us could not be guilty, before they have to ask? You never know what else they may inquire into, once they start."

Mercy looked appalled.

"Not that it would be criminal," Caroline went on. "Just private."

"Of course. Yes, you are absolutely right." Mercy smiled with considerable charm, and a degree of honesty. "I underestimated you, Mrs. Fielding. I apologize."

"Think nothing of it," Caroline said airily, convinced that Mercy would do that anyway. "Will James say the same thing?"

"Ah . . . well." Mercy cleared her throat. "That's it, you see. He was restless and he couldn't sleep. He said he was going to rehearse somewhere where he wouldn't disturb me. So, no, he won't—not exactly the same thing, that is. But it would mean the same, of course."

"Rehearse," Caroline repeated. "Are you avoiding saying that he went back to the stage?"

Mercy was perfectly still. "Well . . . ," she breathed out. "I don't know where he went, do I? I was here. He may have gone to the billiard room. There would've been nobody there at that hour."

"Did he say where he was going?" Caroline pressed.

"I don't think so."

And that was all she could learn. She knew that persisting with Mercy would only make an enemy of her. And of course, if she did not know for certain where James had been, then in reverse, he did not know

174

where Mercy had been, either. That sort of testimony covered both people, or neither. She thanked Mercy and went to look for James.

She found him in the billiard room alone, practicing sinking the balls into the pockets around the table. She bluntly asked him where he had been at the time Ballin had been killed.

"Probably asleep in my bed," he answered, putting the billiard cue down across the table and staring at her. "Why? Do you think I killed him?"

It was a far more aggressive answer than she had expected, and it was interesting, as if he had foreseen the question and was prepared for it. Perhaps he was a better actor than she had given him credit for.

"I find it difficult to think of any of us doing it," she replied. "But the police may not have the same trouble. They don't know us, and to them we are a band of actors, traveling people with no roots and no respectable profession. And it is either one of us who murdered him, or one of the highly respectable Yorkshire people, citizens of Whitby whom they have known for years. What do you think they will be disposed to believe, James?"

His face blanched. For a moment he held on to the edge of the table as if he needed it for support.

"I think you take my point," she said quietly. "Mercy said you took your script and went out of the bedroom to practice, so as not to disturb her. The natural place to do that would be the stage. Is that where you went? If you did, you had better say so now. To lie about it, and get caught later, could be seen as damning."

"I . . . er . . ." He blinked and shook his head, as if he were plagued by flies buzzing around him. "I . . . went to the stage, but it was cold and rather eerie there by myself. I decided not to bother, and I brought the script back and sat in the library. I didn't really want to rehearse so much as think of some way of making my part more heroic at the end. Ballin wasn't in the corridor then, I swear. I could hardly have failed to see him if he had been. Not if he was lying on the floor, as you say."

"No," she agreed. "Thank you. I don't suppose you asked a footman to bring you a drink, or anything?"

"In the middle of the night?" He raised his eyebrows. "I've got more sense than that. I don't want to be on the wrong side of Netheridge."

She believed him. "Thank you."

176

"Mrs. Fielding?"

She was almost to the door. She turned. "Yes?"

"Who the devil *was* Ballin? Does anyone know? And where's his body gone to?" His face was white in the pale daylight of the room.

"Someone must know who he is," she answered him. "You don't sharpen a broom handle into a dagger to kill a stranger in the middle of the night, especially when you are snowed in with an entire group of people."

He put his hands over his face. "Oh, God! And the body?"

"I have no idea. Have you?"

"Me? No!"

"I thought not. Thank you, James."

Vincent Singer was no more help. Caroline went to him next because it was the encounter she looked forward to least and she just wanted to get it over with. She had little confidence that she could persuade him to talk, still less that she could trick him into saying anything he did not wish to, certainly not to reveal anything that would betray a vulnerability on his part.

She found him in the library, reading Netheridge's copy of Gibbon's *Decline and Fall of the Roman Empire*.

"Decay always fascinates me," he observed, putting a piece of paper into the book to mark his place before closing it. "You look troubled. Are you also afraid that Ballin is perched upside down in the rafters somewhere, waiting for nightfall to come and suck our blood?"

"I think he is far more likely to rot in the warmth, and attract rats," she said tartly.

He gave a long sigh. "What a curious woman you are, all sweetness and respectability one moment, and violent imagery of the charnel house the next."

"If you think that is surprising, then you know very little of women," she retorted. "Especially respectable ones. We usually only faint to get out of a situation we find embarrassing. I am surprised so many people believe it. Well, that, and on occasion, there are those who lace their corsets too tight."

"How extremely uncomfortable, and faintly ridiculous," he replied. "Though I don't believe that's what you came to say. You have a look of purpose about your face. No doubt it is a grim purpose."

"Extremely. The police will come and investigate Mr.

Ballin's death, when the snow thaws. I think it would be very much more pleasant for us if we could solve it before then."

Vincent's eyes widened. "Really? And how do you propose to do that? I do remember you saying, several times, that your son-in-law was some kind of policeman. Did you take lessons from him?" He made no attempt to hide his sarcasm.

She sat down in the chair opposite him. "If you disagree, I am perfectly happy to see if we can clear everyone else, Vincent. It may be one of the servants, although I think that is very unlikely. Or one of the Netheridges, of course. Whom do you think the police will suspect? Mr. Netheridge, owner of the coal mine and the jet factory and philanthropist to half the county, or someone from a group of London actors here to perform *Dracula* for Christmas?"

Vincent stared at her, his face pale and tight as he realized immediately the truth of what she said.

"You have a tongue like a knife, Caroline," he observed, but his voice was shaking, in spite of his usual inner control. "I can't prove where I was at the time he was killed, which was obviously after we all said good night, and whenever it was you went back to the theater."

"Midnight," she told him.

"I was in bed, but no one can prove it for me. Thank God I won't be the only one in that situation."

The next person Caroline saw was Douglas Paterson. She found him on the landing, staring out at the snow. He turned as he heard her footsteps. He looked withdrawn and anxious.

"Good afternoon, Mrs. Fielding," he said, almost without expression. "Not long till dark again. Do you think we'll have more snow tonight?"

She stood beside him and looked at the sky. The light was fading quite rapidly. It was barely past the shortest day of the year, but there was considerable color in the sunset. Banners of cloud streamed across the west, and the red of the sinking sun blushed on the snow.

"No, I don't," she answered. "I think we might even get a thaw soon, at least enough to allow people to reach us, perhaps in time for Christmas."

"You can't put on that play now, you know," he said with just a trace of satisfaction.

Caroline was caught by an intense desire to both protect Alice's dreams, and deflate this pompous young man.

"Not here," she agreed. "At least certainly not this Christmas. But she has made such a good job of it that I think we may wish to perform it some time in the provinces, or even in London. After all, *Dracula* is a most popular work all over the country. And we could always bring it back to Yorkshire at a more appropriate time." She saw his face pale and smiled at him sweetly. "Knowing how you love Alice and want her to be happy, I hope that is of comfort to you."

He looked back at her with a fury that he was momentarily helpless to express.

"I am hoping we may forestall the police, at least to some extent," she continued. "They are bound to ask us all where we were when Mr. Ballin was killed. Some of us are fortunate enough to have been with someone else at the time, and therefore our whereabouts are vouched for. Would that be true for you as well?"

She saw the anger turn to satisfaction in his eyes.

"Yes. I was with Miss Rye," he said instantly.

There was nothing funny in their situation; still, she

could not help allowing her eyebrows to rise as if in horror, though in truth she was not at all surprised. "Really?" she said in a breathless whisper. "And will Miss Rye be willing to say that publicly, do you suppose? I doubt Alice will be amused, and Mr. and Mrs. Netheridge will be most displeased indeed."

His satisfaction vanished. He blushed scarlet with embarrassment and real, deep outrage.

"Your mind is most . . . deplorable, Mrs. Fielding!" His voice shook. "I dare say it is the company you keep."

"I was with my husband, Mr. Paterson," she replied, angry in turn now. "Or do I mistake you? Perhaps you had a chaperone you omitted to mention? Alice herself, even?"

He swallowed hard, his face still burning. "No . . . no, we were alone, in the morning room. We . . . we were discussing Alice's love of the theater, and Miss Rye was assuring me that it is not nearly as glamorous as Alice assumes. She herself is weary of it, and envies Alice's opportunity to settle down to a happy married life in a respectable society, with a husband and family."

And money, Caroline thought, but she did not say so. It occurred to her how much more suitable it would be for everyone if Lydia married Douglas, and Alice came to London with the players. Lydia's roles could be filled easily enough by another aspiring actress, and Alice would be an asset to the writing and producing side of the business. More important for both of them, and for Douglas, they would all be happier.

"It seems as if Lydia and Alice each desires what the other has," Caroline said more gently. "Perhaps they should exchange places."

"I can't marry an actress!" Douglas said in horror. But even as the words left his lips there was a change in his attitude, a new brightness in his eyes. The anger seeped out of him as if by magic.

"Well, she isn't an heiress, of course," Caroline agreed. "But that has its advantages as well. There is something very liberating in owing no one, Mr. Paterson. I made a very rash judgment in marrying Mr. Fielding, but I have never regretted it, even for an hour. I have had some difficult times. I have been cold and hungry and very far from home, but I have never been bored or lonely, or felt as if my life had no meaning. I have lost certain friends—or perhaps in truth they were really no more than acquaintances—but I have gained friends who are of worth, and I have contributed to something of value. I don't think I have ever been so happy before, even when I had considerable money, social position, and a very beautiful house. But then one person's happiness is not necessarily the same as another's."

He lowered his eyes very slowly. "I apologize, Mrs. Fielding. I was extremely rude. I am afraid of losing what I know, and have always believed I wanted. I was afraid of Mr. Ballin because he lured Alice away from me into another kind of world, but I did not kill him. I was with Lydia. If you ask her, I'm sure she will tell you." He gave a rueful smile and met her eyes again. "If I was with her, then she was also with me. We were in the morning room until you went back up the stairs again to your room to tell Mr. Fielding about Ballin. I know that because we heard your footsteps and I looked out the door to see who it was, so we could go upstairs unobserved. We had not realized how late it was, and we felt it would be indiscreet to be seen."

"So it would," she agreed. "What was I wearing?"

"A . . . a pink dressing robe, and your hair was loose down your back. It is rather longer than it looks to be."

She nodded slowly. "It is fortunate you chose that particular moment to look. Thank you."

"I . . . er . . ."

"You have no need to explain yourself further," she told him. "I shall confirm it with Lydia, and we shall be able to keep the police from bothering you—I hope."

"Mrs. Fielding!"

"Yes?"

"Thank you."

She said nothing, but smiled a little bleakly and nodded.

*I*t was after dark. Outside the wind had dropped, and the frost was bitter when Caroline spoke to the housemaid who usually changed her bed linen and tidied the room. She had come in to give Caroline clean towels, but after she had put them on the rail she stopped a moment, clearly wishing to speak. She was a handsome girl, but her face was troubled. She kept moving her hands, rubbing one with the other softly.

"What is it, Tess?" Caroline asked. She was almost certain what the girl was afraid of, and she sympathized with her.

"Is 'e ill wi' summat catching, ma'am?" she asked.

"No," Caroline answered. She thought Eliza Netheridge might not forgive her, but the truth had to be told some time. "He is not sick. I'm afraid he met with what may have been an accident, and he is dead. We did not tell you because we didn't wish everyone to be frightened, nor did we want to spoil Christmas."

Tess's face flooded with relief, until the truth sank in that a man was dead. Her expression crumpled to sorrow. "'E were a nice man, even if 'e were a bit odd, like. I'm sorry as 'e's dead, ma'am."

"I think it happened very quickly." Caroline tried to keep her imagination of the scenario out of her mind, the violence, the pain, and the blood; even if it had been brief, it hadn't been painless. But she put the image out of her mind; she would never have a better chance to speak to one of Netheridge's servants. She had to get a hold of herself, focus, and learn what she could from Tess.

"The police are going to ask us what happened, because they have to know," she went on. "The poor man's family must be told."

"I'm terrible sorry . . ."

"Of course. We all are. We are not quite sure what happened, and it would be better if we knew. Were you upstairs late in the evening?"

Tess nodded. "I din't stay. Mr. Netheridge were . . . not 'isself."

"He was ill?"

"No, ma'am, but 'e an' the mistress were 'avin' a disagreement."

"What about?" Caroline did not make any excuses as to why she wanted to know. There were none that would not sound completely artificial. "The play?"

"Oh, no, ma'am. It were about the drawin' room, an' such like, the dinin' room, too. It'll all need redoin' pretty soon. Come the spring, at the latest. The master says it'll all be the same as 'is mam 'ad it. It always is. The mistress says as she'll 'ave it 'er own way this time, like she wants it. 'E says it's always been like 'is mam 'ad it, and she says it's time it was changed. They went on an' on like that, an' I know it wasn't no use askin' 'er anythin' about anythin' else that night, so I just went."

"What time was that?"

"Just before midnight. I waited around, like, but it wasn't goin' to get any better, so I gave up."

"How long do you think they argued?"

"'Alf hour, maybe more."

"So I don't think they could have seen what happened to Mr. Ballin."

"No, ma'am. They was too angry to see anythin' else but the curtains an' walls an' the like."

"Were they going to redecorate the bedroom as well?"

"Yes, ma'am. An' the mistress says as it in't goin' to be brown this time." She looked pleased. "Wot lady, 'ceptin' 'is mam, wants a brown bedroom?"

"None," Caroline agreed. "Mine is mostly pink and red, and I love it."

Tess breathed out in a sigh of pleasure. "Cor! An' your husband don't mind?"

"If he did I wouldn't have done it. The pink is very pale and cool, and the red is hot. He likes it."

Tess went out smiling so widely that Caroline heard the other maid on the landing asking her what had happened. The tale of Caroline's bedroom would be all over the house in an hour.

The last person Caroline spoke to was Alice herself. She found her alone after dinner in a long gallery overlooking the snowbound darkness of the countryside. There was nothing to see except an occasional light in the distance where the city lay, shrouded in snow, just like them.

"I shall miss you when you're gone," Alice said quietly. It was simply a statement. She did not seem to be expecting a reply. She took a deep breath. "And I miss Mr. Ballin. Do you think it was Douglas who killed him, Mrs. Fielding?"

"No," Caroline replied without hesitation. "Nor was it your father."

Alice turned to face Caroline. Even in the candlelight and shadow of the gallery, Caroline could see the shock and shame in Alice's face.

"Were you not afraid of that as well?" Caroline asked her. "You know if you want to break off your engagement to Douglas and come to London, it will take a great change of heart on your father's part, to allow that." She bit her lip. "And he might be a good deal less inclined to back our company in the future, if he feels that we have influenced you toward that."

"But he invited you up here to help me!" Alice protested. "You came. If he then blamed you for what happened as a result, that would be monstrously unfair."

"Not really. He has no obligation to back us."

"But that is why you came?"

Caroline felt the heat in her own face. But she could not deny it now. "Yes. But things don't always work out the way you expect."

"I have enough money to live for quite a while in London, even if I don't earn anything right away." Alice turned again to stare back out the window into the darkness.

"It would be a very big change," Caroline warned.

"I know. Leaving home always is, but there are all sorts of ways in which I am not really at home here. I . . . I feel that if I marry Douglas I shall have stopped growing, the way a plant does if you put it in too small a pot. The flowers never open, the fruit never forms . . .

that will be what I'll feel like." She looked at Caroline again. "Is it worth dying a little inside, just to be safe from hurt, or failure? And there's more than one kind of loneliness. You could spend all your life with people who only know what they think you are, what they think you ought to be, and never let you be anything different."

"Yes, but growing can hurt, and you don't always get what you want," Caroline warned. "Or sometimes you do, and then find that you don't want it so much after all."

"So is it better to not even try?" Alice asked earnestly. "I was going to say 'to stay at home,' but surely home is where you are yourself, your best self, isn't it? I don't think that for me it is Whitby. Not any more."

"Then perhaps you had better find out where your home truly lies," Caroline conceded.

"Will you ask Mr. Fielding to consider allowing me to join your group? I won't expect anything beyond the opportunity to work. And I won't ask to come with you now. That would be embarrassing for you, after this."

"Of course I'll speak to him," Caroline said quickly. "I think if it is really what you want, then we will find a way to make it possible. But all the same, give it a little longer, perhaps a bit more thought."

Alice smiled. "And I think maybe Miss Rye would be better for Douglas anyway. Haven't you noticed?"

"Yes, of course I have."

"And I don't mind," Alice said with surprise. "When I realized that, then I knew I shouldn't marry him. It would be dishonest, and I don't want to start any undertaking by lying to myself."

"I don't see that possibility in you," Caroline said frankly.

$\mathcal{T}$hey all retired early. There was little to stay up for. It did not seem possible that it was Christmas Eve. Everything was motionless in the icy grip of the snow. No one had the heart to put up wreaths of holly or ivy, ribbons of scarlet, or any of the other usual ornaments. The weather had prevented the delivery of the tree. It would be a somber Christmas, shorn of all the trimmings, haunted by Ballin's death.

Caroline lay in bed wondering what else she could

do. They did not know when the thaw would come, but it could be within the next few days. Then the police would be sent for. The reality of murder would no longer be avoidable. The players would be suspect, and every tragic or grubby secret would be dragged out, examined, and very probably misunderstood. Unless she could find an answer before then.

Eliza had questioned the servants, and they were all accounted for, as Caroline had expected. Joshua and Mr. Netheridge had searched the house again, but they had still not found Ballin's body. Where had they not looked? Why had anyone moved it? It could only be because there was something about it that would reveal who had killed him, and perhaps why.

Caroline was in bed, staring at the ceiling. She thought Joshua was asleep, but she was not certain. As soon as she knew for sure, she would get up and begin her own search for the body. Their only answers lay with Ballin himself. Something that forced the killer to go through the trouble of moving the body.

193

Ballin was quite a big man, and strong; he must be heavy. Inert bodies were not called "deadweight" for nothing. No woman could have carried him alone. Two together would have found it difficult, but perhaps not impossible. One man might have managed, if he was strong and used to lifting.

Joshua was asleep. She was sure of it now. Very carefully she slid out of the bed and crept to the dressing room, feeling her way. Thank goodness they had a separate room for clothes where she could light a candle and dress without wakening him. She must dress warmly, and put on her boots. She might need to go somewhere unheated.

She considered starting with the attics, but they were mostly servants' quarters. No doubt all the rooms would be used, one way or another, and the whole area would be far from private. Also, who would willingly carry a dead body up four flights of stairs? There might be box rooms up there, full of old furniture and suitcases, cabin trunks and the like. Excellent places to hide a body, but not if you were trying to do it alone, in the middle of the night.

She stood on the silent landing in the very faint candlelight, thinking. She must make no sound, or she would disturb someone. She could imagine the furor: the screaming if it were Mercy, or even Lydia; the outrage and suspicion if it were Douglas or Mr. Netheridge; the sarcasm if it were Vincent, or even James.

Of course one of them knew exactly where Ballin was. But that was a thought she refused to entertain. It would paralyze her. Courage. She must use all the courage she had. And for heaven's sake, also the sense.

How long did it take for a dead body to begin to rot, and to attract scavengers, not to mention smell? The rats and flies, so loved of Renfield, would soon give away a corpse kept in a warm place. Therefore it would be somewhere as cold as possible. And she couldn't be squeamish about searching.

They burned both wood and coal in the house fires, so there would be a coal cellar. Very possibly there would also be a place inside for wood, certainly at least for kindling. Had anyone looked there, thoroughly?

The house where the meat and other perishable food was kept would be perfect, but the servants would go in there regularly. They would check all the stores to make sure nothing was spoiling. But they might not go to the icehouse, not in this weather.

She went down to the cloakroom where she had left her outside coat when she had arrived, not knowing then that they would be unable to take walks. She put on her boots. The cellar would be bitterly cold, and dirty.

She lit one of the lanterns that were stored in the cloakroom and set off.

An hour later she was aching, filthy, and shuddering with cold, and she had found nothing that helped in the slightest to figure out what had happened to the body of Anton Ballin.

Think! It had to be somewhere. Was it conceivable that whoever had murdered him had somehow destroyed his corpse? But how? Burning? The only possible place for a fire big enough to get a whole body into would be the furnace used to heat the water in the laundry room. And the maids did the laundry regularly.

Were the fires kept going all night? Hardly likely, at least not hotly enough to destroy a corpse.

Still, she would look.

She went slowly, very reluctantly, to the laundry

room. The fire under the big copper tub in which the sheets were boiled was glowing dimly. One might have burned a rat in it, but nothing bigger. And the smell would have been awful.

She stood in the middle of the room and turned around slowly. Apart from the copper one, there were deep tubs next to the wall, and mangles. On the shelves above, there were many jars for all kinds of substances: soaps, lye, starch, chemicals for cleaning various stains on different kinds of fabrics.

She walked slowly through to the drying room. Long airing racks were suspended from the ceiling to deal with days when it was impossible to dry anything outside.

There was another large tub by the wall. She tiptoed over to it and lifted the lid, her heart pounding. There was nothing inside it but loose, light brown bran. It was useful for lifting certain stains, or for rubbing fabrics that needed extra care. Determined not to have to come back and search the room again, she found a wooden spoon with a long handle and poked it down into the bran. It met no resistance. With a gulp of relief she closed the lid.

There was nowhere else left to look, except the still-room. There were plenty of bottles and jars in it, but a glance told her there was nowhere large enough for a corpse.

So where was he? It must be two in the morning now. Christmas Day. And here she was frozen cold, hunting around her hosts' laundry room for the body of a dead man. And she had told Alice that life in a company of touring actors was fun!

The only place left was the icehouse. It couldn't be there, but where else was there to look? The stables? No, Caroline knew enough of horses to rule that out. Horses smell death and are afraid of it. They would certainly have let people know if there were any sort of decaying body near them. Even in the hayloft the smell would be appalling, and they would have had a plague of rats within hours, let alone days.

There was no choice but to go outside across the yard to the icehouse. She went to the scullery door and unlocked it. Why anyone had bothered with the bolts in this weather was beyond her. Habit, and obedience possibly. They were stiff to move, and the top one was high, but she managed, with rather a noise. She hoped fervently that everyone else was asleep.

She pulled the door open and stepped out, holding the lantern high. She did not completely close the door: She needed the crack of light to guide her back, and somehow leaving it ajar made her mission seem less final.

The air was bitter but there was no wind at all. In fact, it was possible to imagine that it could thaw, just a little bit, by morning. She walked half a dozen steps across the yard. The snow was completely untrodden since yesterday's fall, and there was not a mark on it. It was deep enough to cover the top of her boots and cling to her skirts. When it melted she would be soaked.

The icehouse was ahead of her, half under some trees whose black branches seemed to rest on the roof. There was something else up there: piles of wood like discarded floorboards, half-covered with snow. There were more timbers to one side of the house, and bags of something. Coal? No, there was room in the cellar. Kindling? It would get soaked and be of no use. Perhaps rubbish no one had been able to dispose of properly in the snow.

In spite of the stillness, the wind seemed to sigh a little in the bare branches, and several lumps of snow fell off the trees. She was right: It was thawing, just a tiny bit.

Could the killer have put Ballin's body out here, with the rubbish? How long could it remain hidden? Perhaps they had planned to do something else with it after a few days?

She walked with difficulty, forced to lift her feet unnaturally high in the deep snow. Suddenly she was anxious. Should she look now, or ask Joshua to help her in daylight? But what a cowardly thing to do, when she didn't even know if there was anything here or not. And maybe if whoever killed Ballin saw her footsteps in the snow leading to the side of the icehouse, they would know someone had been there, and move the body before she had another chance to check for it.

She reached the sacks of rubbish, holding the lantern high so she could see. The timber had slid a little, and several pieces were lying over the tops of the bags. She put the lantern down carefully and started to lift the top piece of wood. She put it to one side and lifted the next one.

Then it happened—the shift in the snow on the roof. She looked up. A few lumps dropped off and fell onto the sacks. The stars were brilliant above the pale outline of the ridge, and she could see the ends of wood poking up. A larger lump of snow fell. Then as she stepped back, without thinking pulling the wood with her, there was a roar of sliding snow on the slates. A figure launched itself at her, diving downward, head thrown back, mouth wide open. It struck her so hard she staggered backward, falling into the deep snow as it landed hard, half on top of her. By the yellow light of the lantern she saw the hideously distorted face, glaring eyes, flesh eaten away and sliding off, teeth bared.

She screamed, again and again, her lungs aching.

Nothing happened. No one came.

Ballin's terrible face was inches from her, his body hard as rock. But something had happened to him, beyond agony, beyond death. The flesh of his cheeks seemed to have half-dissolved and slipped sideways, crookedly. Even his nose was rotted away, twisted to one side.

For a moment she thought her heart was going to burst. She was alone in the night with the face of evil, the vampire without his human mask. This thing was a creature of the night, dead and yet not dead.

There was no one to help. She must do this alone. She steadied her breath and forced herself to grab the lantern and look at the body. It was frozen rigid, as unbending as the planks of wood that had held it up there on the icehouse roof.

His face was terrible, as if it were falling apart. How could that happen in the paralyzing cold, and so soon after death?

She made herself look at it again, steadily. Her hand shook, and the light of the lantern wavered over Ballin's face. Caroline stared and stared, and slowly she realized that it was not decay that made him look as if he were rotting and falling apart. His face was literally sliding off his skin. It was actor's makeup. More than greasepaint, he had a thin layer of some rubbery kind of substance, a gum of some nature, to pad out his cheeks and nose. Underneath it she saw the harder, deeper lines of a different face, one that in some half-remembered way was vaguely familiar. She knew him, but she had no idea from where, or when.

And as she understood that, she knew why his killer had moved the body.

Shuddering with cold and horror, she gingerly pushed Ballin away and stood up. She must go and tell Joshua. If nothing else, they must put the body in some decent place, not leave him lying on the ground by the icehouse. None of the servants, rising early to prepare breakfast, must find him.

She tramped back through the snow to the back door. Thank heaven it was still slightly ajar. Her teeth were chattering from the cold.

She walked slowly through the scullery into the kitchen. She was trailing water behind her. Her whole coat was covered with snow from when she had fallen, and her skirt was wet at least a foot above the hem.

Where had she seen Ballin's true face before? It was in a photograph, she was sure of that, definitely not in person. But his name had not been Ballin. She would have remembered that. Anton. Had it been Anton something-else?

She was in the hallway now. Only a couple of candles were alight. The tall clock said it was nearly three in the morning. She reached the bottom of the stairs and started up, holding her soaked skirt high so as not to trip over it.

She was almost at the landing when she remembered. The photograph had been in the green room of a theater: Joshua had pointed it out to her because he felt that the man in it was a great actor. Anton Rausch. A handsome face, powerful. And there had been a tragedy connected to him. He had killed some actress in a murder scene in a play. A knife. It was supposed to have been a stage prop, a harmless thing whose blade would retract when it met resistance. Only it had not retracted, because Anton had replaced it with a real knife.

Or someone had.

It had ruined his career.

She realized she was standing still at the top of the stairs. The cold ate through the fabric of her clothes and chilled her flesh.

She walked to her own bedroom and opened the door. She still had the lantern, and she set it down on the dresser.

"Joshua," she said calmly.

He stirred.

"Joshua. I know who killed Ballin, and why. I found his body."

He sat up, fighting the remnants of sleep. Then he saw her clearly. "Caroline! What happened?" He started to climb out of bed.

"It's all right," she said, her voice steady. "I'm cold, and a bit wet, but I'm perfectly all right. I found Ballin's body."

"Where?" He was up now. He reached for his robe, warm and dry, and put it around her. "Did you say you know who killed him, or was I imagining it?"

"Anton Rausch," she said quietly. She was shivering uncontrollably now.

"Ballin?" he said incredulously. "Oh, God! Of course. I should have known the voice. I saw him play Hamlet! I only met him in person once. Oh, heaven, I see."

"Do you?" she asked.

"Yes. Vincent. He was the other actor involved in that tragedy. He was the lover of the actress who died. Anton Rausch was her husband."

"Then he came here for revenge? But how could he know Vincent was here? And why now? That was years ago."

"Perhaps Anton could prove his innocence now. I don't know."

"But if he attacked Vincent, for revenge, then Vincent is not guilty of murder. It doesn't make a lot of sense," she argued. "And again, how did he know Vincent was here?"

Joshua shook his head. "It wasn't a secret. The theater knew where we would be, the manager, several others. It just wasn't advertised because it was a private performance."

"But if Ballin attacked him—I still think of him as Ballin—why didn't Vincent defend himself?" she asked.

"Because Anton didn't attack him," Joshua said quietly. "Think about it, Caroline. If Anton had attacked Vincent with that sharpened broom handle, then Vincent would have injuries: tears on his skin at least, wrenched muscles where they fought, bruises, perhaps rips in his clothes. Vincent must have attacked Anton, taking him by surprise. He went armed. He intended to kill Anton before Anton could prove who actually changed the knives that night."

She tried to imagine it. "How could Anton prove such a thing, after all this time?"

"I don't know. Perhaps a dying confession. A stage-hand, a prop man. We'll never know now."

"Then why didn't Anton just tell the authorities, and have Vincent arrested?"

"There are lots of possibilities. Perhaps he wanted Vincent to do something for him, a repayment other than having to answer to the law."

"Poor man," she said quietly. Joshua took her hand. "We can't leave him lying in the snow by the icehouse. Should we waken Mr. Netheridge and tell him?"

"Yes. I think so. Since this is his house, he deserves to know. We have taken enough liberties already."

"Have we?"

He smiled. "Yes. Very definitely. And unfortunately we won't even be entertaining his guests on Boxing Day."

"But you will help Alice, won't you?"

"Of course. We might even perform *Dracula* some-time." He smiled with a wry twist of his lips, his eyes very gentle. "But we will have to find another Van Helsing."

❖

*I*n the morning, breakfast was eaten, largely in silence. Then Mr. Netheridge asked the guests to leave the withdrawing room for a certain matter of business he had to attend to, all but Joshua, Caroline, and Vincent. Perhaps no one except Caroline noticed that the butler and three footmen were waiting in the hall.

"Is this about Alice . . . Miss Netheridge?" Vincent asked curiously when the doors were closed.

"No," Netheridge replied. "I think perhaps Mrs. Fielding will explain it best."

Vincent was standing in front of the great stained-glass window. His back was to the magnificent view it partially concealed, even though it was possible to see through its paler sections the sunlight on the snow beyond.

"How melodramatic," he said, looking at Caroline. "You seem to have acquired a taste for acting yourself. But you need more practice. Your timing is poor, and timing is everything."

"Actually, I prefer to work with the lights," she responded. "So much depends on which light you see things in. Anton Rausch has taught me that," she replied.

Vincent paled. Suddenly his body was stiff, his hands clenched.

"I found his body," she added simply. She touched her own cheek. "The makeup had slipped, and I recognized him from a photograph I once saw in a theater. He was a great actor, better than you, Vincent. That's what it was all about, wasn't it? Nothing to do with that actress, beautiful as she was."

Vincent's face hardened. "He came for revenge. He didn't know who had fixed the blade at the time it happened, and of course they jailed him. He must have worked it out, or somebody else did, and told him. He attacked me. He came at me with that broom handle, spiked at the end like the blade of a halberd." He lifted his shoulder a little, his gaze steady on her face. "Wicked-looking thing. I barely had time to defend myself and turn his lunge back against him."

"Vincent, don't make more of a fool of yourself than necessary," Joshua said wearily. "You are at the end of this. There is no way you could have turned a weapon that length against the man holding it. And there are no wounds on you. You attacked him, to keep the truth from coming out. I'm sure he did want revenge, at a price you could not afford."

It was Netheridge who moved toward Vincent. "The snow is thawing. We'll be able to get a man out to fetch the police by tomorrow. Until then we'll lock you in one of the storerooms—"

Vincent sprang suddenly and without any warning. He leaped forward and grasped a light wooden chair. If he smashed it, then one of its legs would make a dagger of hard, sharp-pointed wood. But Caroline was faster; she picked up the onyx ashtray from the table nearest her and threw it at him. He ducked it, caught his arm in the huge velvet curtain, and lost his balance. He fell backward, dragging the curtain with him, fighting hard and panicking. There was a splintering crash and the whole vast stained-glass window buckled and flew outward, Vincent with it. His thin scream echoed back in the air, and then stopped abruptly.

Caroline felt the sudden rush of cold air, and at the same moment heard in the silence the church bells in the distance, ringing out Christmas morning in Whitby.

Slowly she walked over to the gaping space and forced herself to look down. Vincent lay on his back on the paved courtyard two stories beneath, arms and legs splayed like a broken doll in the snow.

She heard movement and felt Joshua's arm around her, holding her tightly, close to him.

"There's nothing you can do," he said, his voice catching a little. "I'd rather it were this way, for Vincent as well as for us."

"I suppose so," she agreed softly. She turned back from the clean, icy air, retreating into the room again.

Eliza was staring at the remnants of the window, her face ashen.

"I'm so sorry," Caroline apologized.

Netheridge cleared his throat and put his arm around Eliza. "Not your fault, Mrs. Fielding. It was a tragedy that just happened to end here. It isn't a quick thing. Mr. Singer let the evil in a long time ago, and it must have been like a rat, gnawing at his soul all these years. I've learned a thing or two from your play, the bits I've seen, and what Eliza's told me about. Made me think I've been holding on too tightly to things I

211

shouldn't have. Kept too many doors shut for too long. Time to open them, time to let the good in, too."

Caroline nodded very slowly, and smiled at him.

Behind her, other church bells joined in the welcome of the day when, briefly, gloriously, all mankind is at home.

A Christmas Garland

For all those who keep hope alive
in the darkness

$\mathcal{L}$ ieutenant Victor Narraway walked across the square in the cool evening air. It was mid-December, a couple of weeks before Christmas. At home in England it might already be snowing, but here in India there would not even be a frost. No one had ever seen snow in Cawnpore. Any other year it would be a wonderful season: one of rejoicing, recalling happy memories of the past, and looking forward to the future, perhaps with a little nostalgia for those loved ones who were far away.

But this year of 1857 was different. The fire of mutiny had scorched across the land, touching everything with death.

He came to the outer door of one of the least-damaged parts of the barracks and knocked. Immediately it was opened and he stepped inside. Oil lamps sent a warming yellow light over the battered walls and the few remnants of the once-secure occupation, as they had been before the siege and then its relief. There was little furniture left whole: a bullet-scarred desk, three chairs

219

that had seen better days, a bookcase and several cupboards, one with only half a door.

Colonel Latimer was standing in the middle of the room. He was a tall and spare man well into his forties; a dozen Indian summers had burned his skin brown, but there was little color beneath it to alleviate the weariness and the marks of exhaustion. He regarded the twenty-year-old lieutenant in front of him with something like an apologetic look.

"I have an unpleasant duty for you, Narraway," he said quietly. "It must be done, and done well. You're new to this regiment, but you have an excellent record. You are the right man for this job."

Narraway felt a chill, in spite of the mild evening. His father had purchased a commission for him, and he had served a brief training in England before being sent out to India. He had arrived a year ago, just before the issue of the fateful cartridges at Dum Dum in January, which later in the spring had erupted in mutiny. The rumor had been that the bullets were coated with animal grease, in the part required to be bitten into in order to open the cartridge for use. The Hindus had been told it was beef fat. Cows were sacred, and to kill one was blasphemy. To put cow fat to the lips was damnation. The Muslims had been told it was pork fat, and to them, the pig was an unclean animal. To put that grease to your lips would damn your soul, although for an entirely different reason.

Of course, that was not the only cause of the mutiny by hundreds of thousands of Indians against the rule of a few thousand Englishmen employed by the East India Company. The reasons were more complex, far more deeply rooted in the social inequities and the cultural offenses of a foreign rule. The bullets had merely been the spark that had ignited the fire.

Also it was true, as far as Narraway could gather, that the mutiny was far from universal. It was violent and terrible only in small parts of the country. Thousands of miles remained untouched by it, lying peaceful, if a little uneasy, under the winter sun. But the province of Sind on the Hindustan plains had seen much of the very worst of it, Cawnpore and Lucknow in particular.

General Colin Campbell, a hero from the recent war in the Crimea, had fought to relieve the siege at Lucknow. A week ago he and his men had defeated 25,000 rebels here at Cawnpore. Was it the beginning of a turning of the tide? Or just a glimmer of light that would not last?

Narraway stood to attention, breathing deeply to calm himself. Why had he come to Latimer's notice?

"Yes, sir," he said between his teeth.

Latimer smiled bleakly. There was no light in his face, no warmth of approval. "You will be aware of the recent escape of the prisoner Dhuleep Singh," he went on. "And that his guard, Chuttur Singh, was hacked to death in the course of Dhuleep's escape?"

Narraway's mouth was dry. Of course he knew it; everyone in the Cawnpore station knew it.

"Yes, sir," he said obediently, forcing the words out.

"It has been investigated." Latimer's jaw was tight, and a small muscle jumped in his temple. "We know Dhuleep Singh had privileged information regarding troop movements, specifically regarding the recent patrol that was massacred. We also know the man could not have escaped without assistance." His voice was growing quieter, as if he found the words more and more difficult to say. He cleared his throat with an effort. "Our inquiries have excluded every possibility except that he was helped by Corporal John Tallis, the medical orderly." He met Narraway's eyes. "We will try him the day after tomorrow. I require you to speak in his defense."

Narraway's mind whirled. There was a chill like ice in the pit of his stomach. A score of reasons leaped to his mind why he could not do what Latimer was asking of him. He was not even remotely equal to the task. It would be so much better to have one of the officers who had been with the regiment during the siege and the relief do it, someone who knew everyone. Above all, they should have an officer who was experienced in military law, who had defended men dozens of times and was known and respected by the regiment.

Then a cold, sane voice inside assured him that it was precisely because he was none of these things that Latimer had chosen him.

"Yes, sir," he said faintly.

"Major Strafford will be here any moment," Latimer continued. "He will give you any instruction and advice that you may need. I shall be presiding over the court, so it is not appropriate that I should do it."

"Yes, sir," Narraway said again, feeling as if another nail had been driven into the coffin lid of his career.

Major Strafford's dislike of him dated back to the time before he had joined the regiment. Almost certainly it stemmed from Narraway's brief acquaintance with Strafford's younger brother. They had been in the same final year at Eton, and little about their association had been happy.

Narraway had been academic, a natural scholar and disinclined toward sports. The younger Strafford was a fine athlete but no competition for Narraway in the classroom. They existed happily enough in a mutual contempt. It was shattered one summer evening in a magnificent cricket match, nail-bitingly close, with Strafford's team having the slight edge—until Narraway showed a rare flash of brilliance in the only sport he actually enjoyed. The dark, slender scholar, without a word spoken, bowled out the last three men on Strafford's team, including the great sportsman himself. The fact that he did it with apparent ease was appalling, but that he did not overtly take any pleasure in it was unforgivable.

And Strafford Minor had never been able to exact his revenge on the field, which was the only place he could redeem his honor. Other victories did not count. And practical jokes or barbed wit looked to be nothing more than the spite of a bad loser.

But that was boyhood, two years ago and thousands of miles away.

"Captain Busby will prosecute," Latimer was going on. "The evidence seems simple enough. You will be free to interview Corporal Tallis at any time you wish, and anyone else you feel could be helpful to your defense. If there are any legal points that you need to clarify, speak to Major Strafford."

"Yes, sir." Narraway was still at attention, his muscles aching with the effort of keeping complete control of himself.

There was a brief knock on the door.

"Come," Latimer ordered.

The door swung open and Major Strafford came in. He was a tall, handsome man in his early thirties, but the echo of Narraway's schoolfellow, so much his junior, was there in the set of his shoulders, the thick, fair hair, the shape of his jaw.

Strafford glanced at Latimer.

"Sir." He saluted, then, as he was given permission, relaxed. He regarded Narraway expressionlessly. "You'd better read up on the case tonight and start questioning people tomorrow morning," he said. "You need to be sure of the law. We don't want anyone afterward saying that we cut corners. I presume you appreciate that?"

"Yes, sir." Narraway heard the edge of condescension in Strafford's voice and would dearly like to have told him that he was as aware as anyone else of how they would all be judged on their conduct in the matter. More than that, the future of British rule in India would be flavored by reports of decisions such as this. The whole structure of Empire hung together on the belief in justice, in doing things by immutable rules and a code of honor that they themselves never broke.

Thousands of men were dead already, as well as women and children. If the British ever regained control and there was to be any kind of peace, it must be under the rule of law. It was the only safety for people of any color or faith. Otherwise there was no hope left for anyone. Right now there seemed to be little enough in any circumstances. Delhi had fallen, Lucknow, Agra, Jhelum, Sugauli, Dinapoor, Lahore, Kolapore, Ramgarh, Peshawar—and on and on. The list seemed endless.

"Good," Strafford said curtly. "Whatever you think

you know, you'd better come and see me and tell me at least the outline of your defense." He looked at Narraway closely, his blue eyes curiously luminous in the light of the oil lamp. "You must be sure to mount some defense—you do understand that, don't you? At least put forward a reason why a man like Tallis should betray the men he's served beside all his career. I know he's a quarter Indian, or something of the sort, but that's no excuse."

The tight muscles in his face twitched. "For God's sake, thousands of soldiers are still loyal to their regiments and to the Crown, and fighting on our side. Tens of thousands more are going about their duties as usual. No one knows what the end of this will be. Find out what the devil got into the man. Threats, bribery, got drunk and lost his wits? Give some explanation."

Narraway felt dismay turn to anger. It was bad enough that he was picked out to defend the indefensible; now Strafford required him to explain it as well.

"If Corporal Tallis has an explanation, sir, I shall offer it," he replied in a hard, controlled voice. "I cannot imagine one that will excuse his conduct, so it will be brief."

"The explanation is not to excuse him, Lieutenant," Strafford said acidly. "It is to help the garrison here feel as if there is some sense in the world, some thread of reason to hold on to, when everything they know has turned into chaos, the people they love are slaughtered, and the nation on every side is in ruins." A flush spread up his fair face, visible even in this wavering light. "You are here to satisfy the law so that we do not appear to have betrayed ourselves and all we believe in, not to excuse the damned man! I know you are new here, but you must have at least that much sense!"

"Strafford . . ." Latimer said quietly, interrupting for the first time. "We have given the lieutenant a thankless task, and he is quite aware of it. If he isn't now, he will be when he has looked at it a trifle more closely." He turned to Narraway again. "Lieutenant, we do not know where we shall be by the turn of the year, here or somewhere else, besieged or comparatively free. This matter must be dealt with before then. The women and children need a celebration, however meager. We need hope, and we cannot have that without a quiet conscience. We cannot celebrate the birth of the Son of God, nor can we ask His help with confidence, if we do so with dishonor weighing us down. I expect you to conduct Tallis's defense in such a manner that we have no stain on our conduct to cripple us in the future. Do I make myself clear?"

Narraway took a deep breath and let it out slowly. "Yes, sir," he said, as if he had some idea in his head how to do it. It was a lie, by implication. He had no idea whatsoever. He saluted and left the room.

He walked away from the command building without any notion where he was going. It was totally dark now, and the sky was burning with stars and a low three-quarter moon. There was sufficient light to see the broken outline of the walls and the black billows of the tamarind trees, motionless in the still air. His feet made no sound on the dry earth.

He passed few other people, even on the road beyond the entrenchment. Sentries took no notice of him. In his uniform he passed unquestioned.

Half a mile away, the vast Ganges River murmured and shifted in the moonlight, reflecting on an almost unbroken surface, streaked here and there only when the current eddied.

The prisoner who had escaped and the guard who

had been savagely murdered in the process were both Sikhs. That in itself was not extraordinary. The Sikhs had been on both sides during the mutiny. India was made up of many races and religions, languages and variations in culture from region to region. Internal wars and squabbles abounded.

John Tallis was British, but one set of his grandparents had been Indian—Narraway had no idea, though, if they had been Hindu, Sikh, Jain, Muslim, or something else. He dreaded meeting the man; yet, as soon as he had any clarity in his mind as to how he should approach the subject, he must do it.

The crime had been monstrous, and there could be no defense. The guard, Chuttur Singh, had been hacked to death. It had not even been a simple breaking of his neck or cutting his throat, which, while gruesome, would at least have been quick. The massacre of the patrol was equally bloody, but it was, in a sense, part of war and so to be expected. But it would not have happened had the enemy not known exactly where to find the patrol and at what hour. When Dhuleep Singh had escaped, he had passed that information over.

What had changed John Tallis from a first-class medical aide, a man of compassion and loyalty, into a man who could betray his own?

Narraway was walking slowly, but already he was at the beginning of the street that led into the battered and bedraggled town. In the distance he could see the spires of two of the churches against the skyline. Nearer him, there were a couple of shops with their doors closed. There was hardly anyone around—just a glimpse of light visible here and there from a half-shuttered window, a sound of laughter, a woman singing, the smell of food. The air was chilling rapidly with the darkness. If he stood still, he would become aware of the cold.

He started to walk again, smelling the dampness of the river as he got closer to it. The earth was softer under his feet.

What did Latimer really expect of him? He had implied that he required Narraway to find something that would make sense of Tallis's act. Because people needed to understand, because no one could fight chaos. Maybe a lack of reason is man's last and worst fear, the one against which there are no weapons?

Was Latimer—as the man in command, the one everybody looked toward—trying to create a belief in order, a reason to fight?

Narraway went through the last trees and stared across the surging water, away to the northeast, where he knew Lucknow was, beyond the horizon. Exactly a month before Christmas, General Havelock had died outside the city, worn out, beaten and bereaved. Had he finally felt the consuming darkness of loss and panic and been overwhelmed by it, unable to see hope?

How much is morale affected by the character of a leader? It was a question Narraway had asked himself many times, both at school and, later, in his military training. An officer must know his tactics, must understand both his own men and his enemy, must be familiar with the terrain and with the weapons, must guard his supply lines, must gain all the Intelligence of the enemy that he possibly can. Above all he must earn the trust and the love of his men. He must act decisively and with honor, knowing what he is fighting for and believing in its worth.

Latimer had to deal with John Tallis immediately, and in such a way that no one afterward would look back on it with shame. Victor Narraway had been chosen to bear the burden of defending a man who was totally indefensible. He was strategically and emotionally trapped, exactly as if he were besieged in the city of his own duty, and there was no escape, no relief column coming.

It was already late. There was no point in waiting any longer. The situation would not get better. He turned away from the sheet of light on the river and walked into the shadows again, making his way back toward the barracks and the makeshift prison where John Tallis was being kept until his trial, and inevitable sentence of death.

He must begin tonight.

*T*HE GUARDS STOOD TO ATTENTION OUTSIDE THE PRISON door. In the darkness it was hard to see their faces, so their expressions appeared blank. They looked at Narraway with indifference. One of them held up an oil lamp. They were both young, but they had been in India long enough for their fair skins to be burned dark by the sun. They recognized the insignia of rank on Narraway's uniform.

"Yes, sir?" the taller of the two said with no flicker of interest.

"Lieutenant Narraway, to see the prisoner," Narraway told him. He expected distaste, a forced civility. He saw nothing at all. Was the man genuinely impartial, or—after the siege—had he no feelings left?

"Yes, sir," the man said obediently. "You'll pardon me, but may I have your sidearm, sir? No weapons allowed when you're with the prisoner."

Narraway remembered with a chill that the prisoner who escaped had murdered the guard with the guard's own weapon. He handed over his revolver without demur.

A moment later he was inside the cell, standing face-to-face with John Tallis. The man was tall, a little hunched over; naturally lean, but it seemed the low rations and the exhaustion from first the long, burning summer under siege, and now imprisonment, had left him gaunt. He still wore his army uniform, but the trousers bagged on him. The tunic hung hollow over his chest and pulled a little crookedly at the shoulders. His thick, black hair was lank and his blue eyes startling against the sun-weathered skin of his face. He might have been any age, but Narraway knew he was thirty.

Narraway introduced himself. "I'm going to defend you at your trial," he explained. "I need to talk to you because I have no idea what to say. I know your regimental history because it's a matter of record. Everyone agrees you were one of the best medical orderlies they've ever known."

He saw Tallis lift his chin a little, his mouth twisting into a self-mocking smile. His teeth were white and perfect. "That'll come in useful if I'm ever charged with incompetence," he said, his voice cracking a little. "Unfortunately, it doesn't help now."

Narraway struggled for something to ask that might offer any mitigation. What on earth did Latimer think he could do? There was no defense! He was going to be completely useless.

"Tell me what happened," Narraway said aloud. "Exactly. Give me all the details you can remember. Go back as far as you need in order to make some sense of it."

Tallis looked incredulous. "Sense? When did you get here, yesterday? There isn't any sense. It's a colossal pileup of one idiocy after another. Bullets greased with pig fat, cow fat. It's probably bloody mutton anyway! Nobody's listening to anyone. People are just settling old scores, or shooting scared at anything that moves."

"You must have had some reason for helping Dhuleep," Narraway said desperately. "Give me something, anything at all to say on your behalf."

Tallis's eyes opened wider. A look of terror was naked in their blue depths for a moment; then he concealed it. He swallowed convulsively, his throat so tight he all but choked. "I didn't do it," he answered. "And I haven't any idea who did."

Narraway was at a total loss. Tallis was not justifying himself, not making excuses, not blaming anyone else. He was just giving a sheer, blank denial.

"But there was no one else who could have," Narraway said as calmly as he could manage. "Everyone else's whereabouts are accounted for, one way or another."

"Then someone is lying, or got it wrong," Tallis answered. "I did not kill Chuttur Singh or let Dhuleep Singh go. You have to prove that."

"I've got less than two days," Narraway protested. "Captain Busby's already been through all the details of the night, and Major Strafford. There was no one else who could've done it."

"I didn't do it," Tallis said simply. He gave a shrug of his bony shoulders. "I'm a medical orderly. I only kill people by accident, never on purpose."

Narraway was startled, angry; then suddenly he saw the black humor in Tallis's eyes. In that instant he felt a wave of compassion for the man's courage. In other circumstances, a thousand miles from here, he could have liked him. He licked his dry lips. "Where were you when Chuttur Singh was murdered?" he asked.

Tallis thought for a moment. "If it happened when they say it must have happened, I was in the storeroom, alone. I was counting what supplies we had, and going over what we could possibly get ahold of if any kind of relief supplies came in, and considering what we could make for ourselves with things from the bazaar," he replied. "If I could prove it, I would have already. It's a pretty good mess in there. We've been making do for a long time. I'm just about out of inventions."

"Did you not make lists of anything, inventory, notes about what to get?" Narraway struggled to think of something that could help support Tallis's claim.

"Certainly," Tallis replied, "but I can't prove when I wrote them. I could have done it anytime in the previous twenty-four hours. Believe me, I count those damn things in my sleep, hoping I've got it wrong and that we have more supplies left than I thought. I sometimes even get up in the night and count again, hoping items have got together and bred—like bedbugs."

Narraway ignored the analogy. "Did you know Chuttur Singh?" he asked.

Tallis looked away, and when he spoke, his voice was thick with emotion. "Yes. He was a good man. Silly sense of humor. Always coming up with crazy jokes that weren't funny. But he made me laugh, just because he laughed."

That sounded so normal to Narraway; it was absurd that they should now be talking about murder, thinking about an execution. It was a nightmare he must wake up from. He used to know how to do that, when he was a boy—make himself wake up. "And Dhuleep?" he asked.

"Different altogether," Tallis replied, watching Nar-

raway closely. "Quiet. Never knew what he was thinking. He used to recite poetry to himself. At least I think
it was poetry. It could have been a string of curses, or a
recipe for curry, for all I know. Or a letter to his grandmother." He blinked. "If they hang me, will you write a
letter to *my* grandmother? Tell her I died bravely? Even
if I don't?"

Narraway drew in his breath to remonstrate with
him, tell him not to be flippant or not to give up hope,
but the words slipped through his mind and were all
useless. They were going to hang Tallis in less than a
week, get the whole matter dealt with and out of mind
before Christmas, for everybody's sake—everybody except Tallis and his family back in England, proud of
him.

"If it should prove necessary, and you give me an ad-
dress, of course I will," he said instead, as if it were the
natural answer. But it was also of no help at all.

Narraway knew Latimer was looking for more than
Tallis's surrender. He needed some answers that allowed the men to have hope, which revealed a spark of
sanity amid the senselessness and the fear.

"Somebody did kill the man, and you're the only one

unaccounted for," he pointed out sharply. "Everyone else was busy and in someone else's sight. Look, if you had a reason for killing him, if you know something about him, tell me." He started to say that for Tallis's own sake he should explain the circumstances, but stopped abruptly. Whatever Tallis said, it would make no difference at all when it came to his sentence, and they both knew it. If he pretended that wasn't the case, Tallis would think him a liar or a fool, and it would break the spiderweb-thin thread of connection between them.

He began again. "The regiment needs to know the truth. There's chaos and death everywhere. We need at least to believe in ourselves."

Tallis closed his bright blue eyes. "My God, you're young! What—nineteen? This time last year you were sitting for exams behind some neat, wooden school desk, waiting for the bell to ring and tell you time's up."

"Twenty," Narraway snapped, feeling the color burn up his face. "And I—" He stopped short, stung by shame at the absurdity of getting defensive about his age and experience. Tallis was facing trial for his life, and he had been offered nothing better than the most junior lieutenant to defend him.

Narraway lowered his voice and kept it steady. "Please, for the sake of the regiment, the men you know and who've trusted you—help them make sense of this. Give them a reason, whatever it was. Why did you want to rescue Dhuleep? What did you think he was going to do? If you didn't mean to betray the patrol, or get Chuttur killed, what went wrong? If someone is lying, who? And why?"

Tallis stared at him, started to speak, then stopped again.

"Are you protecting someone else?" Narraway asked sharply. "Is this some debt of honor you owe?"

Tallis was completely stunned. No denial in words could have carried such complete conviction as his silence.

"Debt of honor?" he finally said, incredulously; then he started to laugh, quietly but with a jarring, hysterical note underneath it.

Narraway felt ridiculous and painfully helpless. He had expected anger, despair, self-pity, but not this.

Then Tallis stopped laughing as suddenly as he had begun.

"I did not murder Chuttur Singh to pay a debt of

241

honor," he said quietly, almost mildly. "I'm a medical orderly who just happens to be wearing a soldier's uniform. I save lives—any lives. I'd treat a sick dog if I had one. Any debt of honor I owe is to medicine."

Narraway could think of nothing to say. He did not even know where to begin.

"For God's sake, man, think!" he said desperately. "Who was friendly with Dhuleep? Who might have owed him something, or sympathized with him? Is it possible someone had a . . . a debt to cancel, or a feud with anyone who was part of the patrol that was wiped out? If it wasn't you, then it has to have been someone else."

Tallis's brilliant blue eyes opened wide. "Is that why they're saying I did it? Because I owed someone, or hated someone on the patrol? I'm a medical orderly. I don't even know who was on the damn patrol! I'm one of the few men in the station who never has time to gamble or run up any debts. Half of our medical staff was killed in the siege."

"Then think of anything you've heard, gossip, tales," Narraway urged him. "We've no time."

"I've no time," Tallis corrected him. "The regiment

needs this incident put to bed as quickly as can be made
to look decent. I can't blame them for that." He pulled
his lips tight. "Happy Christmas, Lieutenant."

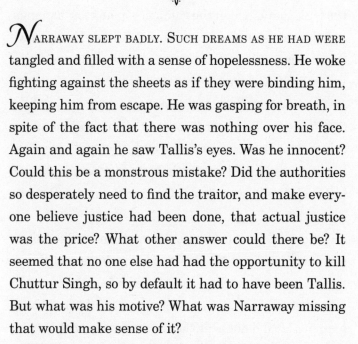

NARRAWAY SLEPT BADLY. SUCH DREAMS AS HE HAD WERE
tangled and filled with a sense of hopelessness. He woke
fighting against the sheets as if they were binding him,
keeping him from escape. He was gasping for breath, in
spite of the fact that there was nothing over his face.
Again and again he saw Tallis's eyes. Was he innocent?
Could this be a monstrous mistake? Did the authorities
so desperately need to find the traitor, and make everyone believe justice had been done, that actual justice
was the price? What other answer could there be? It
seemed that no one else had had the opportunity to kill
Chuttur Singh, so by default it had to have been Tallis.
But what was his motive? What was Narraway missing
that would make sense of it?

He was so tired, his head pounded and his eyes felt
full of grit.

*H*E ROSE EARLY, WASHED, SHAVED, AND DRESSED BEFORE going to the mess and taking a brief breakfast. He liked the fruit they'd had in the summer—mangoes, bananas, and guavas—but there was none left now. He acknowledged other officers but sat alone so he could avoid conversation. He needed to think.

Latimer had given him one day to create some kind of defense for Tallis. An appeal for mercy was pointless. The only answer to a verdict of guilty was execution. Soldiers were killed all the time. Cawnpore was steeped in blood. Death was cheap. One more was barely even noticeable.

After he had eaten, he went outside and walked along the dusty roadway. The low bungalow houses of the officers were ramshackle now: three or four rooms set in extended areas that in better times would have been gardens. He did not hear the silent footsteps behind him and only became aware of Captain Busby when the man spoke, almost at his elbow.

"Morning, Lieutenant," Busby said briskly, not disguising the fact that he had obviously sought Narraway out intentionally. "Good idea to get away from the barracks a bit. Glad you thought of it."

"Good morning, sir," Narraway replied tersely, wondering what Busby wanted with him. He was not ready to discuss strategy yet, or accept any instruction, for that matter.

They came to a crossroads. Busby moved closer, obliging Narraway to accept the tacit guidance and turn along the wider road into the town.

The first building they passed was the library, looking dusty and deserted, its doors closed. There were two women standing on the steps with books in their hands, chatting to each other then glancing up the street toward the tearooms and the bazaar.

A couple of men came down from the breakfast club next to the library and nodded at the women, touching their hats courteously. They looked serious, avoiding anything more than the minimum acknowledgment of Busby and Narraway.

The billiard rooms were deserted this early in the day, as was the Freemasons Lodge with its handsome entrance. Narraway had intended to go toward the river.

He did not want to face the noise and the constant interruptions of the bazaar, with pleas to buy this or that, but Busby was intent on conversation and he could not escape.

"Doesn't look the same as it used to," Busby said ruefully as they passed the doors of the newsrooms. "Everyone's trying, of course, but the memories of the siege are all over the place, and the fear that it will happen again lingers. Every place you look at makes you think of someone who's gone. Thank God it's Christmas soon. Remind us who we are, what we believe in." Busby was talking casually, but his voice was edged with tension. He was a fraction taller than Narraway and perhaps seven or eight years older. His fair skin was burned red-brown by the Indian sun, and he walked with a very slight limp, as if from an old wound. There was a thin scar on the side of his left cheek, hardly noticeable.

"Yes, sir," Narraway agreed. "I've seen some of the children making garlands of colored paper," he added as they passed the theater, where in better times the younger men had performed all kinds of music and comedies for the general entertainment. It was silent now.

Busby smiled. "We must protect the men. They have

a right to expect that of us. We bring them here, thousands of miles away from everything they knew and loved, and expect their total loyalty. We receive it, and sometimes I think we take it too lightly. We owe it to them, especially the wives of those killed on the patrol, to see this trial to a swift end." He glanced at Narraway and then back at the rutted road they were walking along. "I hope you can see that." He said it with a lift in his voice, as if it were, at least in part, a question.

He outranked Narraway, but in the matter of the trial of John Tallis, rank should mean nothing.

"As rapidly as justice allows, sir," Narraway agreed.

"What witnesses do you propose to call?" Busby asked rather briskly.

"I don't know," Narraway admitted. "I only got the case yesterday evening, and I've never represented anyone on trial before."

"For heaven's sake, you're an officer, man!" Busby said dismissively. "I'm not a lawyer either. We're after the truth, not tricks of the law. A loyal Sikh officer has been cut to pieces, and ten of our own men were ambushed out there." He waved his arm in a general southerly direction. "Nine of them are dead. We've got widows, at least half a dozen more fatherless children. Tallis is responsible for that. The legality of it is just for the record's sake; don't harrow up everyone's emotions and open old wounds by asking a lot of unnecessary questions."

Narraway did not answer. There was no point in telling Busby that the colonel had asked him to do more than just tidy it away. Latimer wanted answers, wanted to understand what had gone so terribly wrong.

They walked a few paces in silence. A man pushing a cart of vegetables veered and jolted over a hole ahead of them. Two women—probably officers' wives, from the cut of their clothes—passed on the opposite side, inclining their heads slightly.

"I'm not sure if you are the right man for this," Busby went on, now staring straight ahead. "We might have been better off with someone who'd actually been through the siege and understood the suffering, the deeper issues."

"I think Colonel Latimer chose me precisely because I hadn't been through it," Narraway answered. "He wants this to be fair. If I'd been here through the siege, I'd have loyalties to certain men more than others, perhaps men to whom I owed my life. I might not favor them in any way, but people couldn't be sure of it, of my motivations."

Busby was quiet. They passed a small nondenominational church on the other side of the street. The post office was just ahead of them. They both looked battered, scarred by shells that had exploded too close. A shop nearby was darkened by the stains of an old fire, spreading out like the shadow of a hand.

"I don't know who you're going to call," Busby said suddenly. "No one else could have done it, you know. Don't go trying to raise doubt as to the honor of decent men. Apart from the fact that you won't get Tallis off— and by God, neither should you—you certainly won't do yourself any favors. If you want to make a career in the army, you'll understand loyalty." His voice took on a sudden, intense emotion. "That's what it's all about— courage under fire, steadfastness, and loyalty. You're no damn use to man or beast if your own men don't know that, come hell or high water, they can trust you."

He glanced sideways at Narraway, his eyes sharp. Then, after a moment's penetrating stare, he looked ahead again. "I assume you know that already, and I don't have to tell you? Make a good job of this and the whole regiment will respect you. Filthy responsibility, I know."

"Yes, sir," Narraway agreed, trying to put his words carefully. "My aim is to defend Tallis so that no one afterward—history, if you like—can say he wasn't dealt with fairly. I hope that won't take time, and I sincerely hope it won't necessitate my calling anyone as witness to an event that distresses them more than is unavoidable. But haste now may lead to grief; to dishonor that will later damage the regiment, and even the reputation of the Indian army in the future."

Busby stopped abruptly and swung around to face Narraway. "I think I underestimated you, Lieutenant. You're going to be a damn nuisance, aren't you? But if you think you can teach me the best way to handle this and earn the regiment's loyalty and respect, you are profoundly mistaken. Which I will soon show you."

"Yes, sir," Narraway said with a brief flicker of satisfaction. "I'm sure you will, sir, and with the utmost fairness. You can hardly fail to secure Tallis's conviction, considering the circumstances."

"I don't just want to secure his conviction, damn it,"

Busby said sharply. "I want to get the matter over with, with the least pain to the men and women who have suffered abominations you can't even begin to imagine." He swiveled around and started to walk swiftly back toward the barracks and the entrenchment where the army had been besieged. "Come!" he commanded.

Narraway turned and followed him, catching up with an effort. He did not want to go to the entrenchment again. He knew what had happened there, and could imagine the terror of it all. It was a barren square of ground, a hundred yards or so in either direction, with two- or three-story buildings along most of two sides. The rest was walled by simple earthworks, dug by spade and thrown up to less than the height of a man. During the eighteen days and nights of the incessant bombardment from Nana Sahib and his men, nine hundred people had lived there. Many had died of heatstroke, of cholera, or from their wounds.

Narraway still shuddered as he pictured the people huddled together, terrified, exhausted, trying to protect one another, waiting for relief that never came. He could see the ghosts of them in his mind. He wanted to turn and walk away, but he could not ignore Busby, who was his senior officer. And perhaps even more than that, he did not want Busby to know how deeply affected he was.

He stood silently. If Busby had anything to say, he would have to initiate the conversation himself.

In the distance a dog barked, a woman called out a child's name. There was an echo of laughter, exactly as if everything were perfectly normal—sounds of life, like new green shoots of trees coming up after a forest fire.

"Don't let them down, Narraway," Busby said at last. "You owe them."

Narraway wanted to say something brave, about justice having nothing to do with emotion or personal loyalties, but all the words that came to his mind sounded trite, and they would only anger Busby. Worse than that, he would not truly believe in them himself.

Busby was staring at him, waiting for his response.

"As I see it, sir," Narraway began awkwardly, "the most important thing is that when the mutiny's over and order is restored, India knows that British justice is fair and objective, sir."

Busby shook his head, momentarily taken aback. He started to speak and then changed his mind.

Narraway waited. He longed to leave this place, but he would not go until Busby did.

"I don't envy you," Busby said at last. "I suppose you have to make a show of it. Mind you do just enough."

"I didn't choose this, sir," Narraway answered.

"Nobody chooses their military duty, Lieutenant," Busby said tartly. He stared across the entrenchment. "These poor devils didn't choose to be here either. Just make as much of an effort as you have to so there's no question that the hanging is fair."

"Yes, sir," Narraway answered automatically. He was not sure if he meant it.

Busby turned and began to walk back the way they had come, his shoulders squared, but there was no spring in his step, no vigor.

Narraway waited a few moments longer, then left also, feeling as if he were turning his back on the ghosts, in a way denying them.

He needed to think. At the moment all he had for a defense was to try to discredit the witnesses Busby would call, and that was precisely what Busby had just warned him against. No one needed to tell him that attacking another man would earn him no friends. Most of them had already suffered deeply, lost friends and, in some cases, wives they loved, seen horrors Narraway himself could only imagine. He had been in India a year but he was an outsider to Cawnpore, and no one would forget that.

If his father had not insisted that the army would make a better man of him than a few years at university, Narraway would now be huddling beside a fire in some lodgings at Cambridge, worrying about cramming for an exam, and looking forward to going home for Christmas. His greatest discomfort would be trifling cold, the greatest danger not doing well enough and getting lower marks than he should have.

He had not chosen this. He remembered his last evening at home before taking the train to Southampton and then boarding the ship for what had seemed an endless journey south, around the Cape of Good Hope, into the Indian Ocean. Weeks cooped up, nothing more than a tiny dot on a measureless expanse of water, everywhere he looked nothing but blue. They could have been the only men alive on the earth and there'd be no way of knowing. Even the burning, blazing white stars in the sky above him changed, especially around the southern tip of Africa, before they started north again and re-crossed the equator.

That endless journey—for what? Some of the men he had come to know on that ship were already dead as a result of this savage mutiny—in so many cases, Indian against Indian. He had heard that there were only a little over twenty thousand Queen's troops in India and, of course, far more East India Company men, with all their wives and children—as opposed to Indians num-bering uncounted millions.

Without realizing it, he was walking toward the river. Its swift, brown water was dangerous, full of snakes and other creatures, especially along the banks. But it still held a fascination for him: a sense of width and a freedom that the land did not.

Was that a log floating half-submerged in the water? Or a crocodile? If he watched to see, what else would he miss? Crocodiles sometimes came out onto the banks. He had seen their teeth, like a double row of jagged nails, needle-sharp. They could take a man's leg off in a single movement. He did not believe the stories that they were not aggressive and preferred to eat fish.

As he stared at the water, he wondered whether he was Tallis's best chance or his worst. There was only one possible end for Tallis, really— the gallows. The difference lay in whether it appeared that someone had fought for him, or not. Narraway himself was expendable. If everyone loathed him afterward and he went down in history as the man who had tried to excuse Tallis, that was the price of a swift and unquestioned execution, and the matter laid to rest before Christmas.

And if John Tallis was innocent? Was that even possible?

The log in the river moved and sank gracefully beneath the water, leaving a momentary wake behind it.

Crocodile.

The facts said that Tallis was the only one who could be guilty. And yet when Narraway pictured his face again, recalling it as vividly as if he had seen it just moments ago—the clear, burning blue eyes—doubts arose in his mind. Irrational, but undeniable, doubts.

Then who could be guilty? Who was lying? He could not imagine that several men were all lying to save the man who had really murdered Chuttur Singh and let

Dhuleep go. And if they were, would they allow Tallis to be executed for it?

Narraway could not get rid of the feeling that Tallis trusted him. All sorts of arguments came into his mind as to why it was not trust so much as hope, hope that Narraway could help. Or perhaps it was just a brilliant piece of acting. Or—and this was the easiest to understand—it was a denial to himself that he could have committed such a betrayal, a refusal to face the fact of his own guilt.

But looking at Tallis, that was not what Narraway had felt. He believed he had seen real desperation there, the kind a man has when truth is on his side.

How could Narraway even begin? If Tallis was innocent—and that was the only assumption he could work with—then either someone was intentionally lying, presumably in order to protect himself, or someone had been badly mistaken, gotten the facts wrong. Check everything—that was the only workable possibility, Narraway decided. It would at least provide him with his own set of details. Stand where each man said they had been, prove for himself that they had seen what they said they had, time it all, go over the work they claimed to have been doing. Find the mistakes, the excuses, or the lies.

He turned and headed back through the trees toward the town.

The events of the mutiny were about a year old. It had begun in January, in Dum Dum. Almost every day since then there had been some new disaster, victory and then reversal, siege and relief, a new uprising somewhere else. How ridiculous to be trying one soldier for the death of one guard in the middle of Cawnpore while all over northern India, tens of thousands of men shot and slashed and stabbed one another.

He looked around at the officers' sprawling houses, with their verandas; their wide, scruffy gardens; the tamarind and mango trees, the lazy wind not stirring the leaves. In the summer the heat had been furnace-like, brutal. Now, at night, it was sometimes even cold.

He was not fighting with sword or rifle, although that would come soon enough. Scores of towns and cities were besieged or already fallen. This was only a respite.

In the meantime, as this day dwindled into nothing and disappeared, Narraway must prepare for the hopeless task of pretending to defend John Tallis, for which everyone would despise him, in spite of the fact that they knew he had no choice. He was cast as the second villain in a charade.

He increased his pace a little. He would speak with the witnesses Busby would be bound to call. That had to be the three men who answered the alarm and found Chuttur Singh dying on the floor in a pool of his own blood, and Dhuleep Singh gone.

He was walking past one of the rows of houses where various noncommissioned officers had their homes. They were all built of brick coated with white plaster, in various degrees of shabbiness. Verandas ran around three sides of each one, a flight of half a dozen or so steps leading up to the doors. They each stood separately in their own arid two or three acres, as if space was no object at all.

Narraway knew what they were like inside. The main door led into a wide, comfortless sitting room full of overused furniture—items that looked like they had been salvaged from a secondhand sale and intended only for temporary use, until something worthier could be found.

On either side would be smaller rooms, for beds, and one for a bath. The water for it, when needed, was left to cool outside in a row of large, porous red jars, so the officer's bath might be refreshing.

He looked back at the road and saw ahead of him a woman walking slowly. She had a small child in her arms and a large bundle of shopping carried in a string bag, its handles biting into her shoulder. She was bent under the weight of it and limping slightly, although from what he could see of her slender figure, she was not many years older than he.

Narraway increased his pace and caught up with her.

"Ma'am!" he said more loudly than he had meant to.

She halted and turned slowly. Her face was gaunt, and there were smudges of dirt where the child's dusty fingers had touched her cheek, but her skin was smooth, blemishless.

"Yes?" she said without curiosity. There was anxiety in her eyes, a shadow not unlike fear.

"May I carry the bag for you?" he asked. "I'm going

the same way you are. Please?" he added. He smiled at her. "My day has been fairly useless so far. I'd like to do something to make it better."

She smiled at him, suddenly and radiantly. It took away all the weariness and showed that she was indeed probably no more than thirty at the most, and pretty.

"Thank you, Lieutenant." She accepted, making a move to put the child down so she could unhook the bag and pass it to him, but he eased it off her shoulder and took it without her needing to. Its weight startled him. No wonder she had moved so slowly. The strings of the bag must have hurt her.

They started to walk again, still fairly slowly.

"You are new here," she observed, looking straight ahead of her. The child in her arms looked to be less than two, probably well able to walk, but not far or fast. It regarded him solemnly with long-lashed eyes of golden brown. Its hair was curly, and long enough for Narraway to be uncertain if it was a boy or a girl.

"Does it show so much?" he asked, referring to her observation of his newness. "Or do you know everybody?"

"I know most everybody," she replied. "Of course,

261

people come and go a lot, just at the moment." She made a sad little grimace. "But you look a bit paler, as if you weren't here during the heat." Then she blushed at her lack of tact in having made so personal an observation. "I'm sorry."

"No reason to apologize," he replied. "I never thought of that. I suppose I stick out like a row of sore thumbs."

She laughed at the image of such a thing. "Next time I see you in the parade ground, I shall think of a row of sore thumbs," she said cheerfully. "That will be a new insult for the sergeant major to think of. Except I see you're a lieutenant. I don't suppose you do a lot of marching around to orders."

"Not in the way you mean," he replied. "Although I feel rather a lot as if I'm marching round and round, to orders, and accomplishing nothing."

She looked at him curiously. "A lot of army life is like that. At least my husband always used to say so."

He heard the past tense in her speech and saw the moment of pain, the tightening of her arms around the child. There did not seem to be anything he could say that would help, so he walked beside her in silence for twenty or thirty yards. Then a hideous thought occurred to him. Had her husband been among the soldiers of the patrol that Dhuleep Singh's betrayal had killed? Suddenly, intensely, he realized that he could not afford to know the answer. He could not tell her who he was, and he was ashamed of that. It was a new and much harder bite into the soft flesh of his self-belief. How horribly lonely he was going to be after he had stood up to defend John Tallis, never mind that he had been ordered to do it, and that they could not hang Tallis until justice had been formally satisfied.

He had been trying to frame a few questions to ask her about Tallis, anything that might allow him to learn a little background. Now the words froze on his tongue. The strings of the bag were cutting into his hands. He wondered what was inside it. No doubt fruit, vegetables, rice, food for herself and the child. Would she marry again one day and have more children, or was this one going to grow up alone?

He wanted to speak with her. It seemed cold to walk side by side and say nothing, but consciousness of what the next couple of days would bring, and how differently she would see him, kept him silent. How long would it take him to live it down? The man who tried to defend

John Tallis. Is that who he would remain to the people here?

She stopped at a gateway outside a house exactly like all the others, at least from the outside.

"Thank you," she said with a shy smile. She bent and put the child down. It stood uncertainly on its feet before gaining its balance, then sat down suddenly.

"I'll carry the bag as far as the steps for you," Narraway replied. "Then you can carry him." He gestured toward the child, who was making an unsuccessful attempt to stand again.

"Her," she corrected him. "Thank you." She bent and picked the child up.

Narraway followed her up the path. They were still several yards short of the veranda steps when the front door burst open and a boy of about five came running out, a streamer of bright red paper in his hand.

"Mama!" he shouted with triumph. "I made three chains! All colors. And Helena made one too. It's not as good as mine, but I showed her how."

"That's wonderful." She smiled back at him. He had curly brown hair like hers but huge dark eyes that must have come from his father. "Helena?" she called out. "David said you made a chain too. Come and show me."

A girl of perhaps three stood inside the door, looking at Narraway warily.

"Come on!" her mother encouraged her.

Slowly she came across the veranda and took the steps, one down, standing on it, then the next down. She had a bright blue paper chain trailing behind her. She reached the bottom and joined her brother. She held the chain out to her mother, but her eyes were on Narraway all the time, curious but guarded.

He looked at the chain. "It's beautiful," he told her solemnly. "Did you really make it yourself?"

She nodded.

"Then you are very clever," he said.

Slowly, shyly, she smiled at him, showing white baby teeth.

"It's for Christmas," the boy explained. "To put up in the house."

"It will be lovely," he answered.

"Do you have Christmas?" Helena asked him.

" 'Course he does, silly!" Her brother shook his head

at her ignorance. "Everybody has Christmas!" He looked at Narraway. "She's only three. She doesn't know," he explained.

Helena held out the bright blue chain. "You can have it, if you like," she offered.

He drew in breath to refuse, politely, but saw the smile again, and the hope. He glanced momentarily at the woman, uncertain what to do.

"Take it." Her lips formed the words silently.

Narraway bent down a little to reach the chain and touched it. It was smooth and bright, the paper stuck together a trifle crookedly.

"Are you sure?" he asked. "It's very beautiful. Don't you want to keep it?"

She shook her head, still holding it out to him.

"Thank you very much indeed." He took it gently, in case she changed her mind at the last moment and clung on to it. "I shall put it up in my house, near where I sit, so I can see it all the time." She let it go and it fell loose in his hands.

The woman picked up the baby and carried her to the top of the veranda steps; Narraway handed the bag to her, then waited as they all went inside, the two older children still watching him as he turned and walked down the path again, holding the blue paper chain in his hand.

THE PRISON WHERE DHULEEP SINGH HAD BEEN HELD faced a large, open yard with buildings on three sides and an open dogleg way out, which was where most of the observation had taken place. Men had been working at various jobs of maintenance and repair, the sort of routine necessities that occupied most of a soldier's day when he was not in battle or marching from one place to another. They were tedious tasks but better than standing idle. It was easy to imagine leaving such a post, and then having to be a little imaginative with the truth in order to cover your absence.

Narraway stood in one place after another, checking the angles of sight, the possibilities of error or invention. Could any man have been so absorbed in his work as not to notice someone else pass by him? He did not believe it.

Had anyone left his stated position and then had to

cover his absence? It seemed like the only answer. Proving it would be almost impossible. Even the attempt to prove it would earn him enemies.

*H*e began his questioning with Grant. He had been the first man to reach the prison after Chuttur Singh had raised the alarm. He was not yet on duty now, having been on guard most of the night before. Narraway went to see him, feeling mildly guilty for waking the man when he must be tired. But lack of time left him no alternative.

Narraway went in through the gate, past some ponies picketed near a magnificent mango tree. He walked briskly to the veranda and up the steps, and knocked on the door. He knocked a second time, not really expecting an answer, then pushed it open and went in.

"Corporal Grant!" he called clearly.

There was silence.

Rather than call again, he crossed the sitting room. There was a large, rickety table in the center with a half bottle of brandy on it, four empty soda water bottles, and a corkscrew. Used glasses sat where four card players had obviously been the previous evening. There was also a box of cigars, a few odd magazines, a rather ornate inkstand, a bundle of letters, and a revolver.

The rest of the furniture he ignored, going past more chairs, a battered Japanese cabinet, and a corner stand with assorted hog spears, buggy whips, and a shotgun. He did glance at the various pictures hanging on the wall, hoping they might give him some idea as to Grant's origins and character. There was a school photograph. There was also a painting of a soldier with a woman in clothes of perhaps twenty or twenty-five years ago, judging from the style of the woman's hair and the line of as much of her dress as he could see. They were probably Grant's parents.

"Corporal Grant!" he called again, more loudly. He did not want to intrude into the bedroom. It would be ill-mannered. He would not appreciate a senior officer doing the same to him. Also he wished to make an ally of the man rather than an enemy, at least to begin with. "Corporal Grant!" he repeated.

There was a stirring from the room beyond, then the sound of feet on the floor and a rustle of fabric. A moment later Grant appeared in the doorway, tousle-haired, still half asleep. His trousers had been hastily pulled on, and his tunic was not yet fastened.

"Yes, sir. I am Grant," he said.

"Sorry to disturb you," Narraway began after introducing himself. "I wouldn't waken you now, except that I have only today to speak to everyone about the Tallis case. I've been detailed to defend him. Since you were the first on the scene, I thought I should begin with you."

Grant blinked. He was a good-looking young man, perhaps four or five years older than Narraway, with a slight country burr to his voice. Narraway placed his accent as Cambridgeshire, or a little farther north. His hair was brown with a touch of auburn, his skin burned by at least one Indian summer.

"Oh." Grant sighed. "I see. Well, I can't tell you anything more than what I've already told Captain Busby. Sorry."

"Finish dressing." Narraway made it more a suggestion than an order. "I'll make us tea."

Grant gestured toward the third room. "Kitchen's there. There are servants somewhere. Probably left me to sleep. I hate having them fussing around when I'm . . ." He did not bother to finish the sentence. Narraway already knew he had woken him.

Ten minutes later they sat in the central room with tea in front of them on the table. Grant was in full uniform and freshly shaved. But he still looked tired, and there were dark smudges around his eyes. He seemed nervous, but Narraway attributed that to the stress of remembering a shocking experience and having to recount it, knowing that it would end in the execution of a man he had possibly known quite well and certainly trusted.

"I don't know what I can tell you that makes any difference," Grant said.

"Just tell me what happened," Narraway replied. "If I know what you're going to say to Captain Busby, at least I have the chance to prepare for it."

Grant shook his head. "It won't make any difference," he said unhappily. "I don't know what the devil got into Tallis. I always thought he was a decent chap. In fact, I liked him. Everyone did. Well . . . one or two of

271

the officers thought his sense of humor was a bit off." He looked at Narraway quickly. "They just didn't understand. When you deal with illness and injuries every day, if you don't laugh sometimes, even at crazy things, you go mad."

"You have been out here long?" Narraway asked, looking at Grant curiously, wondering what his experiences had been that caused him to speak with such feeling.

"Couple of years," Grant replied. "I was in the Crimea before that."

Narraway winced. The disasters of that war, the fatal mistakes, were legend already. "Balaklava?" he asked, before he thought of the possible inappropriateness of the question in the present circumstances.

Grant pulled a wry face. "Thank God for Colin Campbell," he said briefly.

Narraway was impressed, in spite of himself. "Were you there with him?"

Grant straightened in his seat a fraction, some of his weariness disappearing. That was an answer in itself. "Yes. Another damn stupid war we got into by accident because we didn't look where the hell we were going!" He rubbed his hand over his brow, pushing the heavy hair back. "Sorry. There are times when I'd put the whole damn government on horseback and order them to charge the enemy guns—with bullets coated in pig grease! Mixed metaphor. Sorry. I lost friends in that too."

Narraway sat silent, thinking of all the young men who had died needlessly because someone didn't know, or didn't think about, what they were doing. Every one of them had been somebody's son, somebody's friend.

Grant rubbed his hands over his face and drew in a long breath, letting it out in a sigh. "Perhaps Tallis did go mad, poor bastard. I hate this more than facing the enemy in the field. But I can only tell you what I know."

Narraway jerked himself back to the present.

"That's all I want," he said quietly. It seemed odd to be in this silent, rather shabby house, sitting over cups of tea, talking about betrayal and murder conversationally, but with hands that trembled and voices that every now and then rasped in the throat. "You heard the prison alarm," he prompted. "Where were you?"

273

"About a hundred yards away, in one of the outbuildings," Grant replied. "I was checking munitions stores. I dropped what I was doing and went outside—"

"Did you see anyone else?" Narraway interrupted.

"Not ahead of me, and I didn't look behind. It's sort of cluttered there . . . sheds, outhouses, that sort of thing. There was a pony and cart off to the left. I just noticed it out of the corner of my eye as I ran to the prison."

"Anybody else moving? Running?" Narraway asked.

"No. I must have been the nearest person."

"When you got to the prison block, the outside door was open?"

"No. It's a makeshift prison. The real prison was too badly shelled. This does pretty well because it was a magazine of some sort. Not hard to make a couple of cells inside, and the whole thing locks only from the outside. Ideal, really. Escape-proof, without help."

"Any other prisoners there at the time?"

"None except Dhuleep." Grant looked down at his lean, sunburned hands on the table. "Before the mutiny there would be the occasional insubordination, drunken fights and things, maybe even a theft or two. Since the

siege and the massacre, no one steps out of line. Those
of us left are . . . close." He looked up, hoping Narraway
would understand without the need for explanation.

Narraway nodded. "What had Dhuleep done?"

"Dereliction of duty. Off his guard post at night. I
thought he'd just gone to get some sleep or something
like that. We're all tired, a bit jumpy." He sighed. "But
of course he could have been anywhere."

"Most likely trying to find information about the patrol," Narraway replied.

Grant looked down at the table again. "Yes—I suppose so. Looks like it now, doesn't it?"

"How did you get in?"

"It's easy enough from the outside. The key's there."

"What did you find when you entered?"

Grant's face tightened, his eyes suddenly bleak.
"Chuttur Singh was on the floor in the main room outside, lying near the door. He must have used his last
ounce of strength to reach up and pull the alarm. The
cell door was open. There was no one inside, just Dhuleep's bedding on the floor and a plate of food, spilled . . .
and blood. Lots of it. There was a trail of blood from the
cell across the floor to where Chuttur had crawled. He

was in a terrible state, his uniform slashed half to pieces, scarlet with his own blood. His face was gray, what I could see of it. He could hardly move." He stopped speaking for several seconds, emotion choking him at the memory.

Narraway waited.

A clock ticked on the mantelpiece. Somewhere outside a child shouted, its voice innocent, happy.

"He was dying," Grant went on with an effort. "He told me Dhuleep had escaped and to go after him. He had to be stopped because he knew about the route of the patrol. I wanted to stay and help him. He was . . . there was blood everywhere!"

He looked up at Narraway, agony in his face. "I should have stayed," he said hoarsely. "I left him and went after Dhuleep. I—I was desperate that he shouldn't get away, because of what Chuttur said about the patrol."

"How long had Dhuleep been in the cell?" Narraway asked.

"A day or two, I think," Grant replied.

"So they didn't know he had this information, or

they would have changed the patrol route, or time, or something?" Narraway said.

"Can't have," Grant agreed miserably. "But the patrol was ambushed. I know that for a fact."

"How?"

"Tierney told me."

"Tierney?"

"The one man from the patrol who lived, although he's in a bad way. He said they were taken totally by surprise and pretty well massacred. That's what letting Dhuleep go did. That's why they'll hang Tallis." His voice cracked. "God, it's a mess. Not that Tallis doesn't deserve it for what happened to poor Chuttur Singh. Regardless of what happened to the patrol, no one should die lying on the floor, alone. I shouldn't have left him." Grant stared into the distance, perhaps into a place inside his head rather than beyond the walls of the small, shabby house. "We didn't even get bloody Dhuleep anyway!"

"Did you find any trace of him?" Narraway asked, although he could not think what difference it would have made in the end.

"Not then. I suppose we thought we were on his heels and we'd catch up with him if we went fast enough. Damn lot of use that was." He sank into a silent misery, slumped in the chair, his tea ignored.

"So the others arrived soon after you? Attwood and Peterson?" Narraway continued.

"Yes."

"How long were you alone before they came?" Narraway asked.

Grant chewed on his lip. "About half a minute, maybe more, maybe less."

"Tell me what you did again, exactly."

"I went to Chuttur Singh." Grant was concentrating intensely, his mind back in those first awful moments. "I . . . I saw all the blood, and I knew he was fatally wounded. I just wanted to . . . I don't know. To say 'save him' is ridiculous. There was so much blood on his clothes, on the floor, it was clear he was beyond help. I suppose you don't think. You just . . ." He stopped. His face was ashen.

Narraway tried to keep the image from forming in his own mind, and failed. "You went to Chuttur Singh on the floor and realized he was past help. Then what?"

"He said . . . 'Dhuleep's gone,' I think. Something about someone else coming in, took him by surprise. Let Dhuleep out. He was mumbling, choking. I remember he said 'gone.' And then, 'Get him, he knows the patrol.' The man must have gone in the time it took Chuttur to crawl from the cell to the alarm." Grant was sweating, as if in his imagination he had made that desperate crawl himself.

"Then what?" Narraway asked.

"Then I looked into the cell, and he was right . . . of course. Dhuleep was gone. There was nothing there except blood and the heap of bedding, blood on that too. That was when Attwood and Peterson came."

"You told them what had happened?" Narraway pressed him.

"I told them that Dhuleep knew about the patrol and we had to catch him. Someone—I don't remember who—kneeled to see if he could help Chuttur, then we all went outside to hunt Dhuleep."

"Did you go together or split up?" Narraway was still clinging to the hope that one of them might have seen someone else.

Grant's voice took on a weariness. "We started within

sight of one another, but when there was no sign of him, we split up. I went west. I think Attwood went south and Peterson went down to the river, but I'm not sure."

"Did you draw others into the search? Ask people? Send anyone else out?" Narraway asked.

"Yes, of course. Anyone we spoke to."

"Did you find any sign of him?" Narraway went on. "What were you looking for anyway? Footprints? How would you recognize his? Anyone who'd seen him? Who else was around? Soldiers, women and children, civilians? Who could have seen him? Surely someone must've, with the knowledge of hindsight?"

"Of course," Grant agreed with a twisted smile. "With hindsight! A Sikh soldier in uniform. Not remarkable on any military station in northern India. No one knew that he was escaping. They probably didn't give him a second look."

"He'd just slashed a man to death," Narraway pointed out. "Those long, curved swords the Sikh soldiers carry are lethal! You said there was blood everywhere. Poor Chuttur bled to death. Dhuleep wouldn't have escaped without a mark on him. His trousers might have kept out of it, being draped and tight at the ankles as they are, and if they were dark or striped, you might not have noticed. But his tunic would be light, and they're loose and long-skirted." He waited expectantly, watching Grant's face.

"Perhaps he took it off?" Grant replied after a moment or two. "He'd have had to. You're right, there must have been blood on it. But he did get away, and it doesn't matter now. He'll be miles from here. God knows where. I certainly don't."

"You said you didn't find any trace of him then." Narraway was not ready to give up. "Did you later?"

"Yes." There was no light of satisfaction in Grant's face. "There was blood, just splashes here and there. And stains against a wall and a doorpost. Didn't help. I'd like to think some of it was his, but I don't know whether Chuttur even got a blow in or not."

He lowered his eyes, his mouth pulled tight. "I'm sorry. I liked Tallis. He seemed to be one of the best. But if he engineered Dhuleep's escape, then I'll be happy to see him hanged. I don't have to do anything but tell the truth for that. Someone came in from the outside. Had

to. No other way. That person must have struck Chuttur, stunned him at least, and then let Dhuleep out, and
maybe gone with him, leaving Chuttur to die."

"And you're sure you can't open that door except
from the outside?" Narraway asked.

"Yes. Didn't I say that?" Grant bit his lip. "Chuttur
couldn't even get out himself. All he could do was raise
the alarm and wait, poor devil. You can't save Tallis,
and you shouldn't." He faced Narraway squarely. There
was sadness in his eyes but no doubt at all.

NARRAWAY FOUND ATTWOOD, THE SECOND SOLDIER TO
arrive at the prison, working in the magazine. He had to
ask his superior officer for permission to release him for
as long as Narraway required him. It was given grudgingly, and Narraway and Attwood stood in the shadow
of the magazine's huge walls to talk. Narraway could
not help wondering why General Wheeler had not chosen this for his entrenchment, rather than the miserable earthworks.

Attwood was in his late twenties, a career soldier with a scar down one cheek and a finger missing on his left hand. He was short, solid, and barrel-chested, and had a vigorous Yorkshire accent. He regarded Narraway, who was from the south of England, with good-natured contempt.

"Nothing to help you, sir," he said briskly. "Heard the alarm. Ran to the prison. Got in behind Grant. Found the poor lad kneeling on the floor with Chuttur Singh, the prison guard. Damned good man. Best soldiers on earth, that lot, them and the Gurkhas."

"And Dhuleep Singh?" Narraway asked.

Attwood gave him a hard stare. "Gone, o' course. 'E's not going to hang around, once the door's open, is 'e? Look, I know you've got to put up some kind of a defense fer Tallis. It's the law, or we can't 'ang the bastard. But you're on a fool's errand. Not that we're short on fools around here," he added grimly.

Narraway's temper flared. "Anybody particular in mind, Sergeant?" he said sharply.

"Whichever damn fool put grease on the cartridges in Dum Dum, sir. Any idiot who'd served with Indians

could've seen that one coming. Offend every last bleedin'
one of 'em in one go!" He shook his head. "Don't tell me
it was some genius who actually wanted this bleedin'
chaos from Delhi to breakfast time!"

Narraway recalled what Grant had said about ignorance, but he could not afford to agree with Attwood, at
least not openly.

"Fool's errand or not," he replied, "I have to do the
best I can."

Attwood grinned, showing a broken front tooth.
"Don't make a mess of it—sir," he said cheerfully. The
"sir" was definitely ironic. "We don't want to have to do
it all again, so as we can 'ang 'im with a clear conscience.
Honor of the regiment that you fail nobly. Sir." In his
own mind—and probably that of most soldiers'—his
own three chevrons were worth more than the one pip
on Narraway's shoulder. "But you'll fail, either way. No
question to it," he added.

"Then help me to do it as nobly as possible," Narraway snapped. "When you were inside, what did you
see, apart from Grant on the floor beside the dying
guard?"

"No one else, sir," Attwood answered dutifully. "I

looked into the cell where Dhuleep had been. No one there, just bloodstained bedding on the floor."

"Lot of blood?"

"Quite a bit. As if there'd been a bit of a struggle, like someone—Dhuleep or Tallis—slashed at Chuttur, one man armed with one o' them long Sikh swords—edges like a razor, they 'ave—the other one trying to defend 'imself and not making much of it. Bloody murder, it was. Hardly a battle at all. Thank Tallis for that. Must 'ave caught Chuttur a hell of a whack before 'e ever let Dhuleep out. Damn coward, if you ask me—sir."

Narraway kept his temper with difficulty. It was not that he objected to what Attwood was saying, or to his contempt. He was angry with his own helplessness, and there was a degree of frustration inside him because he resented the fact that he had liked Tallis, that Tallis had even made him believe, for a moment, in the possibility of his innocence.

"Did you hear what Chuttur Singh said to Grant?" he asked aloud.

"No. Grant told us. Don't remember the words exact, but 'e said that someone 'ad come in an' caught Chuttur by surprise. Chuttur didn't tell 'im 'oo, of course. Maybe 'e didn't even see. Poor devil was dying when we got there. 'E'd been cut to bits." Attwood's face was bleak with anger and grief. He was a battle-seasoned soldier, but he was not immune to pain or the loss of a fellow soldier, even after the hundreds of deaths he had encountered and the whole brutal savagery of war.

"Couldn't 'elp 'im," he went on. " 'e told Grant to go after the prisoner. Said 'e knew the patrol's route an' that we 'ad to get 'im. We didn't, but by God, we tried." He clamped his mouth shut and glared at Narraway out of tear-filled blue eyes, defying him to offer pity.

"Yes, Sergeant, I know that," Narraway agreed quietly. "Corporal Grant said you found traces of blood, and boot prints. Although I suppose the prints could have been anyone's. Nobody saw him, is that right?"

"Nobody that's saying so," Attwood agreed.

"He must have had blood on him," Narraway pointed out.

"To some people, one Sikh soldier looks like another," Attwood said drily. "And some folks are too scared, keeping their eyes shut to what they don't want to see. Everybody's frightened and sick and too tired to see where they're going half the time, never mind tell one

Sikh from another. Lost too many people, sir. Too many women and children. What kind o' people kill women an' children, I ask you?" He blinked, glaring at Narraway. "Don't you string this thing out, sir. We need to finish it. Get it all squared away before Christmas. Remember 'oo we are and why we're 'ere. Get me?"

"Yes, Sergeant, I do," Narraway answered him. "But it'll never be over if we don't do it properly."

"Then do it properly—sir," Attwood said abruptly. "Now, if you'll excuse me, I'll be getting back to my duty." He saluted and, without waiting for Narraway's permission, turned on his heel and marched back up toward the magazine.

❧

NARRAWAY FOUND PETERSON, THE THIRD MAN TO ARRIVE at the prison, sitting at ease under a tamarind tree. He was off duty for another hour or so and was smoking a cigar alone, staring into the distance. He was a private soldier of two or three years' experience. When Narraway stopped in front of him and asked his name, he scrambled to his feet and saluted.

"Sir," he said obediently, stubbing the cigar out with reluctance.

"At ease, Private Peterson," Narraway replied. "I don't think I'll take up much of your time." He looked at the dry grass the man had been sitting on and decided it looked comfortable enough. He sat down gingerly and waited until Peterson did also.

"Tell me about the escape of Dhuleep Singh," Narraway said.

Peterson looked at him with as much distaste as he dared show. "You the officer who's going to defend Tallis?"

"Someone has to," Narraway replied.

"You're new here, aren't you?" He added "sir" after a moment's hesitation. It was not outrightly rude, but bordering on it.

"I've been in India nearly a year," Narraway replied. "I've only been in Cawnpore for a couple of weeks. Why? Is there something I should know?"

Peterson kept his expression as bland as he could. "Thought so. You wouldn't defend Tallis if you'd been here any longer."

"Why not? Don't you think he should be tried?"

Peterson remained silent.

"You'd rather we just hang him and be done with it?" Narraway asked. "You're right, I haven't been here very long, not long enough to realize we'd sunk that far, anyway. Is there anybody else we should hang, while we're about it?"

Peterson flushed. "No, sir. I just meant . . . I don't know how you can defend the man, that's all. The whole patrol was wiped out—all but Tierney, and he'll likely not make it. That's all down to Tallis, because if Dhuleep hadn't escaped, that ambush wouldn't have happened. If they'd been attacked out in the open, it would've been a fair fight."

"There's nothing fair about war, Private Peterson. I thought you would have known that, after three years' experience. But trials are supposed to be fair. That's the whole point of them. Justice, not revenge. We're meant to be above hanging a man just because we think he might have done something we don't like."

Peterson swiveled around to face Narraway, his eyes blazing. "Something we don't like?" He all but choked on the words. "He let Dhuleep out to betray the patrol so they were butchered. And one of them slashed poor

289

Chuttur Singh to death. I think 'don't like' is a bit pale—sir!"

"Yes, it is," Narraway agreed. "And after we are satisfied that he is the one who is responsible for all of it, we'll hang him from the strongest branch and leave him there to swing. But after—not before."

"He's the only one who could have," Peterson responded. "Captain Busby questioned everyone. There's no one else it could be."

"Then we'll have no problem proving that at trial," Narraway said, surprised that he was still reluctant to give up hope that there was some other explanation. "Tell me what happened when you got to the prison after the alarm went off."

Peterson essentially repeated what Grant and Attwood had said. He chose slightly different words, more from his own vernacular, but the facts and emotions were the same. When he had finished, he kept his eyes fixed on the middle distance, where two young women were walking with children by their sides. Narraway thought of the woman he had met earlier, the children with their colored paper chains, Helena's smile.

"We need this finished," Peterson said quietly. He took a long breath and let it out slowly. He was not looking at Narraway, and yet he was very clearly speaking to him, his voice low and urgent. "Everything we thought we knew for certain has got blown away. People we trusted turned 'round and killed us, all over the place. But Christmas is Christmas, anywhere. We've got to remember who we are. What things are like at home. What we believe in, if you"—finally he turned and faced Narraway, meeting his eyes—"if you get what I mean, sir?"

"I get exactly what you mean, Private Peterson," Narraway said, with an upsurge of emotion that took him by surprise. Peterson had appeared so ordinary, even tongue-tied, and yet he had explained the heart of what was needed better than any of the officers. "I'll do the best I can." He said it as if it were an oath. Then he stood up, and Peterson scrambled to his feet to salute him.

$\mathcal{F}$INALLY, NARRAWAY WENT TO THE HOSPITAL TO SEE THE surgeon, Major Rawlins.

Perhaps the only point in speaking with Rawlins was to be aware of what Busby might draw from him, although Narraway knew there was little he himself could do with the information. He was going through the motions, because he had been ordered to. He wished he could forget Tallis's face, his eyes.

He went into the hospital building and walked along its almost-deserted corridors, passing a few orderlies, a couple of soldiers with bandaged wounds, one on crutches. He asked for Rawlins and was directed onward. The place smelled of blood, bodily waste, lye, and vinegar. His stomach clenched at it, and he wished he could hold his breath. How many men and women had bled to death here, or died of disease?

He found Rawlins busy stitching a surface wound in a man's leg. Narraway had to wait until the doctor had finished and could give his attention to the matter that, for him, was far from urgent.

He had a small office, where he invited Narraway to sit down, waving him toward a rickety chair. He perched on the end of a table himself. Rawlins was a little more than average height, broad-shouldered, perhaps in his forties. His fair hair showed streaks of gray only as the light caught it. His skin was deeply burned by many years in the Indian sun. He was a handsome man, far more obviously English-looking than Narraway himself. Narraway had heard that Rawlins had an Indian wife.

"Thought you'd be coming," the doctor observed. "But there's nothing I can say that'll help you. Wish there were. I liked Tallis. He was a bit of a clown at times, but a damn good orderly. Would have made a good doctor, given the chance. Saved a few men's lives with nerve and quick thinking." His face was suddenly sad. "Don't know what the devil happened to him. About the best thing you can do for him is not give him false hope. There's only one way it can end."

"He says he didn't do it," Narraway replied. "The facts say he must have, and yet I find myself hard put not to believe him. Or at least not to think that he believes himself. Why would he do it?"

Rawlins shrugged. "God knows. Why would anyone, unless they sided with the mutineers? But if you were on their side, why the hell would you stay here instead

293

of slipping off to join them? Staying here, he had a good chance of being killed anyway. What a bloody mess. The last thing we need is to lose a really good medical orderly. Ask your questions. It's a waste of time, but I assume you have to go through the motions."

"I don't know what else to do," Narraway admitted. "There isn't any defense for such a thing." He wanted to tell Rawlins how helpless he felt and how totally confused he was by Tallis, but he despised complainers. "Busby's bound to ask you about Chuttur Singh. The way Grant describes it, Chuttur was struck on the head, probably dazed. Tallis let Dhuleep out of his cell. One of them took Chuttur's sword and hacked him to death, to try to prevent him from raising the alarm. Does that fit in with what you observed once Chuttur's body was brought to you?"

"Seems to," Rawlins replied, his face puckered with regret. "Based on the medical evidence, I can't see anything else possible, honestly. Chuttur had the exact injuries you describe. The Court will draw the obvious conclusion: Dhuleep was locked in his cell, so there had to be a third man, someone who got in from the outside. That person struck Chuttur, taking him by surprise or he'd have defended himself, and unlocked the cell so Dhuleep could escape."

"Any idea if Dhuleep was injured as well?" Narraway asked.

"Not a clue. I was told he left blood here and there, but not much," Rawlins answered. "Smudges, smears on a wall, a couple of footprints edged with blood. If he was hurt, if it wasn't just poor Chuttur's blood from his clothes, then he wasn't hurt badly. I'd like to think he was dead, lying out there in the scrub somewhere, or on one of those stony riverbeds, being picked apart by the carrion birds. But he was well enough to get as far as the rebels, because he told them where to ambush the patrol."

His face was tight with a sudden wave of emotion. If someone had brought the bodies back, Rawlins would have seen them, perhaps identified them before burial. And he would have treated the one man who came in alive but later died from his injuries—and also Tierney, the lone survivor. Being a soldier was easier, Narraway thought, than being an army surgeon. Even trying to defend Tallis was better than Rawlins's job.

"I don't suppose it matters anyway," he agreed. "As

you say, the facts allow for only one explanation. How is Tierney doing? Will he make it?"

"Could do," Rawlins replied. "Lost a leg. Wish I could have saved it, but it was shattered. You can see him if you want, but I doubt he can tell you anything. No question they were betrayed by Dhuleep, not that it makes any difference to your case either way. I wouldn't waste your time, and the Court's, even raising that question."

"I'd like to see him, if he's up to it." Narraway rose. "But I don't want to . . . upset him . . ."

Rawlins also stood. "He might be glad of someone to talk to. He's still in a bad way, just lying there alone most of the time. We do what we can for the pain, but he's not a fool. He knows everyone's clinging by our fingernails, as it were. We could all be dead in a few months if we don't turn this tide. The news is bad, isn't it?"

"Yes," Narraway confessed. "Far as I know. But we've got Campbell. He could turn the tide, by Christmas. Remember the Crimea, Balaklava?"

Rawlins grinned lopsidedly. "The Heavy Brigade: 'Here we stand, here we die.' " He paraphrased Campbell's famous exhortation to his men. "Not exactly what I had in mind."

"He won," Narraway pointed out.

"Yes, why shouldn't the tide turn?" Rawlins agreed. "I'll take you to see Tierney, if he's awake. This way."

Rawlins led Narraway into a small hospital ward where only one bed was occupied. A man lay slightly propped up on a pillow. His face was almost colorless and his cheeks were sunken, the bones sharp and protruding. His skin was stretched over them, papery and fragile. He might have been any age from twenty to forty. The bedding was draped over a frame above his right leg and the empty space where his left leg should have been.

Narraway wished immediately that he had not come, but it was too late to retreat. How did Rawlins deal with this sort of thing day after day and stay sane?

Although they had moved with very little sound, Tierney must have sensed their presence because he opened his eyes and looked at Rawlins.

"Hello, Doc. Come to see if I'm still here?" He gave a very faint smile.

Rawlins smiled back at him. "Only full-time patient I've got now. Have to see you," he replied cheerfully. "If I have nothing to do, they might not pay me. Then how will I buy a decent cigar?"

"That's what I'd really like," Tierney said huskily. "A decent cigar."

"I'll bring you one," Rawlins promised. "But if you set the bed on fire, then you can damn well lie on the floor."

Tierney laughed. It was a rough, croaking sound. "Like I'd know the difference! What've you got in this mattress? Sand?"

"Gunpowder," Rawlins replied. "So don't drop the ash, either." He gestured toward Narraway. "This is a brand-new lieutenant—at least, new to Cawnpore. Tell him about the place. We have decent mangoes here. And tamarinds, if you like them, or guavas. Nothing much else is worth anything."

"Any news?" Tierney asked, still looking at Rawlins.

"Nothing that I've heard," Rawlins replied. "If we win, I'll tell you, I promise. If we lose, you'll find out anyway." He gave a mock salute and left, walking back into the corridor, leaving Narraway alone by the bed.

Narraway lost his nerve to ask Tierney anything about the ambush of the patrol. It wouldn't make any difference to the trial anyway. It didn't matter where

Dhuleep Singh had gone or what he had told anyone. The murder of Chuttur Singh was enough to damn him.

"Where were you before here?" he asked conversationally.

"Delhi, God help me," Tierney answered with a downturned smile.

"I imagine it was pretty bad," Narraway sympathized.

"All so bloody unnecessary," Tierney replied, a trace of bitterness in his voice. "The Indian soldier's a damn good man. If we'd just listened, instead of always thinking we knew everything better. Took their loyalty for granted. Damn idiots should have seen it coming. Stupid bloody mess! You?"

"Calcutta," Narraway answered, thinking back to his arrival in India, confused, excited, and afraid, hearing rumors of unrest already. "Nearly a year ago. Glad I'd escaped the English winter!" He gave an ironic little laugh.

"Wouldn't mind a dusting of snow for Christmas," Tierney said. "Where are you from? You sound like Home Counties, but that could be education, I suppose.

I see you're a lieutenant, and you can't be more than twenty."

For no particular reason, except that he was eager to speak about something that had nothing whatsoever to do with India, mutiny, betrayal, wounds, blind stupidity, or trials, Narraway told Tierney about his home in the softly rolling hills and wide valleys of Kent. He spoke of long rides on horseback over the Weald in the early morning, with the light on the grass, which rippled like water in the wind.

"So what are you doing out here in the dust, eating yet another curry and wasting time waiting for something to happen?" Tierney asked with a slight, stiff shrug of his shoulders, his eyes smiling.

"Escaping boiled cabbage, gray skies, and biting wind with an edge of sleet in it," Narraway replied cheerfully. "And my father's wrath," he added.

"Which makes you much like the rest of us," Tierney commiserated. "Tell me more about Kent. Do you like the sea? I miss the sea, the smell of it and the cold, sharp spray on your face."

Narraway stayed and talked for close to half an hour, until he could see that Tierney was exhausted. Even then the soldier did not want Narraway to go. It was not until he unwittingly drifted off into a fitful sleep that Narraway walked softly away, grateful to have two feet to stand on, no longer even aware of the smells of blood and carbolic and other odors he would rather not name.

$\mathcal{H}$E NEEDED TO BE ALONE TO THINK. HE WAS TOO FILLED with emotion. The futility of it all was overwhelming him. Everyone knew at least something of the needless waste of the Crimean War and questioned the purpose of it. The army that had beaten Napoleon at Waterloo had rested too long on its laurels. It was now cumbersome and sorely in need of updating.

The idiocy of the grease on the bullets, which had fired a whole nation's mutiny, was still being excused by some. But it could've been avoided so easily! Was there no communication, no Intelligence from which to foresee such errors and avoid them? Didn't the army speak to the government, or listen?

This was such a small part of the whole, and yet thinking of a few greased bullet cases, Narraway saw the enormity of even the smallest thoughtless act. One match could light the flames that consumed a nation, especially if the earth was already tinder dry—and no one had noticed that, either.

For everyone's sake, he must do the job that Latimer had commanded him to do. If he did not defend Tallis sufficiently well, if the Court could not say honestly that he had been properly represented, then Tallis's execution would in a sense also be murder. It would seem to others as if the regiment had convicted him in order to appear to have dealt with its own failure—vengeance rather than justice. They would look weak, not to be trusted; more than that, history would judge them to be without honor.

He continued walking, his feet making little sound on the earth and the thin winter grass. He passed walls broken by shellfire. They were crumbling away now. Ahead of him was a small, grassy mound with a few tangled bushes at the base of three trees. They were spindly, graceful. One was leafless and clearly dead. The other two still had rich evidence of life and in spring would no doubt have leaves, perhaps even blossoms.

A few yards beyond was a round stone-rimmed well. There was nothing there with which to draw water, no covering to keep falling leaves out, no rope or pulley, no bucket of any kind.

He stopped and looked at it curiously. There was an air of desolation about it.

"You can't want to stand here, sir."

He turned and saw Peterson a few feet away from him.

"Can't I?" He was curious. Peterson's face was white, his eyes hollow, without life. "Are you ill?" he asked suddenly. "You look—"

Peterson shivered. "That's the well, sir—that well. You don't want to stand here."

" 'That well'?" Narraway repeated.

"Bibighar. They massacred the women and cut them up, cut their heads off, and their . . ." He made a helpless gesture, half indicating breasts. "That's where they threw the bodies. Then their children after them. Scores of them, not all of them even dead. Filled it right up. You don't want to stand here, sir."

Narraway thought for a moment he was going to be

303

sick. His stomach clenched, and the outlines of the trees blurred in his vision. Sweat broke out on his skin. He turned to face Peterson.

"No," he agreed. "I didn't know it was . . . this well." Carefully and a little unsteadily he put one foot in front of the other and walked away, Peterson a yard or so behind him.

He had heard the story in whispered pieces, conversations that trailed away into silence. Cawnpore had been relieved on July 17, about five months ago now, but the ghosts of the siege were everywhere. The heat had been appalling, over 120 degrees in the shade. The horrified soldiers of the relief had found the corpses of more than four hundred men, women, and children.

In the Bibighar—the huge, two-roomed house in which Nana Sahib had kept the women of his pleasure during his occupation of the town—the soldiers had found the walls scarred low with the marks of sword cuts where women had been beheaded while on their knees. It was littered with hair and the combs that held it dressed, children's shoes, hats, bonnets, the torn pages of Bibles and prayer books. They had looked down to find their boots submerged in blood.

"I'd slit him open and pull his entrails out," Peterson said quietly, staring into the distance. "And burn them in front of him, still attached."

Narraway found his voice with difficulty. "Nobody would charge you for it," he said, coughing a little to clear his throat. "But if they did, I'd defend you. You wouldn't need any better skill than what I've got to get you off. I don't know how anybody here is still sane."

"Maybe we aren't," Peterson replied. "I wonder sometimes if I am. I wake up in the middle of the night and I can still smell it. Funny that, isn't it? I can't always see it, but I can smell it, and I can hear the flies. Do you believe in God?"

Narraway was about to answer automatically, but then he stopped. Peterson deserved better than that. Narraway himself needed more than a trite response.

"Well, I certainly believe in hell," he said slowly, selecting his words. "So I suppose I must believe in heaven, too. And if there's a heaven and a hell, then I think there must be a God. All this is unbearable if there isn't."

Peterson shook his head. "It's not the same as good and evil. Nobody doubts that. But is there anybody in control of it? I wonder sometimes if there isn't. If it all just happens, and that's all there is. Is there any sense, any justice? Or is it up to us to make sense and justice?"

"That's a hell of a question, Private Peterson. But I suppose Bibighar is as good a place as any to ask it."

Narraway thought for a while. It was also a place that demanded answers to such questions, not just for Peterson, or the Court that was set for tomorrow, or Tierney, or John Tallis. He needed them for himself.

Peterson waited.

"If there was somebody in control, you'd think they'd make a better job of it, I suppose," Narraway began. "What happened here seems beyond ordinary human evil. It's as if someone opened a door into . . . something else. But if hell were not more despicable than anything a sane man can imagine, then maybe heaven wouldn't be higher than even our most exquisite dreams."

Peterson shook his head slightly. "Wouldn't you accept heaven a little lower if hell could be . . . not this bad?"

"I don't think anybody asked me," Narraway replied seriously. "But if they had, I don't know what I would have said. After all, we haven't seen the heaven part of it—only this."

"But you believe in it?"

Narraway suddenly remembered the blue paper chain, and all the women who were going to celebrate Christmas, for their children. "Yes, I do," he answered. "Lots of people do, no matter what happens. We pick up the pieces and start again, for the sake of those who believe in us. If we can do it, then the best in us is trusting in something, reaching toward something. And that's what's important."

"Reaching toward God?" Peterson asked. "Sir?"

"I think so. Something that is as good as this is awful. Believe it, at least until you wake up dead and find it isn't true."

Peterson's face relaxed in a smile. "I didn't expect you to be so honest. Thanks. But I'd still leave this place, if I were you." He motioned to the well in the distance.

Narraway agreed, and with a brief salute he walked away from the Bibighar and its ghosts.

KNOWLEDGE, THAT WAS THE KEY. NARRAWAY SAT ON THE stone buttress of the old armory, now little more than a pile of rubble. The wind was rising, cold-edged, tossing the leaves on the trees. Information was what mattered, and how it fit together to form meaning. Everything was a matter of putting the pieces into the right order.

One of the difficulties was that you never knew if you had all the pieces or if something vital was still missing, something that formed the center of the picture.

What had he overlooked? Because so far, it all made no sense. He was a soldier, not a policeman, not a lawyer. But he should still be able to understand it if he tried hard enough. He knew the people, he knew the events. Did he know them in the wrong order? Was it something missing that was wrong, or one cornerstone point that was a lie? What one change would alter it all so it fit?

There had been no one inside the prison except Chuttur and Dhuleep. The door opened only from the outside. Grant had found it closed, had gone in and discovered the dying Chuttur, who told him that Dhuleep had escaped—that someone had engineered his escape—but he had not said who. Attwood and Peterson had then arrived, perhaps a minute later, and passed no one. Chuttur died without ever speaking again.

The three soldiers had gone looking for Dhuleep, but found only traces of his escape, signs of where he had been. The patrol had been ambushed and killed, all but Tierney.

The only man unaccounted for was Tallis. Tallis swore he was innocent. What was missing? Where was the lie?

It had to be Tallis—didn't it?

What was the information, the knowledge that Narraway did not have? He hated the chaos that had spread like madness across India, and the tiny piece of it that jumbled and boiled in his own mind, senselessly. He hated the internal darkness of it.

*H*E WAS ALLOWED IN TO SEE TALLIS WITHOUT QUESTION, although the guards' faces reflected a coldness, as if they imagined he was defending him because he wished to, not because he had been commanded. He hesitated, wanting to tell them how much it was against his will, then realized that would be childish. Half of what anybody did in the army was against their will. You still should do it to the best of your ability, and without complaining or trying to justify yourself. He was an officer; better than that was required of him. The fact that just over two years ago he had been a schoolboy was irrelevant. Many of these men had been soldiers in combat, shot at, acting with courage and loyalty at eighteen. Respect had to be earned.

He thanked them and went into Tallis's cell.

Tallis stood to attention. It hadn't been a day since Narraway had seen him, but he looked leaner, even grayer in the face. He was a man with only two or three days to live, and the shadow of that truth was stark in his eyes.

Time was too short for niceties. They stood because there was nothing in the cell to sit on, except the floor.

"At ease," Narraway said. Otherwise Tallis would be obliged to remain at attention. "I've spoken to the three men who answered the alarm and found Chuttur Singh. He didn't name you, but he said there was a man who came in and took him by surprise, and let Dhuleep out. And given the situation, that's the only answer that makes any sense. Dhuleep couldn't have opened the door from the inside himself."

"I know that," Tallis said quickly. "We all know there had to be someone else, but it wasn't me." His voice was level, but there was desperation in his eyes. "I was counting bandages and checking what medicines we had left in the storeroom. I can't prove it because no one else even knows what was there. I wouldn't have been counting them if I knew myself what was there! It's the only time I'm sorry we didn't have some poor devil sick, in need of medicine!"

"Ever treat Dhuleep?" Narraway asked. "Do you know anything about him?"

"I suppose I could always invent something," Tallis said with mock cheerfulness. "How about rabies? I let him go so he could infect the entire mutineer army. No good? I could say—"

"Tallis!" Narraway snapped. "I want to know if you knew the damn man. Did you ever treat him?"

Tallis looked slightly surprised. After a moment, he spoke seriously. "Yes. He had a bunion on his left foot. I'm intimate with it. I could draw you a picture. Couldn't cure it, of course. But I cured his indigestion. It doesn't exactly rate as a friendship. I cure people I don't like exactly the same as people I do. That's what medicine is about." He gave a sad, self-mocking smile. "Just like you defend people whether you think they're guilty or not . . ."

Narraway was temporarily robbed of words. He had not intended to be so transparent. "Give me anything to argue with," he begged. "What was Dhuleep like? Why did no one expect him to escape? Why was there only one guard? Who would want to help him? Who did he associate with? Who would want him free? If you didn't do it, then someone else did. For heaven's sake, man, help me!"

"Do you think I haven't lain awake trying to think?" Tallis asked. "Nobody likes a telltale, but I'd outdo the best actor on stage with stories that'd curl your hair if I knew any. I thought he might know something that was worth his freedom, but who would he sell it to? Latimer? Then I wondered if he was a double traitor, to us and then to the mutineers. Maybe he was let go on purpose, like a disease, to spread lies." He shrugged. "But as far as I know, he was just one more Sikh soldier who seemed to be loyal to us. Some are, some aren't. We can't afford to do without the loyal ones. I mean, look at it!" He swung his arm around, indicating the immeasurable

land beyond the cell and the compound. "We're a hand-
ful of white men, a few tens of thousands, half the world
away from home, trying to govern a whole bloody conti-
nent. We don't speak their languages, we don't understand their religion, we can't stand their bloody climate,
and we have no immunity to their diseases. Yet here we
are, and we expect to be liked for it! And we're all taken
by surprise when they stick a knife into our backs. God
help us, we're fools!"

"Don't say that in court tomorrow," Narraway said
drily, although he was startled by how much he agreed
with Tallis.

"Never let the truth spoil a good defense," Tallis said,
paraphrasing with a crooked smile. "I haven't got a
good defense, except that I didn't do it. And I haven't an
idea in hell who did. I'm trusting you because I haven't
got anything else. If you'd asked me a month ago if I
believed in some kind of divine justice, or even in a man-
made honor, I'd have laughed at you, probably made a
bad joke." He shrugged his thin shoulders.

Suddenly his face was totally serious. The laughter
had vanished; even the self-mockery was gone. "You see

313

courage that's sublime. People enduring pain, disfigurement, losing parts of themselves so they'll never be whole again—and yet not complaining, still keeping the dignity that's inside them intact. People care for others, even when they know they're dying themselves. They keep faith even when it's idiotic, even when everything's gone and they know it's gone."

Narraway wanted to shout at him to stop, but he couldn't.

"I know they'll convict me, though I didn't do it," Tallis added, his eyes never leaving Narraway's. "But I still believe you'll find a way to prove that I didn't. Unfair, isn't it?" He grinned. It was a brilliant, shining smile, as if in spite of all that his brain told him, he had a kind of happiness he refused to let go of. He would not accept reality. "You should try being a doctor sometime. See this after every battle, every skirmish. They carry them in one after another, people who look to you to save them, and you can't, but you try anyway. One thing you learn, Lieutenant: You can't tell who's going to live and who isn't. You learn there's something bigger than you, bigger than anything sense tells you. I believe in the impossible, good and bad. I've seen lots of it. I did not kill Chuttur Singh, nor did I let Dhuleep go. I wasn't even there."

Narraway wanted to have an answer, something brave and wise to say. He wished, with a hunger that consumed him, to believe in the impossible, but he could not. So he did the only thing he could bear: He lied.

"Then I'll believe in miracles too," he said quietly. "And I'll find you yours."

He did not remain. He had already asked all the questions he could think of. He left the prison and walked outside into the dark. The vast night sky arched over him, brilliant with stars. The faint wind stirred through the branches of the few trees, a black latticework against the sheen of light. And he felt just as boxed in, as locked and shackled, as Tallis.

He walked for quite a distance. He knew that before he turned in he should report to Colonel Latimer, but he was putting it off as long as possible. He had learned nothing useful in the time he had been given to look into the case. Quite honestly, he did not believe any extension of the time would make a difference. It would just be putting off the inevitable and prolonging the misery for everyone, including Tallis himself.

He turned and went in the direction of the officers'
mess, where he knew Latimer would be at this time in
the evening. Probably Busby and Strafford would be
with him, which would make it worse.

He passed a couple of small buildings and heard
someone tapping nails into wood. He wondered what
they were making. Household furniture? Mending a
chair or a table? Or maybe working on a toy for a child,
a Christmas present? A wagon with wheels that turned,
perhaps? He could dimly remember one in his own
childhood. Only fifteen years ago he had been the right
age to play with such a thing.

Would the widow's little boy have a wagon, or colored
bricks this Christmas? Perhaps Narraway could make
sure that he did. He didn't have to give it to the boy
himself; that might only embarrass her, make her feel
obligated to him, and he did not want that. Would the
boy even like a wagon? Wasn't it worth trying? The little
girl, Helena, had given him the blue paper chain, certain that he would like it because she liked it. He should
find something for her too. He would have to ask somebody. A woman would know.

He stopped and knocked on the door of the building where the banging came from. After several moments, a man in a leather apron came to the door. "Yes, sir?" he said politely. He was Indian, dark-skinned, black-haired.

"Are you a carpenter?" Narraway asked.

"No, I just mend things here and there. If you have a chair that is broken, perhaps I can help?"

"Actually . . . what I want is a small wooden wagon . . . for a child," Narraway replied, feeling foolish.

The man looked surprised. "You have a son? You want something for him for a gift, sir?"

"No . . . and yes. He's not my son, but he's lost his father. I just thought . . ." He trailed off, his confidence draining away.

"I can do that," the man said quietly. "I will make you one. Come back in a few days. I have many small pieces of wood. And red paint. It will not cost much."

"Thank you," Narraway replied. "I'd like that very much. My name's Lieutenant Narraway. I'll be back."

As he walked past the next open door he heard a woman inside, singing. Her voice was soft and filled with music. He had no idea who she was, but she was singing to someone she loved, of that he was certain. Probably it was a child. Reluctantly he moved on, out of earshot, toward the officers' mess.

At first Narraway was almost relieved not to see Latimer, and he had half turned to go when he noticed Strafford in a corner, and then Latimer beside him. He pulled his tunic a little straighter and squared his shoulders, then walked across the floor, threading between the tables and chairs and rickety stools, until he stood to attention in front of Latimer.

"Sir."

Latimer turned toward him as if he had been expecting this moment, and not looking forward to it any more than Narraway himself.

"Are you ready, Lieutenant?" he asked. His face was pale and tired. He nursed a glass of whisky in his hand as if it could feel his touch, his fingers caressing it.

"Yes, sir," Narraway replied. They both knew it was a lie, but it was the answer expected of him.

"You've spoken with Tallis?" Latimer pursued.

"Yes, sir."

"Any help?"

"Not much."

Latimer smiled; for a moment it softened the lines in his face. "Like him?"

Narraway was not prepared for the question. "Ah . . . yes, sir. I couldn't help it. Would have preferred not to."

"If you'd said 'no,' I wouldn't have believed you." Latimer sighed. "One thing you'll have to learn if you're going to make it in the army, Narraway. Know when to lie to your superiors and when not to. Sometimes we know the truth, but we don't want to hear it."

"Sorry, sir. I didn't know this was one of those moments."

"It wasn't. Your judgment is quite right. He's a likeable man. We need the kind of humor he brings, and the unreason, the ability to hope when it makes no sense. I wish to hell it had been anybody else but him. You can't save him, but for God's sake, make it look as if you're trying."

"Yes, sir." Narraway fell silent. He felt stupid, but there was nothing else to add.

"Busby'll give you a hard time. Expect it, and don't lose your temper, no matter what he says. He lost a life-long friend in that ambush. He'd served with Tierney a long time too. That's the fellow who lost a leg."

"Yes, sir, I know. I spoke to him. A good man," Narraway replied.

"Did you?" Latimer looked slightly surprised. "Tell you anything useful?"

"No, sir. Just thought I should speak to him."

"Well, you'd better go and get a decent night's sleep— or as decent as you can."

"Yes, sir. Good night, sir."

Latimer lifted a hand in a slight salute. "Good night, Lieutenant Narraway." Then: "Did you make any sense of it yet?" he asked suddenly.

Narraway felt the coldness deep inside him. "No, sir, but I will."

"That was the lie I wanted to hear," Latimer said with a faint smile.

*N*ARRAWAY COULD NOT SLEEP. HE LAY ON HIS COT. IT WAS comfortable enough, better than many places where he had slept perfectly well over the last year, but restfulness eluded him. He turned one way, then the other, sometimes with his eyes closed, sometimes staring up at the ceiling, which was pale from the starlight through the window. Tallis's face came back to his mind, regardless of all his efforts to banish it away. This was an inescapable burden, suffocating him.

It was not only Narraway's career at stake, it was the whole regiment's honor, its belief in justice as an abstract, a perfect and beautiful thing that every man strove for. Except that that was nonsense. Some men strove for it. Many merely used the word as an excuse.

Narraway had not been among the soldiers who had relieved Cawnpore after the siege. He had been farther north. But he had heard about it. What the soldiers arriving had seen had driven them almost out of their senses. The vengeance had been appalling. No one had bothered with justice then.

Had he not seen the emotion in the men, the stunned look in their eyes, the sudden clumsiness in movement, as if they lacked coordination? The horror and the grief were too enormous to recover from in just a few short months. Maybe those men would never again be quite the same men as they had been before.

Right now, faced with the immediate decision of what to say at the trial in a matter of hours, Narraway dared not think about his future, but that time would come. He could not win; it was only the measure of his loss that counted. Some would judge him for trying at all, even though the soldier in them would know he was obeying an order he could not refuse. Reason would defend him, but emotion would not.

Again and again, he came back to reason. He could see very easily why Latimer needed to understand. It was not simply a matter of morale. Without understanding, they would commit the same errors over and over again in the future. For all he knew, they might be committing them right now.

What was he misreading? Was there something in the puzzle that did not belong? He must have some plan before morning.

He went over it again in his mind and came up with the same answers. There was no one it could have been, except Tallis. Tallis had sworn his innocence. And no one, not even Busby, could come up with a *reason why* Tallis should have wanted Dhuleep to escape.

Reason—that was the missing piece.

He could not think of anything that would justify letting Dhuleep escape. His hunger to see sense was growing more powerful, the need for an overall intelligence that promised future control.

He could hear no sound in the night air except his own breathing and the whine of an insect somewhere.

Then a thought struck him. Perhaps the act made no sense because it was not the result Tallis had intended. What if he'd wanted something quite different? Might he have known that Dhuleep had information about the patrol, and intended to kill him because of it? The original charge against Dhuleep was not serious, so in a few days he might well have been let go anyway. Maybe Tallis hadn't wanted to risk that? And the plan had just gone wrong when he reached the cell?

But how would Tallis have known Dhuleep had such information? And why not plan to kill him in some more discreet way—medically, to make it look more or less like a natural death—instead of just barging into the cell?

Or might Chuttur secretly have been a traitor as well? These days, nobody knew who was on which side. People crossed from one to another. After all, it was a mutiny, not a war with clearly defined lines. So maybe *Tallis* had been the one to kill Chuttur, but Dhuleep had managed to get away in the process.

But why would Tallis not mention such things if they were true? Was someone else involved, someone else he could not betray? Were there further traitors he must not warn? Narraway could not forget that Tallis had said he trusted him. Would he spend the rest of his life measuring himself against this one failure? Would he even have the courage to fight his hardest for Tallis, knowing he could only lose? And when it was all over, would he have the courage to watch the hanging, knowing that he had been the one hope Tallis had had?

Why the hell did Tallis not trust him with the entire truth, and yet believe he would still help, pull off some kind of miracle? They did not even know each other. Narraway had never represented anyone at trial before; he had no reputation for such a thing.

Maybe it was not Narraway that Tallis trusted, but British law? Then where the devil did he grow up, that he did not know there were miscarriages of justice at home as well?

A trust in the British? After the atrocities on both

sides of the mutiny, that would be absurd. And Tallis had surely seen the worst of all that. He was a medical orderly—no one could tell him about a horror that he had not already seen.

Narraway turned over again and pulled the blanket after him. He was cold and tired, and his head was pounding, but he was no nearer sleep.

Perhaps it was God Tallis believed in. That did not require reason. When circumstances were extreme enough, sometimes that was all there was to believe in. Tallis was a young man. He had chosen a noble path in life: healing others, even when it meant risking his own life. If he had stayed in Britain he could have been comfortable, respected, and safe. So maybe he had a right to expect something of God?

Was that the way he saw it? God would help him?

Why? God had not helped the thousands who had been murdered in the mutiny. He had not saved the women and children at the Bibighar well.

He turned over to the other side, then on to his back, eyes open, watching the starlight on the ceiling.

What did he believe in himself? What did he trust? That called for a harsh review. He had been brought up to attend church. Most of the men here had. Did he believe in its teachings, its doctrine? Did he even believe in the God the church taught?

He realized with a sudden chill, as if someone had snatched his blanket away, that he had never really looked far enough into himself to know what he believed. If he had to answer now, tonight, staring at the starlight on the ceiling of his bedroom in this battered and rather shabby house, did he believe in God?

He certainly did not *disbelieve*. But he did not believe in the grand and rather distant God of the churches he had been to. If He was a God for everyone, then He must be equally so for the Indian, or the Chinaman, or the African.

And yes, that God he did believe in. Maybe it was because he needed to. For everything on earth to be pointless, accidental, and without love or purpose was a sterility he would not entertain. It left no room for true laughter, beauty, or even love. It did not allow for hope, for that in man that forgives, nor for that in woman that nurtures endlessly, that will sacrifice to save her children without ever thinking of the cost.

For what did he trust God, the good parent?

Mercy? Perhaps at Judgment Day, if such existed, but there was scant evidence of it now.

Justice? There was scant evidence of that, either. But then, if there were, if good were rewarded with good and evil with evil, would either of them really exist? Would there be anything more than enlightened self-interest? No true virtue, simply a system of barter?

That was a world so ugly, so barren and eventually hideous, that he thrust away the idea. It was a kind of universal death.

No justice, then; except what man himself strove to make.

No biblical promise that he could recall had ever said that justice would come without pain or loss: simply that in the end, it would be worth it.

Faith? Certainly. But blind faith that did not expect immediate reward, a trust that did not look to be vindicated and explained at every step along the way? Was that what he believed?

Yes, perhaps it was.

Could he live up to it? That remained to be seen.

But a plan was beginning to form in his mind, a way to discover the missing pieces that would make sense of both Tallis's act then and his silence now. The truth must lie in the characters of Dhuleep and Chuttur themselves; something Tallis knew of them and Latimer did not.

Gradually he drifted into an uneasy sleep, filled with nightmares that ballooned and faded, sometimes acutely sharp.

THE TRIAL OF JOHN TALLIS BEGAN THE FOLLOWING MORN-ing. Only the necessary attendees were present. Latimer had wanted as little attention brought to the details as possible. He sat at the top table with two officers Narraway did not know. Busby was at a small table on one side of the room with his papers spread in front of him, and Narraway was at the other.

Tallis, in uniform rather than his medical working clothes, sat beside Narraway. They had no suitable handcuffs or chains in which to keep him, but there were armed soldiers at the door, and in the room beyond where various witnesses were waiting. A couple of junior officers appeared to be ushers, and a third sat at a small table off to one side, pen poised to record what was said. How on earth he would keep up with the conversation, Narraway had no idea.

As soon as the formalities were dealt with, Busby began by calling his first witness. It was clear even from the brisk way in which he spoke, from the neatness of his uniform and the immaculate way his hair was brushed, that he intended to observe the letter of the law.

Of course, he knew he was going to win. There was no battle, only the pretense of one.

Grant was called. He came in straight-backed but looking curiously tired. He faced Busby, waiting.

Busby stood, speaking quietly, as if there were only the two of them in the room.

"I'm sorry to have to take you through all this again, Corporal Grant," he said gently. "I'm sure you understand the necessity. We must do justice here, not only to the dead and their families, but also to the living. It must also be seen by others, far beyond this regiment, or Cawnpore itself, that murder will be punished, fairly and justly, and that our actions are not taken out of revenge."

"Yes, sir," Grant responded, straightening his shoulders a little more.

Step by step, Busby led him through the events of the night in question: hearing the alarm, dropping what he was doing, and running toward the prison. He had him describe exactly what he did, what he saw, never dwelling on unnecessary horrors to give Narraway a chance to object that he was playing on emotions rather than facts.

"Thank you," Busby said when Grant had come to the end of his description. "Please wait there in case Lieutenant Narraway has anything to ask you."

Narraway stood up slowly. He was disgusted to find that he was shaking. It was absurd. He was going to lose. The battle was over before it began.

He cleared his throat. "Corporal Grant, when I spoke to you yesterday, asking you about this tragedy, you told me that Chuttur Singh was fatally wounded when you found him."

"Yes, sir," Grant said too quickly. He also was nervous, his body tight under the fabric of his uniform, his shoulders high and rigid. He had liked both Chuttur Singh and Tallis. This was clearly painful for him.

"We appreciate that there was nothing you could do for him, Corporal," Narraway said as gently as he could. "You said to Captain Busby that Chuttur Singh told you the prisoner had escaped and that recapturing him was more important than anything else, is that correct?"

Busby moved impatiently.

Latimer held up his hand to silence him.

"Yes, sir," Grant agreed.

"He told you to leave him and pursue the prisoner, Dhuleep Singh?" Narraway persisted. "Because he knew the route and times of the patrol?"

"Yes, sir."

"Do you know how he knew that?"

Grant looked slightly surprised. "No, sir."

"Yet you did not question it?"

"No, sir."

"You told me that Chuttur had said someone had come into the prison from outside and attacked him. I asked you if Chuttur Singh had told you who the other man was, and you told me he had not. Is that correct?"

Grant let his breath go slowly. "Yes, sir. That is correct. I . . . I don't think he knew."

"It isn't that he told you, and for some reason or other you are concealing it?" Narraway pressed.

Busby rose to his feet. "Colonel Latimer, this is—"

Latimer held up his hand. "Perfectly fair, Captain. Thank you, Lieutenant Narraway. We have established that Chuttur Singh did not tell Corporal Grant who attacked him, and we may safely presume it was because he did not know. Have you anything further, Lieutenant, perhaps regarding Dhuleep Singh's knowledge of the patrol?"

"Not at this time, thank you, sir." Narraway sat down with relief washing over him, his knees feeling like water.

Busby then called Attwood, who said much the same as Grant had. However, his words were not so identical as to make it seem as if they had conferred. Narraway could think of nothing to contest, and he did not want to risk making a mistake that could cost him credibility.

Finally Busby called Peterson, who added nothing of value, except in his careful and clearly honest description of how he had left the prison block and gone searching for Dhuleep Singh. It was he who had found faint traces of blood showing the path of escape. Busby obtained all the details from him, making the scene seem real and urgent, terribly familiar to those listening. It was Peterson who had gone in the direction of the Bibighar Gardens and the well.

"Did you search the Bibighar building for this man?" Busby asked.

Peterson was white-faced. "Yes, sir. He wasn't there." He was shaking very slightly.

"You looked inside the house?" Busby persisted. "You didn't avoid it . . . because . . ."

Narraway knew what Busby was doing, and he could not bear it. He stood up, facing Colonel Latimer.

"Sir, Captain Busby is suggesting that Private Peterson failed in his duty because of the horror of what happened there, and possibly out of his own personal grief. Private Peterson has told the Court that he looked. He is an honorable man and a good soldier. He is not charged with anything, and should not have his courage or his honesty brought into question here."

There was a murmur of approval from the man to Latimer's right, and both the men acting as ushers nodded.

"Thank you." Latimer nodded at Narraway. "Captain Busby, we are satisfied that Private Peterson has answered your question. No one found Dhuleep Singh, as is only too evident to all of us. If you have nothing further to ask him, then when Lieutenant Narraway has spoken, we will adjourn for luncheon."

Busby sat down, his face faintly flushed.

"Thank you, sir," Narraway acknowledged. "I think what happened after the alarm was sounded is very clear. I have nothing useful to ask Private Peterson."

Latimer nodded, his face expressionless.

"We are adjourned until two o'clock," he told them.

Narraway left alone, not that he was offered much choice. As he walked away across the open space, the cold wind striking him through his uniform, he felt something of a panic. No one openly snubbed him, but neither did anyone speak to him. In a way he was grateful. He needed time alone in which to think. The answer did not lie with any of the soldiers questioned this morning. He was becoming more and more convinced that it had to do with Dhuleep and Chuttur, and the information about the patrol. If only he could grasp the missing fact that would make sense of it. How did Dhuleep know? Was Chuttur involved after all? Was it Chuttur who knew, and was tortured for it?

That answer did not help Tallis's case at all though. He was still missing the key!

In the officers' mess he found a place in a far corner and sat eating absentmindedly. He had no hunger, but he knew that if he ate nothing he would regret it later. How could something as rich as a curry seem tasteless?

He left the plate half-finished and went to look for the sergeant who had spent the most time with the Sikh troops, Gholab Singh. He found him in a small office in one of the barracks still largely intact.

"Yes, sir?" Gholab Singh said courteously, rising to his feet.

Narraway introduced himself and told the sergeant to be at ease.

"What can you tell me about Dhuleep Singh?" he asked as soon as the man was seated again. "Other than what I have read in his army record."

Gholab looked uncomfortable. "I am ashamed for him, sir," he said quietly. "To rebel openly I cannot fault him for, at least not greatly. But to betray behind the back is another thing, altogether different. He was a sneaky bastard, sir. Very clever. Always listening and adding up in his mind, that one."

"It doesn't surprise you that he knew the times and routes of the patrol?" Narraway asked.

Gholab shook his head sadly. "He was a tricky one. He darkens all our names."

"And Chuttur Singh?" Narraway asked.

"A good man," Gholab said without hesitation. "I know his brother and his cousin. Good men, all of them. Maybe a bit too trusting. Not a bad fault in a man. Better than deceit." He shook his head. "Cousin to a snake, Dhuleep. May he eat the dust."

Narraway stayed a little longer, asking questions as they came to his mind, but Gholab could tell him nothing further. He had no idea if either Chuttur or Dhuleep had any personal acquaintance with Tallis.

*T*HE AFTERNOON BEGAN WITH BUSBY CALLING RAWLINS. The room sat in total silence. Tallis stared white-faced into the distance as the surgeon described the injuries to Chuttur Singh.

Busby's expression was one of shock and deep grief. No one could imagine it. Each man in the room had seen the injuries of war, seen soldiers cut down beside them, friends, people with whom they had shared jokes and food, and dreams of home. This was different. Civilized men fought for their ideals, for their countries, sometimes whether they believed them right or wrong. To betray a man who had trusted you was an act that deserved no mercy. Indeed, if the law was to stand for anything, if it was even to survive, such an act must be punished. And Tallis knew that.

"Did Chuttur Singh fight back, Major Rawlins?" Busby asked.

"There were deep slashes on his arms, which suggest he may have tried to defend himself," Rawlins replied. "And I believe there was a degree of blood on his own sword. I can't tell you what that means because his sword may have been used against him."

"To sum up," Busby said grimly, "There was a blow to the back of his head, hard enough to have stunned him, after which he was hacked to death with at least fifteen violent blows from a sword, most likely his own."

"Yes," Rawlins said with a catch in his voice.

"He bled to death?" Busby pressed.

"Yes."

"Have you ever seen wounds like this before?" Busby continued.

Rawlins looked, if anything, even paler. "Of course I have," his voice grated. "I was with the regiment that relieved Cawnpore after the siege. I stood almost ankle-deep in blood at the Bibighar, where the women and children were hacked to pieces. Some of them were the families of my friends. I refuse to describe it for you. Those who saw it will never forget, and those who did not can look at the faces of those who did and thank God for their escape."

Busby looked at him with surprise, then glanced around at the other men in the room. Narraway followed his eyes and saw what he must also have seen. Every other man there had, at one time or another, received help from Rawlins. He had relieved their pain, sat with them through times of agony that could not be helped, comforted them when they feared maiming or death, mourned with them over loss. Busby would be a fool to challenge him.

"And the men of the patrol that was ambushed," he said, changing his line of approach. "Did you see their bodies when they were brought home . . . those that were?"

"They were buried where they fell," Rawlins replied. "The two who were alive—yes, I saw them. One died shortly after being brought back. The other looks as if he will recover, but he has lost the greater part of one leg."

"The dead, they too were hacked to pieces," Busby said, making it a conclusion rather than a question.

"They were ambushed and died in battle," Rawlins snapped. "You have no business, sir, to suggest that they did not fight back."

Busby retreated. "I apologize. I did not mean to imply such a thing at all. They were surprised, betrayed, but I imagine they took a good few of the enemy with them—unlike poor Chuttur Singh, who was betrayed in quite a different manner, and outnumbered two to one."

Rawlins said nothing.

Busby moved only slightly. The room was small, and there was no space to spare.

"Is there anything else that you can tell us of this terrible event that might help us bring the matter to resolution and allow justice to be done?"

Rawlins leaned forward a little, staring at Busby.

"Captain, it is not my job to judge any man, only to heal him if I can. I do not know exactly what happened in that prison, who did it, or why. I have told you what the injuries were to Chuttur Singh, who I examined after he was brought to the medical wing. I cannot deduce anything more than I have already told you."

"Thank you, Major Rawlins. I had assumed as much." Busby seemed about to add something further, then changed his mind and turned to Narraway. His expression was bland, polite even, except for a bright spark of anger in his eyes.

Narraway rose to his feet, knowing this was his last chance. He still had a small, gnawing pain inside him that he could not ignore. What if Tallis was innocent? What if there was still some different question none of them had thought to ask?

He turned to Rawlins. He was limited now. This was not his witness—he could only revisit the issues Busby had raised.

"How long have you been a surgeon with the regiment, sir?"

Busby was still standing. "Are you questioning Major Rawlins's qualifications?" he asked incredulously.

"Of course I'm not!" Narraway said extremely tartly. "I am trying to establish his very considerable expertise. Do you think I should be questioning his qualifications?" He invested the same haughty disbelief into his own voice.

"For God's sake, man!" Busby exploded.

Latimer banged on the table. "Captain Busby! We will not have the Lord's name taken in vain in this court. We may be far from home, but that is all the greater reason to conduct ourselves with dignity. You will please allow Lieutenant Narraway to ask his questions. If they are inappropriate, then I shall tell him so."

A flash of anger spread up Busby's face, but he sat down.

Narraway was about to thank Latimer, then thought better of it. It would be rubbing in the point, probably unwisely. He merely inclined his head and turned again toward Rawlins.

"How long have you been a surgeon with the regiment, sir?" he repeated.

"Seven and a half years," Rawlins replied.

"And have you always had medical orderlies, such as John Tallis?"

"Yes, of course."

"How long have you had John Tallis, specifically?"

"Approximately two years."

"How has his conduct been, during that time?" Narraway could feel his heart pounding in his chest and his breath catching. He did not know what Rawlins's answer would be.

Rawlins stood a little straighter, squaring his shoulders. A tiny muscle ticked in his temple. His fair skin was sunburned, in places badly. He looked desperately tired.

"I found him undisciplined," he said quietly. "His sense of humor was unreliable, to put it at its kindest. He was frequently insubordinate. He was also the best medical orderly I have ever had, and I tried to encourage him to qualify as a doctor. He is highly skilled. He never gave up on saving a man's life or attempting to save a limb. His compassion is extraordinary. He drove some of the more rigid officers to distraction, but I never met an ordinary man, Indian or white, who did not like him. I realize that is not necessarily what you want to hear, but it is the truth."

At the table, Latimer closed his eyes. His face was bleak, reflecting the hurt of betrayal that he felt.

Narraway did not know what to say. The air in the room seemed too heavy to breathe in. His own mouth was dry. He could not look at Tallis. Rawlins clearly not only thought unusually highly of Tallis, he liked the man. This made Tallis's perceived betrayal a profoundly personal one, perhaps even more than it was professional, to the army and the country they both served.

Everyone was looking at Narraway, waiting for him to continue.

He gulped. He must say something.

"Did Corporal Tallis know Dhuleep Singh, as far as you are aware? Did he ever mention him, or did you see them together, Major Rawlins?"

"No."

"Can you imagine any reason whatever why Tallis should want to rescue Dhuleep Singh?"

"No."

"Corporal Tallis is charged with this crime not because we believe he did such a thing, but simply because it does not appear possible that anyone else could've. It is an accident of exclusion and not something we understand or can trace back to any behavior of Corporal Tallis. Do you know of any other reason why we should think him guilty?"

"No."

"Had he any hatred toward any of the men on the patrol that was ambushed?"

Rawlins was startled. "Good God, no!"

"Did he even know who they were? Is he given that information?"

"No! We deal with them when they come back, not before they go," Rawlins said bitterly. "I don't know what the hell you're trying to suggest, but it is rubbish."

"That is exactly what I am trying to suggest," Narraway answered. "There is some major element to this that we have not yet grasped."

"If you are looking for sense in war, then you are even younger and more naïve than I thought," Rawlins said wearily. "If you outlive the disease, it will cure itself."

Narraway could think of nothing to say to that. He thanked Rawlins and sat down.

It was still early, but Busby asked permission to delay calling Major Strafford until the following day, as he had a great deal of evidence to give. There might be a way, with some consideration, of shortening it without impairing the course of justice. Latimer agreed, and they adjourned by half-past four.

Narraway walked out into the waning afternoon. He felt dazed, and he ached as if he had been in a physical fight. He had only this evening in which to come up with any witness to call for a defense when Strafford was finished testifying as to his investigation.

Tallis himself was no help. He still insisted that he had no idea who could have helped Dhuleep Singh escape, only that it hadn't been him.

Unless he could find that missing piece tonight, Narraway had nothing left except to challenge the witnesses Strafford's questioning produced. He could imagine how successful that was likely to be. No one was going to admit to mistakes or go back on what they had first said. Continual repeating of it would have made it indelible in their minds, even if it had originally been tentative. Uncertainty would be wiped out by saying over and over again "I saw" or "I was there." Even if doubt came, who would admit it now, with the Court looking on and the whole regiment watching?

He was walking across the open space beyond the rooms where the trial was held. The sky in the east was darkening, and little whispers of wind were stirring up eddies in the dust. Children were shouting in the distance, playing a game of some sort. A group of women stood close together, heads bent as they talked. Someone laughed: a soft, startlingly agreeable sound.

"Narraway!" a voice called out abruptly from behind him.

He turned and saw Strafford a dozen yards away, moving quickly, his boots sending up spurts of dust.

"Yes, sir?" Narraway answered obediently. This was a confrontation he would dearly like to avoid, but Strafford outranked him and so he had no escape.

Strafford reached him and stopped. He looked awkward, but the muscles were tight in his jaw, and clearly he was not going to be put off.

"I intend to call the witnesses tomorrow who can rule out every man in Cawnpore, apart from Tallis," he said without preamble. "Don't drag this out any longer than you have to. You can question each one as much as you like, and I appreciate that you have to make it look as if you are attempting to defend the man. But you're new here—relatively new to India, for that matter. These men have been through hell. Every one of them has lost people he served with, people who've stood side by side with him in the face of the enemy." He swallowed. "Maybe you don't know what that means yet . . ."

Narraway stiffened. "I'm not a lawyer, sir, I'm a soldier," he said sharply. "I've fought in the line just like anyone else. I've seen men die—and worse than that, I've seen them horribly wounded. I don't mean to be insubordinate, sir, but you have no grounds and no right to assume that all I do is defend soldiers in a back room in some military post. I'm doing this because I was ordered to, not because I chose it."

"I know that, Narraway, damn it!" Strafford said angrily. "Who the hell do you think chose you? Latimer

347

doesn't know you from the clerk who writes up the dispatches home."

"Then he should bloody well look at the pips on my shoulders!" Narraway snapped.

Strafford almost smiled but stopped himself. "Would you prefer it if I said he doesn't know you from any other newly commissioned young officer fresh off the boat? I do, however, at least by repute."

Narraway's heart sank. Here was the issue of Strafford's brother again, the whole school record, the teasing, some of it less than good-natured, the inner contempt from the "swot" who preferred classics to sports—except cricket.

"Is that why you suggested to Colonel Latimer that he have me defend Tallis?" Narraway asked bitterly.

Strafford's eyebrows rose. "Did you think I picked your name out of a hat? Of course it is. You're a stubborn bastard, and you won't be beaten until you can see it so close in front of you you'll hit your nose if you take another step. Every man, no matter what he's accused of, deserves someone to speak for him. And right here and now, in this gutted town with its ground still reeking of blood, we need to be sure we're hanging the right man, and then we need to do it quickly. Fight, by all means, but when you're beaten, which will be tomorrow, give up. Don't give Tallis false hope. That's like a cat playing with a mouse. Let the end be quick and clean."

Narraway looked at Strafford, searching his face. He saw dislike in it, but not deceit.

"Are you absolutely certain Tallis is guilty?" he asked.

"Yes, I am," Strafford replied without hesitation. "I've looked into every other possibility, and it could have been no one else. Damn it, Narraway, the man may be an insubordinate clown, but he's one of the best medical orderlies I've ever seen. Men respect him. He's probably saved as many lives over the last couple of years as Rawlins himself. Do you think I'd pin this on him if there were any other man it could have been? I want the truth—and I wish this weren't it, but it is."

"Why?" Narraway asked stubbornly. "Why would Tallis rescue Dhuleep Singh? They didn't even know each other. If they did, you'd have produced a witness to say so."

"I don't know," Strafford admitted, miserable but not disconcerted. "Why do people do half the desperate or

349

idiotic things they do? When you've been here another year or two, you won't ask questions like that. Where were you during the summer? Not here! Not watching men you know dying of heatstroke or cholera, getting weaker day by day, sharing what food and water there was, protecting the women, desperate to save them. You weren't here crouching behind that pathetic wall of earth, with nothing to shield you but a few bits of wood planking and some boxes, knowing that devil Nana Sahib was massing his hordes around you, growing closer every hour."

Narraway wanted to interrupt him, but he dared not.

"Some of these men have seen hell in a way few people ever do," Strafford went on. "Look in their faces sometime, Lieutenant. Look in their eyes, then come back and ask me why they do crazy things, or forget who they are or why they're here. Imagine what Tallis has seen, and ask me if he could have gone mad and acted in a way that makes no sense. Maybe he thought Chuttur Singh was Nana Sahib, or some other monster who cut up women and children. Maybe he simply lost his mind for a moment. I don't know. I just know that no one else could have done it. Believe me, I wish they could have. I tried to find any other answer."

Narraway felt as if he had suddenly tripped and fallen, or that the ground had risen up and struck him. Of course men who had endured what these men had could not be expected to keep the grip on sanity that men sitting comfortably at home could.

Tallis's clear blue eyes did not look insane. Desperate, perhaps, lit with an occasional, wild, mocking humor; but was that madness or the ultimate sanity? The only way to survive might be to take life a minute at a time, laugh when you could, weep when you had to.

"I saw the bodies of the men on the patrol," Strafford went on, his voice cracking from his effort to control it. "They were cut to bits too. I knew every one of them. I'm the one who had to tell their wives, lie a little and say it was quick, pretend they hadn't bled to death out there knowing no one would come for them or perhaps even find them before the animals had destroyed their bodies."

"I spoke to Tierney," Narraway said. "Actually, I spoke to him for quite a long time. Told him about Kent, where I come from, and he told me about his home. But sir, everything you said—all these terrible things that happened—I'm not going to add to that. I'm not going to give up until I don't have another step to go."

Strafford's face was grim. "My brother said you were a stubborn sod."

"Yes, sir," Narraway replied, standing to attention. "I don't suppose you want my opinion of him?"

"No, I bloody don't!" Strafford's face eased slightly. "I've got my own, better informed than yours."

Narraway relaxed a fraction, but not quite enough for Strafford to be certain of it, he hoped.

Strafford stared at him for a moment, then turned and walked away. He disappeared in another swirl of dust as the wind eddied more sharply, the bare branches of the trees above him clattering, a host of dry seedpods falling lightly to the ground.

Narraway also turned, but instead he walked farther away from the shattered barracks and the entrenchment, away from the Bibighar Gardens and the clustered outbuildings and the beginning of the houses. He must think of something to say tomorrow. Strafford Minor had called him stubborn but not fit to make a good soldier, all brains and no courage, no steel in the soul. He knew that because he had said it to Narraway's face, at Eton.

Well, he would prove that Strafford Minor was wrong.

*I*N THE MORNING, BUSBY CALLED MAJOR STRAFFORD TO give evidence. He began by establishing that it was Strafford who had been commanded to investigate the murder of Chuttur Singh, which was a direct result of Dhuleep Singh's escape.

Then he drew in a deep breath. "I regret the necessity for going into detail in this, but you were the officer entrusted with conducting the investigation into this act that has cost the lives of ten men and will yet take the life of whoever is guilty of perpetrating it. Colonel Latimer has known you and your record for years, but his companion judges may be less familiar with exactly what manner of man you are. I say this because they are going to accept your honor, integrity, and diligence as evidence of other men's actions and pass their verdict accordingly."

Strafford did not reply.

"It is a matter of record that you have served in the Indian Army for eleven years, with distinction. Were you here during the siege last summer?"

Strafford stiffened, and his face paled. "Yes."

"You must have seen an appalling amount of suffering and death."

"Yes."

"During that time, did you know the surgeon, Major Rawlins?"

"Of course."

"And Corporal Tallis, his medical orderly?"

Strafford was clearly distressed by the question. He licked his lips and coughed before replying.

"Of course I did. Before you ask me, he was an excellent orderly, often performing duties far beyond the requirements of his office or his training. Any man here will tell you that." He took a deep breath. "Believe me, I hate having to conclude that he is guilty of orchestrating Dhuleep Singh's escape. I did everything I could to find any other answer at all. I failed, because there is no other."

Busby stood ramrod stiff, carefully avoiding Narraway's eyes and Latimer's.

"Major Strafford, I need to ask you, so no one is in any doubt whatsoever regarding your personal feelings: Have you at any time had cause to dislike Corporal Tallis? We are all aware that on occasion he has been known to be . . . insubordinate, to have a sense of humor that is somewhat unfortunate, given to rather childish practical jokes on those he considers to be . . . stiffer in their command than he judges to be warranted. Has he ever played any of these rather childish jokes on you? Perhaps caused others to have less respect for you than is right? In other words, have you ever been the butt of his humor? Have you been laughed at, made fun of, had your authority belittled?"

"No."

"I see. Major Strafford, I know it is difficult, but can you describe your experience of what happened here at the end of the siege?"

A dull flush spread up Strafford's lean face. "For God's sake, man!" He all but choked on his words. "We were both there when Mrs. Greenway came with the note from Nana Sahib, offering on oath and treaty to give safe passage for the wounded, the women and the children, across the Ganges and then to Allahabad. In return he asked for and was given all the money, stores, and guns in the entrenchment." His voice shook, and he had difficulty continuing.

Narraway sat frozen, not in misery for Tallis but for Strafford himself.

Busby waited.

Strafford controlled himself with a fierce effort, drawing in breath again and again. His face was ashen.

"On the morning of the twenty-seventh, those of us left went from the entrenchment to the boats. There were Indian soldiers lining the banks."

Busby shifted his weight. No one else in the room made even the slightest sound.

"You know what happened after that," Strafford said, his voice so constricted in his throat that he could barely form the words. "Tantia Topee ordered the bugle sounded, then two guns were pulled out of concealment and opened fire on the boats, with grapeshot, followed by the muskets." The tears were running freely down his face now, and he made no effort to conceal them. "The thatch on the boats caught fire. The wounded and the helpless were burned to death. Some of the women, including my own wife, leaped into the river with their children. They too were shot, or cut down by the sabers of the troopers who rode their horses into the water and slaughtered all but a few. The men who made it to the shore were killed there, the women and children taken prisoners."

The room was silent.

Finally, Latimer spoke. "Nothing we can say will ease such horror. It is all a man needs to know of hell. I presume you have some purpose, Captain Busby, in obliging Major Strafford to relive his loss?"

Busby swallowed. "Yes, sir. Major Strafford, during all this horror, and afterward, what was Corporal Tallis's role, to your knowledge?"

Narraway was stunned. He had no idea what to do. The course of the trial had slipped uncontrollably out of his hands. He looked at Tallis and saw tears on his face also.

"He was with the wounded and among the last to embark," Strafford answered. "He did everything he could to help those further attacked. No man exhibited more selfless courage than he did."

"So it must hurt and dismay you, as much as it does Major Rawlins, to be forced to come to the conclusion

357

that Corporal Tallis, and only Corporal Tallis, could have released Dhuleep Singh? And that it is possible that Corporal Tallis could've been the one to murder Chuttur Singh?"

"Yes."

Busby gave a slight shrug. "Just in case anybody should think of it, is there any chance that Chuttur Singh was part of that hideous massacre? Could Tallis have had revenge for it in his mind?"

"No," Strafford said flatly. "Chuttur Singh was loyal all his life. I know that for a fact. No one could have thought differently."

"Thank you. Now let us continue with your detailed evidence of the day of Dhuleep's escape and Chuttur's murder," Busby continued. "What evidence did you find that immediately implicated anyone?"

"None," Strafford replied. "Chuttur Singh had died without naming anyone, and the men who answered the alarm were too late to catch sight of anyone, even when they went after Dhuleep."

"So what did you do?" Busby asked. They all knew what Strafford was going to say.

Strafford sounded tired, and there were lines of fatigue in his face. "I started questioning the other men who had been on duty—or off duty, but in the general area—at the time. They could all account for their whereabouts, except Corporal Tallis." His jaw was tight, as if every muscle was clenched.

Busby looked apologetic. "Since Corporal Tallis has denied any involvement in either the escape or the murder, I'm afraid that obliges me to ask you for the details of your investigation. Lieutenant Narraway has informed me that he will not accept your assurance, as I had hoped he might, and save us this miserable exercise. God knows, we have enough else to do."

Narraway rose to his feet, driven by anger rather than sense. "Is Captain Busby suggesting that we hang a man for a crime of which he may be innocent, in order to save the time it takes to go through the procedure of a trial, sir?"

Latimer's lips thinned, and his hands on the tabletop were rigid. "Of course not!" he snapped, turning to Busby. "Captain, your choice of words was clumsy, to put it at its kindest. It is you who is wasting time with this grandstanding. Move on."

Busby flushed with anger. He dared not retaliate,

but neither would he apologize. He turned to Strafford again.

"Would you please give us an account of the various steps you took in your investigation, and how you ruled out all the possible suspects apart from Corporal Tallis?"

In a flat voice Strafford obeyed, listing all the men he had confirmed were in the immediate area of the prison. He had a sheet of paper with names, and he read them aloud.

"We know to the minute the time of the escape," he continued. "Most of these men were within sight of several people, and it was a simple matter to be certain beyond any possible doubt that they could not have been anywhere near the prison. In all cases the officer in charge at the time will swear to those accounted for, if you wish."

Before Busby could say anything, Latimer spoke.

"If that satisfied you, Major Strafford, it satisfies the Court. Who did it leave unaccounted for?"

Strafford looked at his list. "Corporal Reilly, Lance-Corporal McLeod, Privates Scott, Carpenter, and Avery, and Corporal Tallis, sir."

"Thank you. So that Lieutenant Narraway might question them also, if he feels there is some point to it, perhaps we had better hear from them directly." He glanced sideways at Narraway, as if to be certain the Court knew that it was Narraway who was dragging out the proceedings unnecessarily.

"Yes, sir, if you please," Narraway replied, as if it were Latimer who had asked.

Scott was the first called. In response to Busby's careful direction, he accounted for his duties and his movements on the day of Chuttur's death. He had been across the open yard and around a dogleg from the prison. But anyone coming or going would have had to pass him, because that was the only access to the front, and there was no door at the back of the makeshift prison.

"What were you doing, Private Scott?"

"Working on mending a storeroom, sir. Door and windows had been smashed by shellfire during the siege. I was making it weatherproof again."

"With your back to the courtyard, then?" Busby asked.

"No, sir. During that time I was making a new frame

for the door. Had the wood up on a bench of sorts, planing it to fit."

"So you could see anyone passing in either direction?"

"Yes, sir."

"Could anyone see you?"

"Yes, sir. Lance-Corporal McLeod and Private Avery."

"And no one passed you? You swear to it?"

"Yes, sir."

"And you were there for that entire hour, Private Scott?"

"Yes, sir. It took me longer'n that to finish."

"And could you see Corporal Reilly from where you were?"

"Yes, sir."

"Did he move at all?"

"Yes, sir. 'E came over ter me ter see 'ow I were doing, an' 'e told me I weren't doin' it right. 'E showed me 'ow to."

"And then what?" Busby pressed.

" 'E went off be'ind me, to see 'ow the rest were gettin' on. Then 'e came back."

"In the direction of the prison block?"

"No, sir, other way, back toward the river."

"Is there a way he could have gone around—in a circle perhaps—and got to the prison block?"

"No, sir, not without passing the squad 'oo were over at the end o' the entrenchment, sir."

"And Private Carpenter?"

"He was opposite me, working with Corporal Reilly."

"All the time?"

"Yes, sir."

"Thank you." Busby turned to Narraway with a slight, ironic gesture of invitation.

Narraway accepted, playing for time rather than because he had any questions in mind. He hoped that something might come to him. Testimony had shown Tallis to be exactly the sort of man Narraway had thought him: brave; irreverent, with a completely irresponsible sense of humor; intensely compassionate; dedicated to medicine. But it also had been damning, because it was clear that if Strafford could have found any other answer, he would have.

Narraway stood facing Private Scott. Detail by detail, the soldier accounted for every move he had made, repeating what he had said before, not in parrot fashion, but as if clearly seeing it again in his mind's eye. Narraway achieved nothing at all.

It was exactly the same with Corporal Reilly, and then with Private Carpenter. Busby asked each of them where they had been. They each gave a sober account, in very slightly different words but amounting to the same evidence. In each case they supported one another, proving that none of them could have left their position, and the other's sight, long enough to have reached the prison block and gone inside it. Narraway began to feel as if he was wasting everyone's time, and he could see the truth of it in the growing impatience on the faces around him.

Tallis was looking more and more desperate, struggling to keep his composure and an appearance of some kind of hope. Narraway could only guess at the courage required for Tallis to sit there silently. Was he wasting everyone's time, drawing out the tension and pain pointlessly?

He thought of what Strafford had said of that terrible crossing with the boats on fire, the drowning and the dead, and Tallis wading in and risking his own life without a backward glance. Narraway could not give up yet, not until he was so beaten he had nowhere else to go.

Lance-Corporal McLeod came to the stand, and Busby questioned him also.

He was perhaps twenty-two, fair-skinned, pale. His eyes were hollow, staring far beyond Busby as if he saw something else, something printed indelibly on his memory.

"And where were you exactly, Corporal McLeod?" Busby prompted.

"On the corner, sir, just beyond the building that was pretty well smashed."

"In the southwest, correct?"

"Yes, sir."

"And you could see the door to the prison from where you were?"

"Yes, sir."

"Were you looking at it all the time?"

"No, sir. I was paying attention to what I was doing."

"Which was what, Corporal?"

"Mending a cart, sir. Shaft was broken."

"Was anyone helping you?"

"Yes, sir, Private Avery. Too heavy for one man, at least when it comes to lifting it together to weld."

"And could you see Corporal Reilly and Private Scott working on the storeroom?"

"Yes, sir."

"All the time? Are you certain?"

"Corporal Reilly could have gone the other way, sir, but not past me toward the prison, sir. Private Avery or I would have seen him."

"Thank you. Please stay there so Lieutenant Narraway can ask you . . . whatever it is he needs to." Busby did not hide the fact that he regarded this as a cruel and pointless waste of not only time but emotion. All around them was the air of danger, of hate, the bitter knowledge that fighting was going on just beyond their hearing and sight. All of northern India was in turmoil. Friends and allies were dying to save what was left of British rule, and here they were, locked up in this tiny room, arguing over a truth everyone knew perfectly well. All it really needed was to be faced, the bitter acceptance made and dealt with. Courage was necessary, not more talk, more weighing and measuring of what they all knew. In a sense it was like vultures fighting over a corpse. Busby had not said so, not in so many words, but he had more than implied it.

Narraway did not ask McLeod anything. He knew he had tried Latimer's patience as far as it would go.

The last witness was Private Avery.

Busby stood and faced him patiently.

"Private, would you describe to us exactly where you were at the time Chuttur Singh was killed? We have been over this before. All you need to do is recall what you told me then and tell me again, so the Court can hear you."

Obediently, as if he were reciting some ritual litany, Avery told him exactly where he had been and what had occupied him. He seemed stunned. Narraway thought that the man blamed himself for not having seen something that could have saved Chuttur Singh, as if it had been his fault that he had been so near and done nothing to prevent the killing.

When it was Narraway's turn to question him, he felt like he could not ask the man to repeat it all again—it would be brutal.

"Think carefully, Private Avery: Have you left anything out? If not, there is no need for me to go over it again."

"Nothing, sir," Avery answered. "That's how it was. I'm sorry, sir."

"Just one thing that Captain Busby didn't ask you: Do you know Corporal Tallis?"

Avery's face went even paler. "Yes, sir."

"How do you know him?"

"I got a bullet wound in the arm, sir. Not very bad, but it bled a lot. Corporal Tallis stitched it up for me."

"Corporal Tallis did, not Major Rawlins?" Narraway said with surprise.

"Dr. Rawlins was busy with someone a lot worse hurt than me, sir."

"I see. Did Corporal Tallis make a good job of it?"

"Yes, sir, very good. Healed up real well. And . . ." He stopped, looked at the floor. "There was a lot of blood, sir. I was scared. He made me laugh, and I felt as if it would be all right. It—it was the first time I'd been hit . . . sir."

"So you know Corporal Tallis?"

"Yes, sir." Avery looked so wretched, it was as if he were in physical pain.

"Could you see the door of the prison from where you were working?"

"Yes, sir."

"Did you see him during that hour? Did you see him anywhere near the prison?"

"No, sir."

"Thank you." Narraway sat down again because he could think of nothing further to say.

Latimer adjourned the Court, and Narraway walked out into the late afternoon. The sun was sinking low to the horizon, painting the west with burning color. The coming night had already shrouded the east, spreading a veil of shadow across the sky. He felt as if the darkness were enclosing him, wrapping around him and reaching inside.

It was a time not to be alone.

And yet only in solitude could he even attempt to concentrate his mind. Nothing so far helped. Every piece of testimony proved that no one else could have gone in through the prison door. And more than that, no one had an ill word to say about Tallis. None of them wished to believe him guilty.

Strafford's evidence had been even worse than Rawlins's. He was a good man desperately bereaved, who had nevertheless done his duty without expecting anyone else to ease his burden. He had not wanted Tallis to be guilty. It betrayed everything he had trusted, even the past help that Tallis had been to him personally.

Did all this make Strafford doubt his own judgment now? If he could trust and admire a man and be so bitterly mistaken, could he have faith in himself in any other judgment? If Tallis could be so infinitely less than his estimation, then who else might also be?

And if Strafford, with his knowledge, could be wrong, why on earth did Narraway imagine that he was any better? He barely knew Tallis. He liked his humor and admired his courage. But Strafford had known the man, day in and day out, for years. He had seen his work. They had faced horror and the final, rending grief of loss together. But he'd also had the courage to accept that Tallis was guilty. What must that have cost him?

Narraway could not shake the evidence. No one was lying; no combination of men had conspired to make the situation look this way.

Perhaps Strafford was not being sarcastic when he said he had chosen Narraway because he believed in his

stubbornness and intelligence. Maybe he really did—
and far from ending up feeling furious and duped, if
Narraway could find a way out, a way to restore their
faith in Tallis and thus in their own judgment, Strafford would be intensely grateful?

If that was the case, then by failing he was not only
letting Tallis die, he was also letting down the whole
regiment. It was a lonely and terrible thing to live without the faith you had once leaned on when all else was
broken. Death might not be preferable, but there must
be times, like at two o'clock in the morning, when it
seemed a whole lot easier.

And there were women and children left without
their men—like the widow whose shopping he had carried and whose little girl had given him her blue paper
chain, made for a Christmas her brother had said was
for everybody.

Then, suddenly, he was ashamed of his own self-
absorption. Whoever was betrayed, bereaved, accused
falsely or not, it was not he. He was supposed to be part
of the resolution, the one who fought for justice, whether
that was Tallis's vindication or his death.

He was still walking, aimlessly. He had intended to

go to his own house and spend the evening revising all that he had learned so far, in the hope that some inconsistency would emerge or some new fact or deduction would appear.

However, as he walked along the road, he found himself turning aside from the way to his own bungalow and going instead toward the house of the widow with the little girl who had given him the blue paper chain.

It was almost dusk, and night would come quickly, as it always did in India. There was no lingering twilight of the north here. Soon there would be lights in the windows. Women would begin to cook an evening meal. The comfortable smells of food would fill the air. It would only be after the children had gone to bed that they would sit in the empty rooms downstairs and face the long aloneness of the night.

Helena was sitting on the front steps, holding a doll in her arms and talking to it. She became aware of him standing at the gate and looked up. She smiled at him shyly.

He remained where he was, smiling back at her.

The woman came to the door. He had learned that her name was Olivia Barber. Perhaps she had seen him from the window and had come to make sure her child was safe.

"Good evening, Lieutenant," she said, clearly enough for him to hear her from where he was.

"Good evening, ma'am," he replied. "I beg your pardon for disturbing you."

"It's supper time," Helena said, still staring at him. "Are you here for supper?"

He felt embarrassed, as if he had tried to invite himself in.

Olivia put her hand on the child's shoulder, pulling her back a little. "You are welcome to join us, if you would like, Lieutenant," she said quietly. "I apologize for Helena's forwardness."

He felt even more awkward, but he very much wanted to accept. He wanted the comfort, the normality of it. And he would love, above all else, to forget defeat for an hour or two.

"Are you sure it will not inconvenience you?" he asked hesitantly.

"I'm quite sure," she answered, opening the door a little wider behind her.

He went up the path and inside, Helena watching him carefully all the way. He wondered with a flash of pain if she understood yet that her father was never coming home. Was she too young for that? Had her mother even tried to explain it?

Inside, the house was warm and tidy, full of the smells of cooking, clean laundry and some kind of polish. There were a few toys on the floor, not many. He was pleased to see that there was no wagon. But then, perhaps at five David was too big for such things? Should he ask, or was that clumsy?

The food was not ready yet. He was invited to sit down.

"Aren't you going to play with me?" Helena looked disappointed. "David's reading."

"Helena!" Olivia said chidingly. "The lieutenant has been working all day. He's tired."

Helena's face crumpled.

"I'd love to play with you," Narraway said quickly. "What game would you like?"

He was rewarded with a beaming smile. "Hide-and-seek," she said immediately.

"Helena . . ." her mother began, but the little girl was already running away, giggling with excitement.

Narraway stood up. "Where should I look for her?" he asked quietly. "I don't want to find her too soon. Please tell me where it's all right for me to try."

Olivia laughed and gave a slight shrug. "Anywhere in this half of the house," she replied. "You're fairly safe to try behind all the doors and in the cupboards. She hardly ever hides there."

"Thank you." He set off uncertainly. This was a house in which he was a guest, a woman's house, full of personal and family things. It would be inexcusable to intrude. To start with, he moved tentatively, silently, then he realized it would be no fun for Helena if she could not hear him looking, puzzled, not finding her.

"I'm coming to find you!" he said clearly. He went out into the central entranceway. "I think you're in the coat cupboard." He opened the door and was relieved to see nothing but coats and capes. He closed it again and saw a boot box. "Could you be in there?" he said. "Far too small—but maybe!" He opened it, sighed, and closed it again. "No. Then where can you be?"

He kept it up, with a running commentary, going to one room after another and still not finding her. Finally there was only one room left, which was clearly her bedroom. He opened it tentatively, afraid of intruding.

"She can't be in here," he said aloud. "It isn't bedtime yet." He looked around. The small bed was neatly made, except for a coverlet dropped on the floor. She wasn't here. He was perplexed. He thought he had looked everywhere that had been suggested, excluding only the other bedrooms—Olivia's and the one where David was reading.

"I give up!" he said dramatically. "She's gone!"

There was a giggle from the coverlet on the floor, and very slowly a tousled little girl squirmed out of it, leaving it in exactly the same shape. Her face was alight with victory, eyes shining.

"I won!" she said happily. "You didn't find me! I'm hungry. Let's go down for supper." Dancing from one foot to the other, she led the way.

Narraway followed her to the dining room and took his place at the table, opposite David, already there. He felt awkward then. He appreciated the welcome but was acutely aware that he was in another man's place. So much of the warmth was a pretense, meant to comfort them all for a short time. It was a game that gave a few hours' respite from reality.

They spoke of other times and places, not India. Christmases past, the day with its promise of hope for those with the courage to accept its message and believe it.

But when the housemaid came to take David and Helena to bed and they had all said good night, Narraway remained a little longer in the quiet room. Now that pretense had ended, he could see how tired Olivia was, what an effort it cost her to always hide her grief from them so they would not know how much everything had changed. War raged around them in every direction, but they were not afraid because, to them, she was not afraid.

Suddenly his troubles seemed very small.

"Thank you," he said sincerely. "You have reminded me of the sanity of things that last, and that they are not always bought cheaply."

She looked at him in surprise, not quite sure what he meant. The meal had been simple, mostly rice.

He seized on the first thing that came to his mind. "Have you any more garlands, paper chains? Perhaps I can help you put them up?"

"Lieutenant, they're only—"

"It'll need two of us," he pointed out. "One at each end. Wouldn't the children like to see them all up when they come down in the morning?"

"You don't have to . . ." she began.

"I'd like to. We shouldn't ever forget Christmas, or make little of it. We give presents when we can, but there's no gift as precious as Christmas itself." He stopped, feeling self-conscious.

She smiled at him and stood up. "You're quite right. Of course I'd love you to help hang the garlands up. We have five or six, and there are some wreaths of dried flowers, and ribbons."

She fetched them, and together they put them up with pins and tacks—not always very straight, but an hour later, when they were finished, the room was transformed. As far as Narraway was concerned, it was like nailing your flags to the mast, a statement of hope.

"Do you think they'll like it?" he asked, looking carefully at her face, seeing the light in it again, even a hint of laughter.

"They'll love it," she said without hesitation. "I think I shall pretend to be as surprised as they'll be, if you don't mind?"

"An excellent idea," he agreed.

"Would you like a cup of tea before you go?" she said with a smile.

"Thank you, I really would," he answered, following her into the kitchen while she made it.

Afterward, thanking her again, Narraway went out into the darkness, smiling.

Far above him, a flight of birds crossed the clear night sky and circled down toward the trees. There always seemed to be birds, except over the ruined part of the town—lots of different kinds, unfamiliar to him. He loved their easy flight, which gave an illusion of freedom, an almost magical ability to rise above anything and be wherever or whatever you wished.

He knew perfectly well they were as subject to hunger, cold, exhaustion, and predators as anyone else, but the momentary illusion was still worth something.

He would have to call all the witnesses again and find some discrepancy, some error or contradiction. He hated the thought of arguing and trying to trip them up. The only thing that would be worse was letting Tallis be hanged without giving it the best fight he could.

And that brought him to the fact that he could no longer put off going to see Tallis, perhaps for the last time. The wind was rising a little whispering, murmuring. It was nearly dark, no more birds left in the sky, just a thin ribbon of red fading in the west.

And then suddenly he had an idea—tremulous as the last light, elusive, but perhaps possible!

$\mathcal{F}$OR A FEW MOMENTS, HE THOUGHT THE TIRED GUARD would refuse to allow him in. However, he looked again at Narraway's face, at his eyes, and must have decided that arguing with him would be a great deal more trouble than simply giving in.

Tallis was lying on his back on the bunk, eyes wide open. He stood up as Narraway came in. He was even paler than before, and there were bruises on his skin.

"You look terrible," Narraway said with some concern. "Can I get Rawlins for you?"

Tallis's face broke into a smile. "I like your sense of humor, Lieutenant. I couldn't have done better than that myself. To do what? You have to wait until the patient is dead before you certify it. Or have you given up on proving me innocent, and you're going to smuggle me out as already dead and say I escaped? Stupid, but I like a man who doesn't know when he's beaten."

Narraway heard the edge in his voice, the fear just under the surface. "I was actually going to suggest that he give you something to make you look better, even if you don't feel it," he replied, making an effort to smile back. "I intend to finish the course, whether there's any point to it or not. It's one thing to be beaten; it's another to give up."

"It won't do your career any good," Tallis observed.

"Sit down before you fall over," Narraway told him. "I may need your answers tomorrow."

"It won't make any difference," Tallis assured him. "In civilian life they think twice about hanging a sick man, but in the army they don't give a damn. You can be missing arms and your legs be out cold, and some helpful bastard'll tie you up so they can still put the noose around your neck."

"Thank you," Narraway said wryly. "If I'm ever accused back at home, I'll remember to be ill at the time. Now sit down and try to pay attention."

Tallis sat. In fact, it was more of an overbalancing because he had temporarily forgotten there was no chair, only the mattress on the ground. He looked up at Narraway, a flare of hope in his eyes for a moment before he remembered to disguise it.

"Did you kill Chuttur Singh?" Narraway asked.

"No."

"Did you release Dhuleep?"

"No."

"What do you know about him? And don't tell me 'nothing.' You've treated half the men in this regiment. I need you to tell me everything you know about him, whether you think it's relevant or not. I don't care if it's military-related, personal, or medical. It's not just your life that depends on it; it's the matter of finding the man who did this, if it isn't you. It's about saving some kind of honor for the regiment. Unless you're covering for someone for that very reason."

Tallis looked amazed. Then laughter welled up in him, and died instantly.

"No," he said croakily. "I'm not noble enough to swing on a rope for a crime I didn't commit, if that's what you think. I don't want to be executed out here and my name to go down as traitor." He blinked rapidly, trying to stop his eyes from filling with tears. "I don't want my family to live with that . . . my mother. She was once . . . terribly proud of me . . ."

Narraway found his own throat tight. He refused to allow in thoughts of his last parting with his own mother. She was a woman of immense elegance and quiet, very private but passionate, just as he was.

"Then tell me!" he said in sudden fury, sitting down on the floor, opposite Tallis. "Tell me everything you know about Chuttur Singh and Dhuleep Singh. And be quick. I've only got tonight, and I'd like to get enough sleep to be able to stand straight in court and not need anyone to prop me up. It won't make any difference if you collapse, but it might if I do!"

"No, it won't," Tallis said quickly. "Not really. It'll just look silly."

"Now, Corporal!" Narraway snapped. "Tell me every

last detail you know about Dhuleep and Chuttur. You've got until midnight."

"What are you going to do at midnight?" Tallis asked curiously. "You need a hell of a lot of sleep, for a young and supposedly healthy soldier."

"I'm going to find out more about these men and put the pieces together, of course! Paint a different picture. So, Corporal Tallis, get on with it."

But Tallis could tell Narraway little more than he already knew. He only drew more vividly the horror and the exhaustion of the last few months. There was no anger in him, except at the circumstances that cost young men their lives, and seemingly for so little in return. There was pity and wry, twisting humor here, between the men, snatches of companionship, gulfs of loneliness and, always at the back of it, a courage that climbed up to its feet every time it was beaten down.

Nothing Tallis said made the new theory in Narraway's mind impossible, and at midnight, as he had promised, he left Tallis and began finding the other men, waking them up if necessary, asking the same questions of all of them.

What had Dhuleep been like as a soldier, as a man?

Obviously he was a Sikh. Some Sikhs had remained loyal to the British, some had joined the mutiny. Why had he changed sides, and—more urgently—why had no one noticed? Was he guilty of the charge for which he was imprisoned?

"Yes—and for theft earlier on," one weary sergeant told him, sitting half asleep in the canteen. He was blinking at Narraway with a better temper than Narraway would have shown if he had been woken up at two in the morning by some man senior to him in rank but years junior in experience.

"Theft of what?" Narraway asked.

"Medicines, I think," the sergeant replied. "Quinine, stuff like that."

"To sell? To use on others? Did he need it himself?" Narraway was interested because it was an indication of Dhuleep's character and opportunism.

"Not that much!" the sergeant said with a twisted smile. "God knows what he wanted it for. He wouldn't say. Could have been to sell, or to take to the mutineers, to give to his friends or allies, or simply to rob us of the use of it."

"Could Tallis have been in on it?" It was a question

he really did not want the answer to, but he dared not evade it. "For profit?" he added.

"No," the sergeant said without hesitation. "It was Tallis who reported the theft. If he'd waited, we probably wouldn't have known who did it—or got it back, for that matter."

"So you caught Dhuleep Singh because of Tallis?"

"I suppose so. But it wasn't Tallis as got 'im, it was a couple of regulars called . . . Johnson was one of 'em. I think the other was Robinson, or Roberts. Something like that."

"What sort of a man was Dhuleep, before the theft?"

"Dunno. Ordinary, I think. Bit of a sneaky sod, but a good enough soldier. At least he seemed that way. If 'e ever stole before, 'e got away with it."

"Why was there only one guard looking after Dhuleep?" Narraway asked.

" 'Cos 'e were just a miserable layabout, an' 'e were locked up tight in a cell anyway. Probably wouldn't 'ave bothered locking 'im up, if it 'adn't been the medicines 'e took."

"Thank you." Narraway stood up. "I'd better go look

over all this past evidence and see if I can make any-thing different of it."

The sergeant stood as well, a big man, broad-chested, his shoulders sagging with weariness. "Ye're a tryer, I'll say that for yer. Don't give up, do yer?"

"Not till it's over," Narraway answered, finding the praise both bitter and welcome.

$\mathcal{A}$N HOUR LATER, NARRAWAY HAD GONE OVER ALL THE evidence yet again when he suddenly came across what looked like an inconsistency between what Corporal Reilly had said and Private Carpenter's account. It was very tiny: just something in the order of events. He looked at his notes, reread them to make sure it was not his own hasty writing misleading him.

Corporal Reilly had said that he had been standing at the corner, where he could see Scott on the far side of the courtyard, planing the wood for the new door, and McLeod and Avery in the corner opposite, with a clear view of the prison entrance a hundred yards away to their left.

He also said that Carpenter had been there the entire time with him, as was borne out by all three of the others.

But if Reilly was right, and his account matched Scott's, then Carpenter was lying. He had backed up McLeod and Avery, when actually they must have been out of his sight, in the direction of the prison. It was a very small discrepancy, but they could not all be correct. Was it just an error by a man too tired, too shaken to remember accurately? Did it even matter now? Not if his own idea was right. But what if it wasn't? He could not afford to rely on it. If it was wrong, he must have something to fall back on. They had all sworn that their time was accounted for and that no one else could have gone into the prison before Grant led the response to the alarm.

He must waken Carpenter right now and get some explanation. Tallis's life could depend on it.

Narraway crossed the open space to the remnants of the barracks where Carpenter was billeted and found him with some difficulty. He had to explain to a guard who he was and that his errand could not wait. He expected to find Carpenter asleep. Instead, the man was lying uncomfortably on a straw mattress, tossing fitfully. He sat up as soon as he was aware of Narraway's presence in the room.

Narraway apologized immediately. He kept his voice as quiet as he could make it, so as not to disturb the other men who were within earshot and might also sleep lightly.

"I need to speak to you before the trial resumes tomorrow. Privately."

"What?" Carpenter was dazed. "Lieutenant? You're going to call me again?" He pushed his hand through his hair and sat up a little further. "What for?"

"Can we go outside?" Narraway asked. He phrased it as a request, but it was in effect an order.

In silence Carpenter stood up, pulled on his trousers and tunic, and followed Narraway outside into the night. The clear sky's blaze of stars gave little light, and the wind was higher than before, scraping the branches and rattling the leaves on the tamarind trees twenty feet away.

"What is it, sir?" Carpenter asked, shivering a little.

Narraway went over Carpenter's evidence step by step. He knew it by heart now. He repeated every moment, every word that accounted for someone else. Did it matter? He had no idea. He could not afford to let anything slip.

"Yes," Carpenter said wearily.

Narraway shook his head. "No," he denied quietly. "Not if Corporal Reilly was where he said he was, doing what he said he was doing. In that case, he would have been around the corner, out of sight of the prison. It can't be right. One of you has it wrong. Is that a mistake, or a lie? Think carefully before you decide, Private."

Carpenter stood motionless. Narraway's eyes were used to the dark, but even so he could see no expression on Carpenter's face.

Carpenter blinked several times, as if the dust eddies troubled him. He rubbed his arm over his face. Narraway waited. He felt guilty. There was no arrogance, no anger in the man in front of him, just an inner conflict he could not resolve.

"If you don't tell me the truth, Tallis may be hanged for something he didn't do," he said at last. "A good man, a man we need, will suffer an injustice we can't ever put right. Was it a mistake, Private Carpenter, or a lie?"

Carpenter chewed his lip.

Again Narraway waited. He thought for a moment that Carpenter had fallen asleep on his feet.

"It was a lie, sir." Carpenter's voice in the dark was painful, as if his mouth was too dry to form the words properly.

"Did you leave, or did Reilly?" Narraway asked, chilled now by the fact that what had been only a possibility—a straw to grasp for—had become a reality.

"I did, sir," Carpenter replied. He straightened up until his body was stiff. "I didn't see anything relevant to Dhuleep Singh's escape, sir. Nor did I see Corporal Tallis. I can't help with what happened, sir."

Narraway found that he was shivering too.

"I still want to know where you were," he said aloud.

Carpenter looked resigned, beaten. "I was with Ingalls, sir. Ingalls was . . . ill."

"Then Major Rawlins would know that," Narraway reasoned, wondering why Rawlins had said nothing earlier. Was it possible he did not know of Carpenter's testimony? That seemed hard to believe.

"Private Carpenter!" he said sharply.

"Yes, sir?" Carpenter stiffened.

" 'Yes, sir, Rawlins knows of this,' or just, 'Yes, sir, I am paying attention'?" Narraway demanded.

"Yes, sir . . . I am paying attention. No, sir, Major Rawlins doesn't know. It was . . . it wasn't that kind of illness . . ."

"You mean he was drunk? Why didn't he just sleep it off, like anyone else?" Narraway was puzzled, even disturbed. "Carpenter! You'd better tell me the truth now, rather than have me drag it out of you, and this Ingalls, in court in a few hours' time."

"Yes, sir." Carpenter's body sagged, as if he no longer had the strength or the will to stand upright.

Narraway took him by the arm. The private's flesh was cold even through his tunic. "Here. For God's sake come and sit down, and tell me what was wrong with Ingalls and why you went to him rather than call a doctor."

Carpenter stopped resisting. Together they walked over to a heap of rubble still lying piled up from the bombardment of the siege. For a moment or two Carpenter sat bent forward, composing his thoughts, then he began to speak.

"Ingalls drinks . . . badly. He was right out of it that

day. Jones covered for him. We always do." He did not look at Narraway. "But he couldn't handle this. Ingalls was worse than usual. He was shaking like a leaf and sobbing. Jones couldn't keep him from yelling out. In his own mind, Ingalls must've been miles away, in another world, back in the time when we first came in after the siege. He was one of the ones who found the bodies in the well at Bibighar. They swore an oath then, and he thinks he's betrayed it because he . . ." He stopped, lowering his head into his hands.

"What?" Narraway asked, feeling brutal. He was afraid of what he was going to hear. "I have to know if I'm going to help Tallis," he insisted.

"He would get delirious," Carpenter said. "See it all again, smell the blood, hear the flies. Tallis used to help him sometimes, you know. Made him laugh." He twisted around to face Narraway for a moment. "You've got to help Tallis, sir. I don't know what the hell happened, but he couldn't have done it, unless he had a reason—I mean, one he couldn't get out of, one that . . ." He turned away again and fell silent.

"So you went to Ingalls that day? Because Jones couldn't handle it?" Narraway prodded him.

"Ingalls was out of it," Carpenter said. "He was going to kill himself. Said he'd failed. General Wheeler's daughter was haunting him. He could see her ghost everywhere."

"What?" Narraway gasped. "General Wheeler's daughter? What are you talking about, man?"

Carpenter looked at him.

"Why were you the one to go?" Narraway demanded.

"Because I was there too."

"Where?"

"In the Bibighar. She was one of the women they killed. We found her head. Somebody—I think it was Frazer—cut off her scalp and divided it up, a piece of it to every man. He told us to count the hairs on our piece and swear an oath to kill one mutineer for every hair. Ingalls couldn't do it. He tried . . ."

Narraway sat frozen, unaware of everything around him, the night wind in the tamarind branches, the dust devils stirring across the open ground, the starlight.

Carpenter moved a little, just shifting position. "What have we become, sir? Ingalls doesn't understand anymore. He asks over and over again what the hell we're doing here anyway. Never mind making the Indians into Christians, what are we making ourselves into? And you know what, sir? I can't answer him. I don't know what to do! Tell you the truth, that day I wished Tallis was there. He knew what to say, 'cos he'd make fun of it all and just be . . . gentle."

Narraway sat without moving or speaking. He wanted to save Tallis so badly it was like a physical pain inside him, as if something necessary for survival were missing and the emptiness was going to eat him away.

"Tallis, he wouldn't even say you were going to live if he knew you were going to die," Carpenter went on, his voice seeming almost disembodied in the darkness. "But if you were scared out of your wits, or so drunk you couldn't stand up, and seeing all kinds of things that weren't there, if you'd run away like an idiot and sat angry in a corner, hugging your knees and crying like you couldn't stop, he'd still talk to you like you were a man, and worth something."

"How long did you stay with Ingalls?" Narraway asked.

"Don't know. Until he calmed down and I was sure he'd sleep it off, and not cut his throat. Couldn't very well hide all the knives, could I?" He gave a sharp burst of laughter. "Tallis said that once: 'Let's hide all the knives and guns so no one'll kill themselves. 'Course, then they won't be able to kill one another either, but there are no perfect answers, eh?' And then he gave that crazy laugh of his." He let out a long sigh. "But that doesn't help, does it? I'd have sworn on my life he'd never hurt anyone. Reilly was there, and Scott only lied to save me. And I lied to save Ingalls the humiliation. Makes no difference to the fact that no one but Tallis could have got in there, because he was still the only one who had the chance."

He turned to Narraway, sitting up straighter. "Pity you can't hang Ingalls instead. He'd like it. It'd put him out of his misery. Tallis would've said that, and laughed. Except it's not funny, 'cos it's true. I can't help you, sir."

"I'm sorry for waking you," Narraway said quietly. "I thought for a few moments that I'd find something. Go back to bed. You might sleep. You have to sometime."

For several more moments Carpenter didn't move, then at last he rose to his feet, stiffly.

"Sorry, sir," he said, and before Narraway could reply, he stumbled away into the shadows and was lost.

Narraway sat uncomfortably on the rubble a few moments longer, then he stood up and walked slowly to his own quarters, and a few hours of oblivion before the battle.

*T*HE NEXT MORNING WAS STILL AND COLD. IT HAD NEVER been known to snow in Cawnpore, but it was easy to believe that the shortest day of the year was coming, and Christmas would be only a few days after that.

The small courtroom was grim. No one looked as if they had slept, and the very idea of celebrating anything like Christmas seemed absurd, an idea belonging to a different world.

Busby stood up.

"I have no more witnesses to call, sir." He addressed Latimer but included the other two officers in his gaze. "There is no question that Dhuleep Singh was released from his cell and Chuttur Singh was hacked to death. While it is possible Dhuleep killed Chuttur, I have demonstrated beyond any doubt that there was no one else who could have let Dhuleep out in the first place except Corporal John Tallis. I cannot offer any explanation for why he did so. Whether he was threatened, or bribed, or simply lost his sanity under the pressure of events, I don't know, nor do I believe that it matters. The facts remain."

Latimer nodded slowly, his face furrowed deep with unhappiness. He turned to Narraway. "Do you have anything you would like to say, or to ask, Lieutenant Narraway? It is your duty to offer anything you can on behalf of the prisoner."

Narraway stood up slowly. His brief sleep had been full of nightmares. His mouth was dry.

"Yes, sir." He swallowed. "Captain Busby has presented a powerful case for Corporal Tallis's guilt, but it rests solely on the fact that he was unable to find anyone else to blame. He has not shown that Corporal Tallis was actually seen at the time and the place, that he has behaved like a guilty man, or that he had any mark on him that would prove a fight: bruises, cuts, blood—not even a torn or stained uniform. He has given us no reason at all why Tallis should do such a thing, except in a bout of complete insanity, which must have come on without warning and went again without leaving any mark behind it. As Captain Busby admits, he simply has no one else to blame."

Busby stood up.

"Sit down, Captain," Latimer said grimly. "Your disagreement is taken for granted. Give the man his chance."

Busby's face tightened, but he did not speak again.

"Sir," Narraway resumed, "I believe there may be some explanation for all the facts we have other than Corporal Tallis's guilt, but I need to question the witnesses again, very precisely, before I can be certain. I have already found some errors and dismissed them after investigating more closely, because I found them to be unrelated to Dhuleep Singh's escape. I need now to explore certain other aspects that these errors may have thrown light upon." That was something of an exaggeration. He had no intention of telling them about Carpenter and Ingalls, but he had to make it sound as if he had a better cause for recalling witnesses than speculation, however plausible.

Latimer hesitated, seemed about to say something, then changed his mind. "Proceed, Lieutenant Narraway, but if you stray far from the point I shall stop you myself, never mind any objection Captain Busby may have."

"Yes, sir. I call Corporal Grant again."

Grant was duly reminded of his oath and, looking puzzled, faced Narraway.

The lieutenant was painfully aware that everyone in the room was looking at him with displeasure and a degree of suspicion. He avoided meeting Tallis's eyes.

"Corporal Grant . . ." Narraway stopped and cleared his throat. Suddenly his whole idea seemed absurd. He was going to make a complete fool of himself, ruin his career, disappoint Latimer, see Tallis hanged. He cleared his throat again. "Would you remind us where you were when you heard the prison alarm, and what you did? Please be absolutely exact, and if there is something you don't recall, say so. There is no shame in having your mind so bent in your duty, especially in times of emergency, that you don't notice other things."

Grant did as he was asked, slowly and carefully.

When he had finished, Narraway picked up the thread again, his voice shaking a little.

"The dying Chuttur Singh told you that the prisoner

had escaped," he confirmed. "That he had valuable information regarding the patrol, and that at all costs you should go after him. He himself was beyond help, even had you found a doctor for him, is that correct?"

"Yes, sir," Grant agreed. "I wanted to get help for Chuttur, but he insisted it was pointless and I should go after the prisoner." He looked distressed, his face flushed.

"And then Sergeant Attwood and Private Peterson arrived?" Narraway needed every last detail clear, exact.

"Yes, sir."

"Was it dark in the room? Was Chuttur's face splashed with blood?" He held his breath for the answer.

"Yes, sir," Grant answered, his voice wretched.

Busby rose to his feet, his face grim, his voice grating with anger. "Sir, these men all did exactly what they were trained to do, and what was the right thing. If the lieutenant is trying to suggest now that they were somehow mistaken and should have stayed with the man, when he was beyond all help, he is being cruel and is quite wrong. This only displays Lieutenant Narraway's inexperience, and—"

Latimer held up his hand. "Enough, Captain Busby. Your point is perfectly clear." He turned to Narraway. "Lieutenant, are you trying to suggest that any or all of these men should have tried to assist Chuttur Singh rather than go after the escaped prisoner? It was a judgment made in the heat of the moment, but I believe it was the correct one. Either way, what difference does it make to the guilt or innocence of John Tallis?"

Narraway felt the blood burn up his face. He knew he had sounded brutal, as if he were blaming Grant, but there was no other way. Please God, he was right!

"No, sir," he said, keeping his voice as steady as he could. "Grant, Attwood, and Peterson all behaved exactly as good soldiers should, sir. I intend no criticism at all. I just want to be absolutely certain, beyond any doubt at all, that that's what they did."

"If you do not reach some point soon, I shall be obliged to stop you for wasting our time," Latimer warned. "Get on with it."

Narraway turned to Grant again. "All of you left in pursuit of the escaped prisoner, Dhuleep Singh? You are sure of that?"

"Yes, sir," Grant repeated, his face pale, his distress obvious.

"Thank you. That's all," Narraway said quietly. He hesitated, on the edge of apology, and missed the chance.

Busby declined to ask Grant anything further. His expression reflected his disgust.

It was all hanging on one gamble now. Narraway stood up again. "I would like to call Major Rawlins back, sir."

"Is that really necessary, Lieutenant?" Latimer asked wearily.

"Yes, sir. I believe he may be able to complete my defense of Corporal Tallis, sir," Narraway answered. The hope was taking firmer and clearer shape in his mind all the time. If he was wrong, then there really was nothing left to say.

Latimer agreed. There was a long, tense silence while someone went to find Rawlins. Narraway remained standing, simply because he was too tense to sit down. He did not dare look at Tallis. It was possibly cowardly of him, but the hope was so close, and yet still so far-fetched, that he did not dare offer it.

Busby sat back in his chair, making no secret of his impatience and his contempt. He fidgeted, moved papers, twisted around to see if Rawlins was coming yet.

Latimer waited without moving or looking at either of the officers who sat with him. His dark face was haggard.

The seconds crawled by.

Finally Rawlins arrived. Everyone sat up straighter at once.

Rawlins was reminded of his oath and his position, and he waited, clearly surprised, to hear what Narraway wanted of him now. He too avoided looking at Tallis.

Narraway picked his words with intense care. Everything he said might hold the key to a man's life. He cleared his throat.

"Major Rawlins, you described the injuries Chuttur Singh had received. I don't wish you to do so again. Please just confirm that they were as you told us before. He was struck on the head, but not seriously enough to kill him, just to stun him. And his body was slashed with deep sword wounds from which he bled profusely, so much so that his uniform was sodden with blood. Is that accurate?"

Rawlins's face was tight, bleak with the memory. "Yes."

"He bled to death?" Narraway said.

"I've already said that." Rawlins was angry. "And there was nothing I could have done to save him. To suggest otherwise is not only ridiculous, it is offensive to the three men who found him."

"That would be Grant, Attwood, and Peterson?" Narraway asked. He was aware of an electric tension in the room, almost a prickling. Any moment now, Busby was going to interrupt and break the spell. "Doctor?" he prodded urgently.

"Yes!" Rawlins snapped.

"And those men went after Dhuleep, to see if they could recapture him?"

"Yes!" Rawlins was all but shouting.

"Then who was it who brought the body of Chuttur Singh to you?" Narraway's mouth was so dry he could barely form the words clearly, and yet his body was covered with sweat.

Rawlins froze.

There was a silence in the room that was somehow suffocating.

"Oh, God!" Rawlins cried in horror. "It was a Sikh . . . It . . ."

Narraway licked his lips and forced his voice to be steady. "Could it have been Dhuleep Singh, Major Rawlins?"

Rawlins had known what he was going to say. He stared back at him with eyes wide in his ashen face.

"Yes, it could have been."

Busby sat upright, staring.

Latimer leaned forward, looking first at Rawlins, then at Narraway.

Narraway swallowed hard.

"Sir," he said to Latimer. "I suggest that there is an alternative answer to this tragedy. John Tallis is innocent, as he has always claimed. The assumption that he is guilty arises only from the lack of any other answer."

Now Busby was on his feet. "Are you saying Dhuleep made his own escape, without Tallis's help? That's ridiculous! How did he get out? He was gone before Grant, Attwood, or Peterson even got there."

"No," Narraway said firmly. "No, he was not." He turned back to Latimer. "What if Dhuleep Singh tricked Chuttur, feigning an illness, offering information, or anything else? Then, when he had the opportunity, he struck Chuttur on the head and took his sword and keys. Then when he had killed him, he—"

"In that case, he still couldn't have opened the door, Lieutenant, before Grant got there!" Busby interrupted.

"No," Narraway said again. "You're right. But what if Chuttur was stripped of his guard's uniform and left concealed under the pile of bedclothes? The man Grant spoke to, who told him Dhuleep had escaped with vital information, was Dhuleep himself, with blood smeared over his features, wrapped in Chuttur's bloodstained clothes. We all assumed that someone had opened the door from the outside, and Dhuleep had escaped, closing it behind him. But in fact it was Grant who first opened the door."

There was a sigh around the room, but not a soul moved.

"Dhuleep urged Grant and the others to go as quickly as possible. As soon as they had done so, he took off Chuttur's blood-soaked clothes, re-dressed him, and took him to Rawlins. Then he slipped out and ran away! There was no third man." He took a deep shuddering breath. "That answers all the questions, sir, and it shows John Tallis to be guilty of nothing more than being the only one in the immediate area who happened to be working alone."

Rawlins rubbed his hand across his brow. "You're right," he said with amazement, and with a relief so intense his body shook with it, the color surging back into his face. "I barely looked at the man who brought Chuttur in; I had all my attention on the injured man. But he was definitely Sikh. And the only person unaccounted for other than Tallis was Dhuleep Singh." His voice gained strength and urgency. "But we thought Dhuleep had gone. Of course the three who went looking for him didn't catch him—he was behind them! He went out of the hospital door, in the opposite direction, and got clean away." Rawlins looked across at Tallis. "I'm sorry, John. I was so bloody horrified at what had been done to Chuttur, I never more than glanced at the man who brought him to me."

"He was counting on that," Narraway observed. Then he faced Latimer. "Sir, I respectfully request that

Corporal John Tallis be found not guilty of any wrong-doing at all. There is no villain here."

Slowly Latimer smiled, the light coming back into his eyes, the color to his face. He straightened in his chair and looked first to the man on his right, then the man on his left. Each one nodded, smiling.

"Thank you, Lieutenant Narraway," he said quietly. "This Court finds Corporal John Tallis not guilty in any way whatsoever." He looked at Tallis. "You are free to go, Corporal."

Tallis tried to stand, but he was too weak with the sudden, almost unbelievable turn in his fortunes, and his legs folded under him.

Strafford walked across the courtroom to Narraway, holding out his hand.

"Strafford Minor was wrong about you," he said with intense, burning pleasure. "You're a damn good soldier. There won't be a man or woman in the regiment who isn't grateful to you for this. You've given us back a belief in ourselves. Happy Christmas."

Narraway felt tears sting his eyes. "Thank you, sir. Happy Christmas to you also. I feel a bit more like celebrating now. In fact, I'll go and put some decorations up in my quarters. I've got a blue paper garland I want to hang somewhere special."

Strafford did not ask him to explain. Not that Narraway would have. He simply took the lieutenant's hand and clasped it, so hard he all but crushed his fingers.

"Thank you," he said again. "Happy Christmas."

ANNE PERRY is the bestselling author of
twelve holiday novels: *A New York Christmas,*
Christmas Hope, A Christmas Garland, A
ristmas Homecoming, A Christmas Odys-
A Christmas Promise, A Christmas Grace,
Christmas Beginning, A Christmas Secret,
Christmas Guest, A Christmas Visitor, and
Christmas Journey. She is also the author
two acclaimed series set in Victorian
ngland—the William Monk novels and the
harlotte and Thomas Pitt novels—five
World War I novels, and a work of historical
ction, *The Sheen on the Silk.*

www.anneperry.co.uk

ABOUT THE TYPE

This book was set in Century Schoolbook, a member of the Century family of typefaces. It was designed in the 1890s by Theodore Low De Vinne (1828–1914) of the American Type Founders Company, in collaboration with Linn Boyd Benton (1844–1932). It was one of the earliest types designed for a specific purpose, the *Century* magazine, because it was able to maintain the economies of a narrower typeface while using stronger serifs and thickened verticals.